# Crimson

## Casey Morales

NAmazic Press

# Contents

# Before you begin . .

.

To say thank you for joining me on this journey, I would like to give you a gift, a free copy of my first novella, My Accidental First Date.

Click here to tell me where to send it.

# Disclaimer

T his is a work of fiction.

Names, characters, businesses, events and incidents are the products of the author's imagination. Any resemblance to actual persons, living or dead, or actual events is purely coincidental. In most cases, names of characters are inventions of the author; however, for the purpose of context, certain individuals who were prominent within the historical context of this story are referenced.

Great care has been taken to respect historical events and timelines, such as battles or other significant occurrences during World War II. Any historical discrepancies are unintentional.

# Chapter One

# **Will**

A rthur Wendel Adleman was my polar opposite.

In any other world, we never would have traveled in the same circles, much less become friends. I was athletic and loved to push my body, while he spent most of his waking hours in a library or sitting at a desk, pushing his brain. I was taller than average; his eyes met my shoulder. While we shared an affinity for quiet times, I could turn on the charm when needed, but social settings made him curl into a ball. Our friendship made no sense, and yet, we'd become brothers the moment he'd awkwardly adjusted his bottle-bottom glasses and shaken my hand.

I blew into my cupped hands as I paced in front of the stone step that led into Adams House. Arty sat with his arms folded across his chest, shivering from the frigid air blowing through campus.

"Why does it always take the girls so long to get ready? It's not like she's going on a date. It's just us," Arty said through clenched teeth.

I shrugged. "You're the one with sisters. Women are a total mystery to me."

He chuckled. "Mystery. That's a good word for them."

"Are we ready, boys?" The effervescent voice of our mutual best friend drifted through the now open door, along with a fair amount of warm air Arty appeared to savor. "I believe I won our last two outings. Does that double the bet tonight?"

Janie was sunlight piercing a veiled sky. Her brown eyes glittered beneath deeper brown hair that bobbed as she laughed. Despite coming from one of the wealthiest families among all Harvard students in our class, her smile was warm and bright, shared freely with anyone who'd respond in kind.

The three of us had met in 1938, our freshman year. Some of my earliest memories were of my mom and dad talking about Harvard at the dinner table. I was eighteen and, like so many idiots my age, I thought I could do anything, *be* anything. Attending their alma mater had meant the world to me, but especially to them. My mom tried to hold back tears as she hugged me goodbye that first day. She was never great at hiding her emotions. I remember reaching up and wiping her cheek with my thumb. She'd leaned into my touch, pressing her face against my palm.

That was the last time I saw her.

A month later, I was called from class into the dean's office, where a stately man in pinstripes informed me I was now alone in the world. Thanks to my mom's obsession with candles and scents, my home and my only remaining living family were gone.

I nearly lost myself to grief.

I'm not sure I would've made it through that year without Arty and Janie. They became my rock in ways I'd never known, never needed. Their kindness and compassion, their gentleness, nursed my broken mind and soothed my aching heart.

Arty's dad had one of his employees drive me home. Arty came too, and sat by my side as I sorted through what was left of our uncharred lives. His hand rarely left my shoulder. When I found a framed photo of Mom, Dad and I taken the year before and my chest heaved, he threw himself to the floor and held me until I ran out of tears.

In moments of stillness, I can still feel Mom's face pressing into my palm.

Through it all, Arty and Janie remained steadfast. Their friendship and devotion to me never wavered. I will never understand how I could be so blessed to have such remarkable friends.

For a time, I thought Arty had taken a shine to our Janie. Something in the way he stared a shade too long made me wonder, but in the two and a half years we'd been at college, he'd never asked her out, not even for coffee or a shake. Perhaps it was his own lack of confidence, his social awkwardness, but I doubted that. Janie was our sister, and that was enough.

It was everything.

"Double?" Arty protested as he stood. "I still have to pay for this semester, you know."

She snorted. Arty wasn't the heir to a food fortune like Janie, but his family was far from poor. None of us had struggled a moment of the Depression.

"Ten cents then. You can afford that. Consider it my fee for helping you look good tonight," Janie said, smirking over her shoulder as she led us away from the dorm.

"Helping us look good? I look just fine, thank you very much," Arty huffed.

I elbowed him. Tussling with Janie was a lost cause.

She whipped around, her hair following a split second after her head turned, somehow landing perfectly on her shoulder. "You look fine, but walking in a door with me makes you look fabulous, and you know it."

Arty's mouth dropped, then closed.

Janie winked at me, then wheeled about and continued leading us through the crisscrossing sidewalks that were barely visible under a dusting of snow.

I tried to stifle a laugh, but failed.

"Traitor," Arty grumbled, despite a grin on his face.

We passed a large group of boys headed in the opposite direction, each snug in the thick olive coats of their army uniforms. Like a rippling wave of green and gold, each soldier tipped a cap at Janie, then gave Arty and me a polite nod.

A half-hour later, we strode into the bowling alley, welcomed by blessed warmth and the sound of a half-dozen balls slamming into pins. Candlesticks was one of the oldest bowling alleys in the country. With six lanes, a robust menu, and a well-stocked bar, it was also one of the most popular hangouts for the Crimson elite.

"Come on. Let's get a drink while we wait," Janie said, grabbing Arty by his lapel and dragging him toward the alcohol. I followed on their heels, anticipating the flow of heat a fresh glass would send down my chest.

Janie stepped from the bar, her overfilled sidecar sloshing dangerously in its martini glass, a twist of orange peel threatening to escape with each step. The bartender handed Arty two tall glasses packed with ice, a black tea-looking liquid and a half-dozen lemon slices. I'd never seen the concoction, and cocked a brow in Janie's direction.

She sipped her drink, giggled, and wove her way to a high-top near the lanes.

"I have a bad feeling about this," Arty said, handing me my glass. "She called it a Pimm's Cup, something she heard they served at Wimbledon this year. When the bartender asked what liquor she wanted mixed in, she shrugged and told him to pick for us."

"Great. We could be drinking gasoline."

"Pretty much. Is this how she keeps winning?" He raised his glass, sniffed, then took a sip.

"You didn't grimace or fall to the ground. That's a good sign, right?"

His brow rose. "It's actually good."

"Of course it is," Janie said as we climbed onto our stools. "I'm pretty sure he used brandy, maybe vodka too. I love the spiced fruit."

I took a tentative sip, then a larger draw. "Mmm, this is really good."

Janie raised her glass in triumph.

Two rounds of drinks later, we finally stepped up to our own lane.

"Are the pins supposed to dance like that?" Arty asked, wobbling slightly as he grabbed a ball. "How am I supposed to knock 'em down when they're moving like that?"

Janie giggled. "It's part of the challenge."

"You're a little sneak, aren't you? A dime thief."

She fanned herself with a hand like I'd said something that reeked. "I'm a lady and I'm sure I don't know what you mean. Now, step back and let me show you what a winner looks like."

And she did. Four games in a row.

"Dimes, please," she said, holding out an upturned palm as we racked our balls.

Arty and I fished in our pockets and our tributes clinked before vanishing into her purse.

"I'll use these for our milkshakes. See, you didn't really lose after all."

"She's almost chipper enough to hit with one of these balls," Arty grumbled.

I shook my head and chuckled so Janie couldn't hear. The last thing either of us needed was for her to think there was a rebellion in her ranks. I watched her weave through the uniformed guys toward the desk, her curls bobbing merrily, almost as much as her hips. Nearly every man turned as she passed. She loved the attention, but not as one who craved adoration. Rather, she genuinely loved seeing people smile, knowing *she* made them smile. There were plenty of good people in the world. The war was revealing everyone's character, but Janie stood alone in my mind. She was a beacon of light in a world tumbling toward darkness.

I don't know how I would've made it through the last year and a half without those two. Arty, while entirely too dopey and often curmudgeonly, had a heart of gold and would do anything for his friends. He'd proven that a hundred times. And Janie, well, she was that kind of special that only came along once in a lifetime. If the war didn't tear us apart, I knew the three of us would be great friends for the rest of our lives.

A handsome guy with the silver bars of a second lieutenant stopped her before she reached the counter. His smile broadened as she laughed and her hand reached up and rubbed his arm. Her cheeks colored at his reaction, and I swear her eyes brightened.

Something inside me flared at that touch, at witnessing her affection. It was the strangest sensation. Janie and I had never been anything but friends; a brother and sister, really. Why would the attention of another man stir ... whatever that was?

Arty had found a stool while we waited, so I studied the pair. The man's jaw was square, almost impossibly so. His inky brow formed the perfect frame for his deep emerald eyes. When he smiled, tiny pits formed just beyond the crease of his mouth, something I was sure Janie obsessed over the moment they appeared. By the look of her hand squeezing his arm, he was fit. In his uniform, he was a striking example of duty and honor.

I should've been happy for Janie, for the attention he showered on her, for the respect he showed. I should want her to meet a man who treated her well and offered a brilliant, happy future. So, why did I feel so ... jealous?

*Was* I jealous?

I couldn't tear my gaze away.

Despite winter's grip, the guy's skin still carried a slight tan. He reached up and moved a curl, setting it behind her ear. She giggled, and her eyes fell before returning to his.

My chest flared again.

This was ridiculous. Janie was my sister, my friend.

"Come on, let's save her before we lose our milkshakes." Arty's hand pressed into my back, urging me forward.

"Oh, boys, come here," Janie called with a wave. "Come meet Charles."

Introductions were made, hands were shaken, and Janie insisted the lieutenant call on her at Adams House. Thankfully, she was a mistress in the art of hard to get and spun away, leaving poor Charles staring longingly in her wake.

"That was fun. Milkshakes?" she chirped.

I shook my head again, more to try to free myself of whatever that fit of madness had been than anything else. "Milkshakes sound great. I believe the winner pays, isn't that the Harvard way, Arthur?"

"Oh, quite right, William. Quite right. And we wouldn't want to shun tradition. Horrible business, that."

We'd both adopted our highest-brow accents, sending Janie into a fit of laughter that turned more heads than her hips had moments earlier. Without warning, she took one of us on each side, locked arms, and pulled us out into the night.

Thankfully, though bitterly cold, the snow the skies promised had yet to arrive. We walked, arm in arm, for two blocks to Fisher's Drug Store, where the aforementioned milkshakes waited behind a brightly polished counter.

"God, this is the best milkshake ever," Janie said, losing all pretense and slurping loudly through her straw. Her eyes rolled back almost as much as Arty's had when he'd finished his third drink.

"Do you think they'll accelerate our courses?"

Arty's sudden seriousness jarred me out of the brain freeze that had threatened to drop me to my knees.

"Accelerate? What do you mean? Why?"

He cocked his head like a disappointed parent watching a child lie about homework.

"The war, dummy." He motioned around us. I hadn't paid much attention as we'd entered, but realized nearly every student in the place wore either an army or navy cloak. "They need to make room for more military students. It's all Conant talks about anymore."

"Okay, I get that, and we should do our part, I suppose, but to speed up our courses? Would you even be able to start law school now?"

He shook his head. "That's what I'm worried about. We're not even halfway through. I doubt they'd even take me into the law program without a full-term degree."

Janie sat quietly, watching us without really seeing.

I sat back, suddenly captivated by the countertop.

"When did we become so used to them?" Arty mumbled.

"Used to who?" I asked.

"The army guys. Navy too. I mean, one minute the college is normal, then overnight there are more men in uniform than regular students. You remember how odd it was, seeing them on campus that first month. Now I don't know that I'd recognize the place without them."

Last May, Harvard president James Bryant Conant had committed the college to the national defense on nationwide radio. Since then, the ranks of the Reserve Officers' Training Corps had ballooned, and the school had not-so-gradually turned into a military training institute. Many ongoing research programs were redirected toward military discoveries. Conant even directed much of the instructional curriculum expanded to include aerial mapping, meteorology, camouflage, and a dozen other wartime topics whose names were never listed but were poorly kept secrets from the general student population.

President Conant made sure we kept up with the European conflict. There was no escaping the radio addresses, bulletins, and lectures.

While Poland, Finland, Denmark, Norway, Belgium, Luxembourg, France, Romania, Bulgaria, Yugoslavia, and Greece had fallen, we were still an ocean away, and many couldn't understand why America had to be dragged into a war that could never reach us.

We'd just survived the Depression and were finally enjoying life again. Why would we want to jump into a war?

That was Janie's argument, something I was sure she was simply echoing from her parents as they dined on the finest china, using the most luxurious silverware.

I still didn't know what to think. It all felt so much bigger than any of us. How were college kids supposed to understand war? None of us wanted to.

Arty's heart had been set on law school since before he could speak, and Janie's studies at Radcliffe aimed at her future in her father's business. I still had no idea what I wanted to do with my life, but it didn't include shipping off to fight in someone else's war.

Everything felt poised on the tip of a knife, ready to fall at the slightest breeze. America had resisted calls to enter the war, even struggled with offering arms and aid, but something had shifted over the past year and my gut churned every time someone turned on a radio.

News was never good.

"And what if we get drafted?" Arty's voice nearly trembled with the last word. The draft had begun in 1940, requiring all men between twenty-one and forty-five to register and serve if called. I'd seen a few of our classmates drafted, but Arty and I had been lucky.

"Then our lives change. I don't know what else to say."

Arty glared at me like he wanted to throw something, then his shoulders fell.

Janie steeled herself and somehow managed to sound as bright as ever. "Alright, boys. That's enough war talk. Neither of you is going anywhere, you hear me?"

# Chapter Two

# **Will**

The sun streamed brightly through my window the next morning. Thanks to Janie's magical elixir, I'd slept well past my normal waking hour, allowing the lazy winter sun to rise before me. I rolled over and checked my watch, groaning as I read nine forty-two. Church services started at nine. Even if I rushed, I'd walk into the building to packed pews, annoyed heads turning as I sought a vacant seat, just as the pastor uttered his final words.

"Nothing I can do about that now," I muttered, setting my watch back on the nightstand.

I sat up, scratched my throbbing scalp, and wondered if Janie had made it to mass, then laughed at the ridiculousness of that thought. Janie loved making heads turn, annoyed or otherwise. She was *never* on time.

Arty was Jewish, so the situation meant little to him. The whole matter of religion meant even less to Arty. He'd eat bacon like a champ, play cards on the Sabbath, and break any number of other rules normally required of Abraham's flock. If I had to lay odds, he was currently snug under his covers, giving not a hint of thought to anything outside his dorm.

My bladder clenched, so I stretched and padded into the washroom. Walking felt like a new experience as I banged my shoulder into the doorframe. In that moment, as I rubbed my shoulder, I vowed that Arty and I needed a plan before our next excursion with the playful Miss Janie.

Morning ablution complete, I stood and peered out the window at the soldiers drilling in the courtyard. Perfectly manicured fields now held more brown than green. While temperatures remained near freezing, the snow had still turned to sludge beneath their boots. It seemed a change in student body makeup wasn't the only way the army was leaving its mark on Harvard.

A group of men jogged by, white plumes puffing before them with every breath.

"Great idea, guys," I said, turning to layer on clothing for a morning jog. Nothing cured a night out with Janie like good old-fashioned exercise.

My head gave an unsympathetic throb at the thought of an old fashioned.

A couple hours later, I found myself entering the dining hall, starving and nearly frozen from a run on a sub-freezing morning. Despite losing feeling in my extremities, I could feel the blood pumping faster as my heart thrummed in my chest. There were few things in the world that made me feel more alive than working out.

I glanced around to find Arty sitting alone at the end of a long table.

"You look like shit," he said without a hint of sarcasm or humor.

"Thanks, but you're no sparkling wine yourself."

"Stop, please. No talk of alcohol ever again."

I grunted. "Deal. You done?" I asked, looking down at his nearly empty plate.

"Yeah. It wasn't great today. Stay away from the fish—at least, I think it was fish. I might taste it again shortly."

"You do look a little green," I said, taking an involuntary step back. "You and Janie still up to study this afternoon?"

"Yeah. Right in the middle of the game." His voice sank. The Brooklyn Dodgers were playing the New York Giants, and anyone living on the East Coast would be listening—except for three Harvard students stuck in a library.

"Good. I could use some help with my German."

Arty dropped his fork and glared up. "Seriously?"

I shrugged. "Even if we don't go to war, the Germans run most of Europe now. It's a good language to know for the future."

He rose. "I'll help you with anything math or science related, but Janie will have to hold your hand where Germans are concerned. I want nothing to do with them or their language."

"Fine," I said, holding my hands up in surrender. "Let me grab something to eat and I'll meet you over at Adams."

Without a word, Arty adjusted his black-rimmed spectacles, gathered his textbooks and scurried out of the hall.

The porter arrived and took my order. Since breakfast was still on the menu, he recommended simple fare: eggs, toast, and bacon. Out of curiosity, I asked after the fish. The man's nose wrinkled and his head shook.

I gave him a nod and an easy smile. "Thanks for the tip. I'll stick with breakfast."

Kickoff was at two o'clock.

By some stroke of Crimson magic, Arty had found a study room with a radio and had it tuned to the game when I strode in. Janie was buried in a stack of books and barely glanced up.

"Come on, they just started," Arty practically vibrated. He might've been the nerdiest man on campus, but he loved his football.

I took a seat and listened to a few plays before opening my German textbook. "Sorry, bud, I really do need to study. Can you turn that down some?"

He threw me a look like I'd just shot his dog. "Fine."

I'd barely begun when Arty cranked the volume. "Guys, they've interrupted the game."

We'd grown used to war updates and random announcements, but something in the urgency of the man's voice blaring through the speakers felt different, almost panicked. Janie and I turned toward the radio.

*... to bring you a special news bulletin.*

*The Japanese have attacked Pearl Harbor, Hawaii, by air, President Roosevelt has just announced. The attack also was made on all naval and military activities on the principal island of Oahu.*

*We take you now to Washington.*

*The details are not available. They will be in a few minutes. The White House is now giving out a statement. The attack apparently was made on all naval ... and on naval and military activities on the principal island of Oahu. The President's brief statement was read to reporters by Stephen Early, the President's secretary.*

*A Japanese attack upon Pearl Harbor, naturally, would mean war. Such an attack would naturally bring a counterattack, and hostilities of this kind would naturally mean that the President would ask Congress for a declaration of war. There is no doubt from the temper of Congress that such a declaration would be granted.*

*This morning, Secretary Howell talked with the secretaries of war and of the navy. Now the two special Japanese envoys, Admiral Nomura and Special Envoy Kurusu, are at the State Department, engaged in conference with Secretary of State Howell. Their appearance at the State Department on this Sunday afternoon emphasizes the gravity of the Far Eastern situation, where hostilities now seem to be actually opening over the whole South Pacific.*

*And just now comes the word ... from the President's office ... that a second air attack has been reported on army and navy bases in Manila.*


*Thus, we have official announcements from the White House that Japanese airplanes have attacked Pearl Harbor in Hawaii and have now attacked army and navy bases in Manila.*


*We return you now to New York and will give you later information as it comes along from the White House.*[1]

---

1. Transcript of the emergency radio broadcast at 2:26 pm on December 7, 1941

# Chapter Three

# **Will**

N one of us moved. I don't even remember breathing.

Our eyes remained fixed on the radio as if it were a lion crouched and ready to pounce.

The football game resumed, and the unburdened cheers of the crowd who'd clearly not heard the emergency broadcast grated against my ears. I couldn't decide which felt more surreal, the announcement of the Japanese attack or the way our day was briefly interrupted then resumed as if our whole way of life hadn't just been shaken to its core.

People were cheering as ships sank and men died.

Hawaii had always felt like a distant land, no closer than Europe and her war. That morning, it was one town over, a close neighbor, a friend. It was a family member who'd just been wounded so severely no one knew if they would pull through—so severely, she might take the rest of us with her.

The whole thing felt like a dagger plunged deeply into my flesh. I'd never been stabbed or shot or wounded in any way, save the occasional broken bone as a reckless boy. Neither had America—not in her body proper. She'd inflicted some brutal wounds on herself, but had never suffered at the hand of another.

And now she had.

We both had.

"What does it mean?" Janie's breathless question echoed in the paneled room.

"War," Arty answered. "It means we'll go to war."

"You don't know that," I argued, unsure why I would fight such an obvious statement of fact. "Congress hasn't—"

"Had a spine? Given a shit about what's going on in Europe? Cared about how their indifference is killing people an ocean away?" His voice rose with each accusation.

"Arty—" I began.

"No. Don't you *dare* defend our indifference." He stood and faced us. Janie's eyes widened as she watched our field mouse of a friend morph into some unrecognizable beast of a man. "How much of Europe does Hitler have to control before we wake up, before we realize he won't stop with Europe?"

"He didn't take London," Janie muttered.

"He *hasn't* taken London ... yet. But he's bombed them into a state of perpetual fear. Without Roosevelt's shipments, that bloody flag might already fly over Westminster."

"But—"

"We're going to war. Hell, we're already at war. Japan saw to that." He stormed to the table and slammed his book shut, then shoved it off the table. It banged into the wall and fell with its pages fluttered open.

"Arty—" Janie startled.

"There's no fucking reason to study. We'll be in uniform by the end of the week."

He braced himself on the table with his head hung, then turned to leave.

"Arty, wait," Janie's voice pleaded. "This won't change anything for us."

Without looking back, he said, "Isn't that what the people of London said before the bombs starting falling on them? You two need to open your eyes. This changes everything—for everyone."

I didn't know how to respond to that, didn't even know if I should. Janie looked like she'd been slapped and the sting of it had spread throughout her whole body. I didn't know a person's whole being could become crestfallen until that moment.

When she put her face in her hands and her shoulders began to shake, my heart lurched.

"Janie," I said softly, kneeling beside her with a hand on her shoulder. "Hey, it'll be alright."

That might've been the stupidest thing I'd ever said, but it somehow felt like the only lifeline I had to toss.

"No, Arty's right," she stammered. "It won't."

We tried to study after her tears dried, but neither of us could focus on the mundane subjects that once defined the limitlessness of our futures.

Janie returned to her room, and I, intending to do the same, stepped out into the courtyard, then froze. Hundreds of soldiers stood in rows, their uniforms crisp, their backs erect. The sidewalks sketched the only outlines in the slushy plain not occupied by a man in olive garb. The assembly faced the steps of one of the other buildings, one with a flag pole and America's standard snapping in the breeze.

A lone officer stood beneath the banner.

No one spoke. It felt as if all of Harvard was holding its breath.

I'd seen assemblies like this a hundred times since the military took up residence in our halls, but something about this one felt different, like the weight of the world had settled on each man's shoulders and threatened to drag them under a frothy sea.

But there was something else. I could feel it in my mind's periphery.

As I looked from one man to the next, studied their faces, the set of their jaws, the fire raging in their eyes, I realized what it was—and that it wasn't some feeling on the outer edge of their existence, it was in the soul of their beings.

Determination.

These men had purpose. They'd had it before, but now, purpose had become righteous fury. They had no qualms or doubts about their path. This morning's attack had clarified their futures, defined their direction in ways no other act could. They were the guardians of their homeland and she had been attacked.

If they did nothing, worse would follow.

*Was that what Arty had been trying to say?*

The thought stung like a thorn in my chest. Arty was our bespectacled friend, the waifish boy whose brain was more muscular than any gym rat's arms, while his own arms, well—his brain was strong. I was embarrassed by my friend's conviction, by his anger and indignation, by his clear-eyed vision slicing right from wrong with a surgeon's precision.

Arty saw clearly, and I was ashamed.

He knew what these men knew.

He wasn't standing on some shore, gaping at a storm rising in the distance, lulling himself into some false sense of insulated, *isolated* security.

There wasn't a storm rising. It had risen years ago, when one reckoned the time it took for Hitler to wrest absolute control over his own people and for the Japanese and Italians to thirst for land and wealth.

It had risen and strengthened, then lashed out in its hatred of the peaceful morn.

It had risen while we slumbered beneath our bedcovers' warmth.

The storm had wailed and thrashed and consumed ... while *we* did nothing.

And now, that same tempest was battering *our* door.

We couldn't stand idly by any longer. *I* couldn't.

The officer began speaking, his voice a clarion call to those in ranks. He spoke of patriotism and pride, of duty and honor. He spoke of protecting those who could not do so for themselves. He spoke of sacrifice.

My heart ached at his words, finally understanding their true meaning etched in the faces of his men. Humbled and abashed, I fled the field for the solitude of my room. None of the men's heads turned. No one watched me pass. Still, I felt every eye on my back as they girded for battle and I slunk away.

Hours passed. My books lay unopened at the foot of my bed. I did little more than stare at my walls, listening to my radio in hopes of some correction to the morning's news that I knew wouldn't come. Orchestras played, as they did every Sunday, their bright melodies warring with my melancholy.

My stomach growled, and I finally glanced at my watch. I'd lost the entire afternoon in thought. I'd nearly missed the dinner hours in the dining hall. I reached down and began slipping on my shoes when the music stopped and the familiar voice of the First Lady of the United States spoke.

*Good evening, ladies and gentlemen, I am speaking to you tonight at a very serious moment in our history. The Cabinet is convening and the leaders in Congress are meeting with the President. The State Department and army and navy officials have been with the President all afternoon. In fact, the Japanese ambassador was talking to the President at the very time that Japan's airships were bombing our citizens in Hawaii and the Philippines, and sinking one of our transports loaded with lumber on its way to Hawaii.*

*By tomorrow morning, the members of Congress will have a full report and be ready for action.*

*In the meantime, we the people are already prepared for action. For months now the knowledge that something of this kind might happen has been hanging over our heads, and yet it seemed impossible to believe, impossible to drop the everyday things of life and feel that there was only one thing which was important—preparation to meet an enemy no matter where he struck. That is all over now and there is no more uncertainty.*

*We know what we have to face and we know that we are ready to face it.*

*I should like to say just a word to the women in the country tonight. I have a boy at sea on a destroyer; for all I know, he may be on his way to the Pacific. Two of my children are in coast cities on the Pacific. Many of you all over the country have boys in the services who will now be called upon to go into action. You have friends and families in what has suddenly become a danger zone. You cannot escape anxiety. You cannot escape a clutch of fear at your heart, and yet I hope that the certainty of what we have to meet will make you rise above these fears.*

*We must go about our daily business more determined than ever to do the ordinary things as well as we can, and when we find a way to do anything more in our communities to help others, to build morale, to give a feeling of security, we must do it. Whatever is asked of us, I am sure we can accomplish it. We are the free and unconquerable people of the United States of America.*

*To the young people of the nation, I must speak a word tonight. You are going to have a great opportunity. There will be high moments in which your strength and your ability will be tested. I have faith in you. I feel as though I am standing upon a rock and that rock is my faith in my fellow citizens.*

*Now we will go back to the program we had arranged ...*
1

---

1. Transcript of radio address by First Lady Eleanor Roosevelt on
the evening of December 7, 1941

# Chapter Four

# **Will**

Arty and I met Janie for breakfast Monday morning. The dining hall was packed. Students, both in and out of uniform, milled about, while porters scurried to keep up. It was strange. There was only one topic of conversation: Pearl Harbor and what it might mean for the nation and for each of us. The place felt alive, unlike any morning I could remember, but conversations remained quiet, just above whispers, as though the treachery or tragedy of the event demanded reverence. All the whispers and low murmurs bounding off the wooden walls gave the place an eerie, electric feeling that made my skin crawl.

Reading my mind, Janie said, "This place feels like a tomb. Nobody wants to be heard over the screams of the dead."

"Not sure I'd put it quite that way," Arty said with a raised brow. "But I get what you're saying. I can't tell if people are more angry, sad, or afraid of what's next."

"We're at war. *That's* what's next." I took a sip of tea and stared into my plate, my appetite suddenly gone.

Arty started to say something else, but was cut off by a freckled student with flaming hair and wild eyes. "EVERYBODY! LISTEN

UP!" Another student followed the boy into the hall, carrying a large radio.

"This can't be good," Janie muttered.

"President Roosevelt is addressing a joint session of Congress today," the redhead bellowed. "Midday classes are canceled, and the administration asks everyone to gather in their dining hall to listen."

The boys set up the radio on a table near the door then hurried out, leaving a speechless mass staring at each other over their breakfasts. Like the tickling drops of a spring rain, words began to drip, then fall, then pour. What had been quiet, restless chatter was now a cacophony of agitation.

I could barely hear myself think.

"It's all moving so fast," Janie said to no one in particular.

Arty cocked his head. "Only if you forget what happened in the '30s. Everything's been building to this point, we just didn't want to believe it—or see it. America is brilliant at turning a blind eye when it suits her."

"That's unfair," Janie protested.

Arty crossed his arms and sat back. "Is it? London has been bombed into the nineteenth century, yet here we sit, sipping tea in Harvard's hallowed halls. The whole damn country has sat on its ass while the world burned, while *people* burned."

She refused to surrender. "People—"

"Don't you dare tell me you don't know what I'm talking about. It might not make the news reels on Saturday night, but my people are being targeted by Hitler. His troops are *slaughtering* Jews in Poland and the Soviet Union by the thousands. They don't care if they're women or children, only that they're Jewish."

"Arty—"

"Don't! Don't make excuses or try to soothe poor Arty." He stood and stabbed at the air before Janie. "Do you really think they'll stop there? Who will he kill tomorrow? How many? How many is enough for you to wake up and see there's a rifle pointed at your head? America's too busy feeling good about itself, and most of Europe belongs to him. Who's going to stop him when he decides ..."

It was as though the anger and pain had become lodged in Arty's throat. Moisture brimmed in his eyes. Janie placed a hand on his shoulder, but he shrugged it off as he stood.

"I have class," he said, tossing his napkin and storming out of the hall.

I stared down at my hands.

"Why didn't you say anything?" Janie's tone stabbed.

I glanced up. "What was I supposed to say, Janie? He's right. The whole world's falling apart and we're sitting here on our hands. Roosevelt has to do more. *We* have to do more."

She stared for a moment, as if studying my features, then her mouth set in a grim line. "I have to get to class. Meet back here for lunch?"

"Okay."

I sat numb long after she left, barely noticing the flow of students from the room as they headed to morning sessions.

"Son, are you finished?" An elderly porter bending over my shoulder startled me out of my thoughts.

"Oh, sorry, yes. Thanks," I said, dropping my silverware onto my plate and handing it back to him. "I was just lost in thought."

He grunted. "I've been lost in thought since 1920. Just make sure you find your way out before the world passes ya by."

The man shuffled away to clear the next table. Only then did I look around to find I was alone with two busy porters. Despite the silence in the hall, the thundering of voices battered my mind, and images from news reels of devastated cities and fallen soldiers flared before me like some insidious screenplay refusing to end.

———

At the beginning of the semester, Arty and I had signed up for English literature, the last required course on each of our respective curricula. We'd saved the freshman-level class for our junior year, partly to have an easy subject mixed in with our higher-level work, but mostly to ensure we had at least one class in common.

We usually arrived and sat together, but not that day. Arty was already in his seat in the front row, surrounded by professor-pleasing first years, with no room for his usual classroom companion. This was our last session before final exams, and the first time we'd sat apart.

I took a seat near the back and tried to focus on Chaucer, rather than how Arty was consciously avoiding me for the first time in two and a half years of friendship.

When class ended, I lingered while everyone cleared out, then rose and waited for him to exit. He looked up from the front of the lecture hall, locked eyes, then turned and fled through a door near the lectern. He'd have to wind through the building to exit a side door, then cross the yard to the dining hall, doubling his commute to lunch.

I got why he was mad at Janie, but I'd barely spoken throughout breakfast. They hadn't let me get a word in. It didn't make sense that he was upset with me, and the more I thought about it, the angrier I felt at the unfairness of his ire. Without thinking, I reversed course and ran down the aisle.

"Easy there," I heard the old professor call out as I passed him.

I bolted through the door into a wide hallway. Arty stood at the opposite end, reading something on a notice board. As I skidded to a halt, his eyes remained fixed on the poster.


*IT'S TIME TO ENLIST. AMERICA NEEDS YOU.*


I didn't need to read the rest of the notice to understand what he was thinking. Arty, the least athletic among us, the least prepared to do battle holding anything heavier than a pen, was seriously considering throwing himself into the war.

"Hey," I said, unsure how to even talk to my best friend.

He didn't speak. He didn't move. He just stared at the poster.

I glanced around the empty hallway, thankful at the absence of students and staff. Then I noticed a sign above the door behind us. Neat black ink formed block letters that read, *US Army and Navy Recruitment Office.*

"They already have an office?" I mumbled.

Arty finally turned. "What?"

I pointed. "To enlist. It's really happening."

Arty scrunched his nose and narrowed his eyes, as if not believing what I'd just said, then his features smoothed.

"I'm doing it this afternoon."

"Arty—"

"I have to, Will. I have to help stop him before ... before worse happens."

For the first time that day, something other than anger filled his gaze. I couldn't decide whether to be angry or hurt or scared for him, maybe all three, probably a lot more. I tried to say something, to argue or fight or beg. I tried to speak, but words evaporated before taking flight. All I could do was stare.

Then my friend, my brother, did something rare. He left the protective shell of his personal space and pulled me into a tight, if shaky, embrace. I hugged him so fiercely I thought his bones might snap. It felt like I was saying goodbye, which was silly. Even if he enlisted that afternoon, he wouldn't leave for some time. He wasn't going anywhere.

And yet, there in the halls of Harvard, I truly felt the war's touch for the first time.

The reels that played in my mind began to turn, only this time the broken bodies were no longer distant, no longer obscured. Their faces were no longer featureless.

They were all Arty.

Everywhere I looked, I saw him: his fragile frame shattered against rocks, broken in the mud, snagged against barbed wire. I saw him run into a hail of bullets and fall. Again and again.

Arty fell in my mind's eye, and I began to shake.

His grip tightened around my shoulders as my tears fell.

He didn't shake. He never shed a single tear.

He just held me as I fought waves of anguish and fear for the future we'd already lost.

⸻

At precisely twelve thirty, the three of us sat at the same table in the dining hall. Every seat was filled, and students stood shoulder to shoulder along the walls. Others sat on the floor between the tables. There was no room to walk, and little room to breathe.

The crackle of the radio was the only sound to be heard as President Roosevelt began.

> *Mr. Vice President, Mr. Speaker, Members of the Senate, and of the House of Representatives:*

> *Yesterday, December 7, 1941—a date which will live in infamy—the United States of America was suddenly and deliberately attacked by naval and air forces of the Empire of Japan.*

> *The United States was at peace with that nation and, at the solicitation of Japan, was still in conversation with its government and its emperor looking toward the maintenance of peace in the Pacific.*

> *Indeed, one hour after Japanese air squadrons had commenced bombing in the American island of Oahu, the Japanese ambassador to the United States and his colleague delivered to our Secretary of State a formal reply to a recent American message. And while this reply stated that it seemed useless to continue the existing diplomatic negotiations, it contained no threat or hint of war or of armed attack.*

*It will be recorded that the distance of Hawaii from Japan makes it obvious that the attack was deliberately planned many days or even weeks ago. During the intervening time, the Japanese government has deliberately sought to deceive the United States by false statements and expressions of hope for continued peace.*

*The attack yesterday on the Hawaiian Islands has caused severe damage to American naval and military forces. I regret to tell you that very many American lives have been lost. In addition, American ships have been reported torpedoed on the high seas between San Francisco and Honolulu.*

*Yesterday, the Japanese government also launched an attack against Malaya.*

*Last night, Japanese forces attacked Hong Kong.*

*Last night, Japanese forces attacked Guam.*

*Last night, Japanese forces attacked the Philippine Islands.*

*Last night, the Japanese attacked Wake Island.*

*And this morning, the Japanese attacked Midway Island.*

*Japan has, therefore, undertaken a surprise offensive extending throughout the Pacific area. The facts of yesterday and today speak for themselves. The people of the United States have already formed their opinions and well understand the implications to the very life and safety of our nation.*

*As Commander in Chief of the army and navy, I have directed that all measures be taken for our defense. But always will our whole nation remember the character of the onslaught against us.*

*No matter how long it may take us to overcome this premeditated invasion, the American people in their righteous might will win through to absolute victory.*

*I believe that I interpret the will of the Congress and of the people when I assert that we will not only defend ourselves to the uttermost, but will make it very certain that this form of treachery shall never again endanger us.*

*Hostilities exist. There is no blinking at the fact that our people, our territory, and our interests are in grave danger.*

*With confidence in our armed forces, with the un-bounding determination of our people, we will gain the inevitable triumph—so help us God.*

*I ask that the Congress declare that since the unprovoked and dastardly attack by Japan on Sunday, December*

*7, 1941, a state of war has existed between the United
States and the Japanese empire.*[1]

The radio clicked off, yet no one moved or spoke. A couple hundred students sat in stunned silence. Despite calls by some for America to play a more active role in the European crisis, most were content sending arms and keeping our distance. Only radicals wanted to see our boys crossing the ocean to fight in someone else's war.

But it wasn't someone else's war. Not anymore.

"God, I think I'm going to be sick," someone said at the table behind us.

The scraping of a chair against the wooden floor preceded a blur of motion as the troubled girl darted out of the hall. That simple act somehow restarted time, and students began moving and speaking once more. Quietly at first, then louder, until we could barely hear ourselves.

"I can't eat," Arty said, pushing his plate toward the table's center. "I've got to get out of here."

Janie's brow creased.

"Arty, wait up." I rose and followed our friend as he wove through the remaining students. Janie trailed close behind.

As soon as he set foot on the sidewalk, Arty sped up. There was no aimless wandering in his stride, only purpose. I could see it in the set of his shoulders and how his head no longer dipped as he walked.

"Janie, this is bad. He's made up his mind," I whispered as she joined the pursuit beside me.

---

1. Transcript of President Franklin D. Roosevelt's address to Congress the day after the Pearl Harbor attack

"Made up his mind about what? What are you talking about?"

"Look at him. Look where he's headed."

Her gaze followed where I pointed, toward the administration building where Arty and I had seen the new recruiting office.

"Oh, God, no." She nearly stumbled. "Will, we have to stop him. He'll get himself killed. He's too frail for the army."

"I know. Come on," I said, shifting our stiff walk into a jog.

A dozen strides later, my hand rested on Arty's shoulder. He shrugged it off, but stopped walking and turned to face us.

"Don't try to stop me. I know that's what you're here for. I'm doing this."

"Arty—"

"Don't Arty me, Janie. I know I'm small and weak, but I'm smarter than most of those meatheads in uniform. I can serve in my own way."

"Arty, you're going to get killed." Janie's voice trembled.

"So? What if I do? Hitler is coming for my people. He's going to kill them, Janie. All of them, if he gets his way. I know you think I'm overreacting, but you've got your head buried if you think he'll stop with wrapping barbed wire around a few neighborhoods."

"But—"

"Even if you don't care about the Jews, you have to care about America. The Japanese sank almost half our fleet, and Hitler won't stop with England or Poland. He's probably already planning to turn on the Soviets, despite whatever promise he made. We have to stop him, Janie. *I* have to be part of it."

He looked toward me.

"I get it. Really, I do. After what the Japs did, how can anybody stand by and do nothing? But is *this* the right way? Joining the army? Really? Look at us. Is it the best way for us to help?"

His eyes widened, and his head cocked. "Us?"

I hesitated, feeling the spear of Janie's glare piercing my side. I didn't dare look at her.

"Yeah, us, dummy. You didn't think I would let you do any of this alone, did you?"

His face filled with something; wonder or shock, maybe both.

"You'd really ... you'd come with me? You'd give all this up to—"

I grabbed the arm he was waving around like some freshman tour guide and pulled him into my chest.

Janie's voice cracked like a whip. "William John Shaw, what the hell are you saying? Stop this right now!"

I ignored her, speaking into Arty's ear.

"Arty, it's the three of us against the world, remember? I couldn't let you enlist without me, no more than I could let princess over there do something stupid without hounding her the whole time either."

"Princess?" she screeched.

I gave her a sideways grin and mouthed, "Sorry," then pulled Arty back, gripping his shoulders, so our eyes could meet. I held his gaze so long he started to squirm, then I glanced at Janie. "You're my best friends, both of you. No, that's wrong. You're my family, the only family I have."

I sucked in a breath, bracing myself for what I knew I had to say. "The enemy attacked our home. They didn't bomb some island a million miles away—they bombed *us*. Our whole damn country was attacked, and we can't just stand by and watch. Hell, as soon as we make that decision, we'll get drafted into some infantry unit made for catching enemy shells. They might not listen, but at least this way, we get to suggest how they use us. It'll be *our* choice to serve, not anybody else's."

Arty began to shake. I could feel it in his shoulders before I saw it in his face. When he darted forward and wrapped his spindly arms around me, I nearly tumbled over.

"Thank you, Will. Thank you."

"I can't watch this. I won't." Janie balled her fists and paced beside us. Based on the way her face scrunched up, I thought she might burst into tears at any moment. "Do what you have to, just leave me out of it. I can't—" And she ran back toward Adams House and vanished through the door.

"Three of us against the world?" Arty said as he wiped his nose on his coat sleeve.

I chuckled grimly. "She'll come around. It's a lot to take in, and I don't think she's ever lost ... well, anything, really."

"Probably right." He nodded slowly. His eyes lifted to mine again. "Are you sure about this, Will? You don't have to. Just knowing you support me is—"

"Shut up and walk before I change my mind." I mussed his hair like he was ten.

He grinned like it too.

Then I wrapped my arm around his shoulder and we strode across the slushy yard.

# Chapter Five

# Will

"Don't argue with me, Will. My parents will like you just fine." Arty stood, arms crossed, glaring down as I fidgeted with a book I hadn't opened all morning.

"You're sure? I mean, they don't even know I'm coming, and it's Christmas."

"Hanukkah, actually."

I blew out a sigh. "See, I can't even get that right. They'll think I'm some kind of Jew-hater trying to force them to sing carols or something."

Arty snorted. "You're an idiot. They won't think you're a Jew-hater, because you're my best friend—and I'm a Jew. Unless ... *do* you hate me?"

His voice was tinged with such pain I couldn't help but look up. The smirk on his smart-ass face told me I'd been had.

"Fine. But it's all your fault if they get mad and throw things."

His eyes rolled. "My parents don't throw things; although, after spending a week with you—"

"Ha ha. When did you get so funny?" I stood and shoved him playfully, then turned to finish packing.

"I've always been funny, though I prefer the term clever. It has so many more layers."

"Right. That's you, layered like a cake. Nothing but sugar on top of sugar, sweet cheeks."

He snatched a T-shirt from the bed and hurled it at me.

"Hey! That was folded all nice," I protested.

"Not sure how nice it was. You need more practice." He grinned as he turned. "I'll be downstairs. Driver should be here any time now."

I nodded as the door clicked behind him.

Our freshman year, a few months after my parents died, Arty and Janie left campus to spend the holiday break with their families, leaving me on campus with little more than memories and a racing mind to keep me company. I lost track of the hours as I stared out my window into the wintry yard. Tears fell faster than the Cambridge snow.

When they returned, I was more of a mess than I'd been before the recess. I could barely function, much less focus on the demands of classwork. I'd stopped working out and running, was barely eating, and sleep proved more elusive than a cloudless sky—and those were rare enough in winter. Janie scared the wits out of everyone when she saw how pale and gaunt I'd become in such a short time, dropping her bags and racing to embrace me. Arty's face told the same tale as he scrutinized the set of my eyes. I remember the word he used for them. It chilled me.

Vacant.

Somehow—and I'll never know how—those two got me through that semester.

Janie was more attentive than a mother with newborn pups, coddling and nursing me back to health, practically shoving food in my mouth when I claimed to be full. Arty never went on runs with me, but he did bang on my door each morning until I rose and took my morning laps around campus.

Gradually, I became whole again—or at least less broken.

The terrible twosome, as I began calling them during their conspiratorial period, made a secret pact that I would never be allowed to stay on campus over a break again. I enrolled in classes over the summer of our sophomore year, but when the holiday break rolled around, Janie held true to their promise, dragging me home to spend Christmas with her parents and two younger brothers in New Hampshire. I suppose it was a good thing. Her parents were stiff and aloof, but her brothers latched on, wrestling and playing ball with me for hours in their sprawling yard.

I knew the trip was helpful. My brain understood how much better it was than spending another season alone on campus. But something about the simplicity of that week made my heart ache for my parents all the more. I found myself jealous; not of her family's opulent wealth—I'd inherited enough to never want for anything. No, I was jealous of the richness of Janie's family, of the love that flowed so easily between her and her brothers—even with her parents, as stuffy as they were—and of their time together. I was envious for what I had lost and would never have again.

When Arty and I left the recruiting office that cold December day in our junior year, a recruiter took our paperwork, shook our hands, and told us to report to his office in January. My mind whirled as it tried to imagine what service would be like during a war we'd still yet to fully comprehend.

The holidays were nowhere in my thoughts. Until Arty claimed it was "his year" to host.

I'd never felt like such an orphan, needing to be claimed, to be hosted.

I'd also never been so grateful to have those two in my life.

"Hanukkah? Huh," I said into my empty dorm room as I shoved the last of my clothes into my pack. "What does one do for Hanukkah?"

My parents hadn't been especially religious, claiming to be Christian but never once darkening the doorway to a church. The only thing I knew about Jews was that they had a knack for cold cuts; at least, the old guy who ran the deli across from campus did, and I was pretty sure he was Jewish.

I felt a little like I was visiting a foreign land and hadn't bothered to study the language.

"Come on, the driver should be waiting," Arty said as I entered the lobby of our dorm.

True to his word, the car and driver Arty's dad had sent to retrieve us was waiting in the driveway. The black-capped man nodded, then took our bags as we piled into the back seat. A quick twenty minutes later, the car slowed as we passed through a wrought-iron gate toward a federal-style mansion I later learned was called a "farmhouse."

"Holy shit, Arty," I muttered as I peered out the window at the home that towered before us.

He grunted. "It's just a house."

I turned to catch a flush before it faded from his cheeks.

"You have a misplaced definition of the word *house*. How old is this place?"

Arty's nerd trigger had been pulled. "It was built in 1809 and is on the National Register of Historic Places and Landmarks. We know it was used during the Civil War as a waystation for the Underground Railroad, and legend claims ten presidents have slept under our roof."

"Holy shit."

"You said that already," he said, popping his door open and darting out.

We'd been so consumed with war news and final exams that I hadn't realized how long it had been since I'd seen Arty relax and enjoy himself. I'd certainly never expected that showing off his mansion of a home would make his whole face light up. Unlike the estate before us, humility was one of Arty's most endearing qualities. I couldn't hide a smile as he raced up the stone staircase toward the deeply stained double doors.

I only made it halfway to the staircase when the doors opened and Dina Ableman, a woman of unguessable age and indescribable beauty, flew out, her Rita Hayworth hair somehow never moving as she rushed forward. Her emerald eyes met mine then fixed on Arty.

"Arthur!" she squealed. Her voice was as melodic and youthful as any of the girls back at Harvard.

She grabbed her son by the shoulders and wrapped him in a smothering embrace, and began kissing his cheeks and neck like a mother bird pecking a newly hatched chick. "I've missed you so much, *bubbleleh*."

Arty had fallen helplessly into her arms until that last word, which made him squirm and glance back at me. I made a mental note to ask what she'd called him.

"And you must be William," she said, her raptor-like gaze snapping to me only a second before she bounded down the stairs to wrap me in her viselike grip.

"Arty, help," I squeaked out, earning a deep-throated laugh from his mother that vibrated through me.

"Mama, please," Arty begged.

"Respect your mother, bubblegum," I teased.

Arty's mouth dropped open.

"Bubblegum!" Dina nearly doubled over laughing. "He called you bubblegum, my *bubbleleh*!"

"Yeah, I heard," Arty said dryly.

She stepped back and patted my shoulder. "I like this one. So handsome and witty."

She winked at me, then climbed the steps and draped one arm over her son's shoulders. As they crossed the doorframe without slowing, they reached up and touched an elegant box nailed to the frame. The gesture was so routine, so comfortable, it looked as if their hands rose without any thought. As I reached the door, I looked up to find the box engraved with symbols I didn't recognize. I traced my fingers over them, wondering at the beautiful craftsmanship of the piece.

"You honor Him, and us," a voice like thunder rumbled.

A tall man in a sharp pinstripe suit with perfectly slicked black hair stared as I entered his home. I stretched out a hand. "Hi, Mr. Ableman. I'm Will."

If his voice was iron, Arty's dad's grip was steel. I nearly flinched.

"Welcome to our home, son. It's good to finally meet the boy Arthur has said so much about."

I withered beneath his gaze. "Um, okay. It's nice to meet you too."

He finally released my hand, allowing the blood to return. "Hungry? I think Edna has lunch ready."

"I'm starving."

He gripped my arm and led me past a stairway with a marble handrail and ornately carved balusters. Richly stained panels covered each wall, like some lord's castle in Elizabethan England. If Mr. Ableman hadn't been ushering me through, I would've lost myself in all the art and delicate porcelain displayed throughout. I knew Arty's family was rich, but had no idea they were on par with Janie's regal household.

Reading my mind, Mr. Ableman leaned down and whispered, "Don't let all this get to you. I'm in politics, and appearances matter. We're just a normal family."

I wasn't sure why, but I believed him, and something in his tone warmed my chest.

We rounded a corner, and a long, modern kitchen that stood in stark contrast with the colonial decor stretched before us. Arty was pulling up a stool to an island that divided the cooking area from a round table large enough for six to sit comfortably. Arty had just settled onto a stool beside two boys. A short, round woman stood over a stove littered with bubbling pots. Savory aromas I couldn't identify flooded my senses, making my stomach roar in anticipation.

Mr. Ableman chuckled. "Why don't you go hang out with the boys while Edna finishes up?"

"Won't be but a minute, young man. Go wash up. I told the others to do the same, Mr. A, but I think they need a firmer hand," the woman said with a half-smirk.

"Boys!" he barked, and three heads snapped up. "Hands, now."

The two youngsters scurried from the bar. Arty, a step behind, stopped in the doorway. "Come on, Will, before he learns to order you around too."

Mr. Ableman clapped me on the shoulder, more to urge me on than to be companionable. I took the hint and joined my friend.

In the washroom, I met Arty's two younger brothers. Albert, at fourteen, was the spitting image of his father, with slicked-back black hair and piercing eyes. There was a softness to twelve-year-old Adam, an aura that reminded me of his mother. Where his brother rushed through his handwashing, almost angrily scrubbing the dirt away, Adam was gentle and seemed to enjoy the simplicity of the task. The more I watched the pair, the more I saw a little of each in Arty. He could carry Albert's impatient spontaneity, but could just as quickly revert into himself and lose a day in quiet reflection.

"Want to play football after we eat?" Albert asked as he punished his hands with a towel.

"Uh, sure," I said, glancing at Arty.

Albert laughed. "Don't bother asking egghead over there. He'll have his nose stuck in a book all afternoon."

"Maybe I need to remind you who the older brother is," Arty taunted.

Albert, who was already more muscular than Arty, puffed out his chest and squared off with his brother. "Bring it, big brother."

Adam kept quiet and never looked at his brothers, rubbing his hands until I was sure they'd become raw.

"All of you have names that start with A?" was all I could think to ask to distract them before boyish idiocy got the best of them. All three heads turned toward me with the same stupefied stare.

"You just got that? Arty, maybe your friend's not so smart after all," Albert quipped.

Arty's tension fled with a laugh. "I've been telling him that for two and a half years. He just doesn't listen."

"Wow. They're calling you a dummy," Adam chimed in.

I could feel my ears turning red.

"I see how you three are. Gang up on the new guy." I gave Albert a soft punch on the shoulder. "We'll see how tough you are after lunch."

"Ooh," Adam crooned.

Arty grinned and crossed his arms.

Albert's eyes widened, then narrowed. "You're on, college boy."

Our second day was December 24, 1941, the beginning of Hanukkah. While Albert and I played ball outside during sunlight hours, Arty, Adam, and their mother spent the day spreading holiday cheer throughout the house. I'd never experienced a Jewish celebration, but when we walked into the house surrounded by more candles than I'd ever seen in one place, I knew the Festival of Lights was well represented in this home.

That night, the Ablemans and I gathered around the massive bay window at the front of their home and stacked our hands like some football team before a game as Dina held a long match to the first candle of the menorah. Arty and Albert groused, but Dina insisted the family's tradition be upheld. I would've been content to savor my friend's discomfort from the side of the room, but Dina yanked my wrist and forced me onto the pile. Adam giggled as I squirmed to fit into the pack while keeping my hand atop theirs.

As Mr. A spoke in guttural tones, Arty whispered English in my ear:

*Blessed are You, our God, Ruler of the Universe, who made us holy through Your commandments, and commanded us to kindle the Hanukkah lights.*

When the prayer was complete and the candle lit, I felt everyone's hands offer a gentle squeeze. Dina's eyes glittered with moisture as she looked from one son to the next, then to me. My heart was at once filled at the beautiful oneness of the gesture, and utterly bereft at how I would never again feel that with my own family.

Except for Arty, I was a stranger to these people, yet they made me part of their most cherished family customs. I was suddenly overcome, and my gaze fled to the safety of the flickering light.

When the moment passed, the boys and Mr. A stormed the dining room, leaving Dina and me staring at the flame as it danced. Her voice was soft when she spoke. "You must miss your parents this time of year."

It was a statement, not a question.

"How ..." I was stunned. "I ... Yes, I do."

Her lips pressed together, and her eyes softened. "It's okay, Will. Grieving is how we know the depth of our love. I know the pain is terrible, but it opens a window into our hearts. We only have to look inside to see beauty amid the sadness."

"Beauty?" Something surged in my chest, and I couldn't decide whether I felt more comforted or angry.

"I'm sorry. I read too much poetry. All I meant was that I see how much you loved your parents. It's written all over your face. I see how their loss still pains you, and how our family must remind you of ... of everything. I just want you to know I understand, and it's okay to be sad, even at a time of celebration."

Every emotion I knew clogged my throat.

"Join us when you're ready." She patted my arm and left me alone with the flame.

Three candles burned. The farmhouse no longer felt like foreign territory. The family no longer felt like strangers.

It's funny how quickly things can change.

Arty and I sat at the table by the kitchen eating leftover fried something-or-other, the last remnants of the prior night's dinner. I didn't fully understand the season's obsession with oil, but the food they fried in celebration was everything.

Over the course of the past week, Arty and I had sat through more rounds of dreidel than I could count. When Dina had originally brought out the foil-covered chocolate coins, Albert had groaned. He was at the age of craving adulthood, and even childhood passions now made him grimace. Only when Mr. A pulled out a pocketful of real coins did he join his brother in the furious spinning.

My fears of time spent under the Ablemans' roof had been unfounded, almost as woefully incorrect as the assumptions I'd made that Jewish families were so vastly different from others. Their faith marked them uniquely, but the familial bonds that ran through the core of families of every religion were just as strong in theirs. Their kindness and compassion, their love and respect, the brilliance of their hearts, it all burned as brightly as the candles in their window.

Arty's mom had been right about missing my mom and dad. It was impossible to see this family and not think of my own. And yet, as the days passed, the ache that would never fully dissipate was joined by a joy and warmth I hadn't expected.

Dina hummed as she and Edna whirled about the kitchen, two magicians engrossed in conjuring something new and marvelous. Albert and Adam had left early that morning to spend the day with the children who lived two houses down.

"I've been meaning to ask, do you speak Hebrew too?"

Arty shrugged. "Some. We all do, at least enough to recite prayers and sound out the text."

"Huh. Guess it's like Catholics and Latin."

He rolled his eyes. "Not the same, but an okay comparison for an ape like you."

"Ape? You wound me, good sir." I held my hands to my chest as though stabbed.

"You're such a schmuck."

"Wow, going for the fancy insults," I teased.

"You know what that means, right?"

I cocked a brow. "Didn't realize it had a meaning. I thought it was just a made-up slur."

His grin was wolfish. "It's one of the Yiddish words for dick. Putz means the same thing."

"Jews have two ways to call someone a dick?" I think I was impressed.

He grunted. "We have two ways to say almost everything. Yiddish is a mashup of German, Hebrew, and a bunch of Slavic languages, kind of like how English grabs words from other languages."

We ate and watched Dina and Edna work, then I ventured into deeper waters.

"Have you told them about enlisting?" I whispered.

Arty's glare nearly cut me.

"Shh. No ... not yet."

"Are you waiting until we're on a ship headed to Europe? Arty, you have to—"

"I know that, but this is Hanukkah. Can we let them have the holiday before ruining everything?"

As much as I hated to admit it, he had a point. Telling his parents now would cast a pall over the holidays that even his younger brothers couldn't miss.

"Fine, but we need to tell them before we leave."

"I will. Just ... not yet," he said, a little too loudly.

"Not yet?" Mr. A's baritone filled the kitchen. My back was to the side door that led to the formal dining room, and I hadn't seen him enter. Arty, unable to keep a secret, stabbed me with another gaze.

"Nothing, Papa," he said without conviction.

Mr. A grabbed a chair and dropped into it.

"Why don't I believe you, son?"

Arty's eyes fell, and I knew we were screwed.

"Papa, please," he pleaded. "Can we just enjoy—"

Mr. A's eyes focused like the lens on a camera, zooming in on his son until there was nowhere for him to hide. "No. I think this is the perfect time to tell me what you've been avoiding."

*Damn, he knows,* I thought.

Arty still didn't get it.

"Papa, please—"

Mr. A called toward the kitchen. "Dina, would you come join us? Arty has news to share. I believe Will does as well."

*Shit, this is bad.*

Once Dina was settled snugly beneath her husband's arm, he turned back toward Arty.

"Alright, son, you have our attention. Out with it."

Arty wiped a bead of sweat from his brow and began fidgeting with his fingers. His gaze darted to me, then to his mother, then back to his fingers.

He opened his mouth, then closed it, then opened it again.

Still, nothing came out.

The pitiful, pleading look he gave me nearly broke my heart.

"We enlisted," I blurted out.

The Ablemans didn't flinch. Their eyes didn't widen, and their mouths remained closed, lips relaxed. They didn't speak, simply waited and watched Arty.

*They knew the whole time. How had they known?*

Then my eyes darted around at their home and I remembered Mr. A's comment about being in politics. That sounded like an understatement at the time, but I had no idea how large of one it had been.

*He must keep tabs on Arty.*

Finally, after an interminable span that might've required lighting more candles, Arty looked up and met their gaze. I didn't know what

I expected: anger, fear, frustration? Maybe resentment or a sense of helplessness? That's what every parent felt in moments like these, wasn't it?

But there was none of that on their faces.

I studied them, waited for a crack, some hint of their feelings, but they were stone, monuments to the people who'd sat there moments before.

"I had to, Mama. Our people ... It's terrible over there. People don't get how bad it is, and I couldn't just go to college and live a normal life like it's not happening. I couldn't just do nothing."

Dina finally cracked, reaching across the table and taking Arty's hands in hers. "I'm so proud of you, Arthur. So very proud."

His eyes widened as he stared into hers, then he looked to his father.

Mr. A nodded. "We're both proud, Arty. I know men twice your age who show half your courage and conviction." Then he turned toward me. "You too, Will. I know you didn't want to enlist, but you refused to let our son do it alone. That tells me everything I need to know about you, young man."

Now it was my turn to freeze while my mouth hung open. He'd known *everything*, and he wasn't angry. He was ... proud?

Before I could begin to process the scene, Dina moved to kneel beside her son, taking him in her arms.

"Arty, I love you more than anything in this world, and yes, I'm terrified of what you've done and what you will face. I can't bear the thought of losing my baby boy. But"—she wiped a tear from his cheek—"you wouldn't be my *bubbleleh* if you watched others suffer and stood by. You're doing what is right, and I have never been prouder."

And that did it. Arty's last defense failed, and he began to sob into his mother's shoulder. I felt my heart welling up and tumbling down my face as Mr. A dropped to his knees and joined in the family embrace.

I couldn't tear my eyes away. Through a curtain of tears, I watched as a blessing was given and received with undying love.

"Does Albert know? Adam?" Arty's frail voice asked.

"No," Dina said softly. "We thought you should tell them before you ... before you leave."

Something shifted in Arty's eyes, as though a piece of a puzzle clicked into place, and he looked to his father. "How did you know? We haven't told anyone."

Mr. A grunted as he rose, then chuckled wryly. "I might be the most powerful person in Boston, outside of the mayor, and I work with the President of the United States. How could I *not* know my oldest son had enlisted?"

Arty nodded, as if the answer made perfect sense.

I still hadn't closed my gaping mouth.

Looking back on that day, I'll never know which surprised me more: that Arty's dad was so connected and knew that we'd enlisted, or the unconditional acceptance and love with which they greeted their son's decision, one that would cost so many families the ultimate price. This family—this *Jewish* family—could have easily been frustrated or hostile toward an America who'd refused to see the reality of wartime Europe, and yet, I felt none of that from them. They were proud of their son and their country. Sure, I overheard more than one conversation where they expressed fear of antisemitism's reach spreading across the globe, and even greater fear for the safety of their Jewish family in Europe, but I never heard a word of anger toward their fellow countrymen. They never spoke of American isolationism or indifference. Despite their obvious wealth, Mr. A seemed to understand how most in the US had suffered through the Depression, and how they simply wanted to enjoy life for a moment.

I may have learned more real, honest lessons in those days in the farmhouse than in all my time at Harvard.

# Chapter Six

# **Will**

S aying goodbye carried a heavy significance, especially for Arty and his parents. We understood the weight of our decision to enlist, but for parents to hug their son for what could be the last time was beyond description. So it surprised me when I felt a thrill setting foot on campus again.

Nothing had changed, not really. Harvard was Harvard. It would always be Harvard.

But we had changed.

Our futures would soon be laid before us, and we were both eager to learn what cards fate would deal.

"I bet they send you into the infantry," Arty said.

"Why would you think that? Do I look like a good target?"

He shoved my shoulder. "Yeah, right. Just flap your arms at the Germans and yell, 'Over here! Shoot the big dummy.'"

"Ouch."

"Nah. They need officers, and the infantry makes sense. You're strong and reasonably smart. I've never understood why, but people seem to like you. You'd make a decent officer."

"Thanks. I think."

He nodded like he hadn't just backslapped me.

"Where will you end up?" I asked.

He shrugged. "No idea. I don't want to be shoved in some office doing paperwork, but the thought of seeing real combat terrifies me. I'm not a big brute like you."

"God, all the compliments today. You're amazing."

He laughed. "I know. It's my charm, right?"

"Charm of an adder, maybe."

A group of men in navy uniforms walking in the opposite direction stopped before us. One stepped forward and squinted in the sunlight at a piece of paper in his hand.

"Hey, can you guys point us toward the Geographical Institute?"

Arty and I shared a quick glance. Nobody went to Geo; at least, nobody we knew.

"Yeah, it's all the way over there." I pointed across campus. "In the northeastern corner, a couple buildings down from Andover Hall."

"You guys new?" Arty asked.

"Yeah. Just got here this morning. I'm Ben Meyers." He pointed behind him. "That's Frank, August, and Thomas."

While Arty peppered Ben with questions, Frank and August looked at the surrounding buildings, taking in their new home for the first time, but Thomas eyed me. Unlike the others, his tie was slightly askew, and the knot was loose. Short, almost black hair poked out the sides of his cap as chestnut eyes gripped my gaze. I glanced down, then peeked back up to find a tiny quirk formed at one corner of his mouth.

"Come on, guys. We're already late," Ben said.

They turned, and Mr. Chestnut gave me one last smirk before heading away with his fellow soldiers.

"What was that all about?"

Arty had clearly missed the whole glaring and smirking. "They're sending more uniforms here for training. From what that guy said, Harvard's student body will be mostly soldiers by next year. Navy's doing it too, but mostly it's army guys."

"Huh," I said.

The whole walk to the dorm, I struggled to wrap my head around what had just happened. I hadn't even spoken to this Thomas guy, but something in his gaze unsettled me. What made less sense than his cocky smirk was how my brain wouldn't let it go.

"... the recruiting office?"

"What?"

"Are you listening? You look like you're lost." Arty looked annoyed. "I asked when you wanted to head to the recruiting office. We're supposed to check in. Maybe we'll get some idea of a timeline and our assignment."

The question struck me dumb. I'd been so caught up with the Ableman family and getting settled back into our comfortable routine that I'd forgotten how we'd likely never finish our junior year. The army would decide our futures now; likely already had.

"Shit, Arty, I can't believe ... Now I won't be able to think about anything else until we go. Want to just head there now?"

He stopped walking and stared at the sidewalk. "I guess."

I rested a palm on his shoulder. "It'll be alright. We're in it together, remember?"

He looked up slowly. "You don't know that. They could send you overseas and shove me in a broom closet—or the other way around. Odds are that we won't be anywhere near each other for a really long time."

I hadn't really thought any of this through. He was right. "Jesus."

"Not really our guy, but I agree with the sentiment."

I barked a laugh. "You're impossible, bubblegum."

"I really hate you." He grinned weakly. "Let's get this over with before I lose my nerve."

While we'd been spinning for gold over the holiday break, the military had been hard at work on campus. To our surprise, the recruiting office had been expanded from an office the size of a large coat closet to consume half the floor. Classes weren't scheduled to begin for another two days, but students were already returning, and a long line snaked down the hallway and out the door. The queue led into a door now labeled *Enlist Here*. A dozen paces down the hall, Arty found another whose carefully lettered sign read *Processing*.

"Think this is us?" Arty asked, pointing to the sign.

"No clue, but I'd rather not wait in that line if we don't have to. Let's go in and ask."

He hesitated, then turned the knob and walked in.

A college-age girl with tightly woven hair looked up from behind a small desk. "Hello, boys. Here for processing?"

"Um, maybe. We're not sure," Arty said, earning a bright smile.

"Did you enlist before the break?" she asked.

I nodded. "Yes, both of us. We were told to check in when we returned for second half."

"You're in the right place." She pulled out a large binder and flipped it open. "What are your names?"

"Arthur Ableman."

"William Shaw."

She ran her finger down a sheet filled with hand-printed names until she stopped and looked up.

"Arthur?"

Arty raised his hand, earning another smile.

"You can go in there." She pointed to the door to the right of her desk, then began scrolling again, stopping at my name. Her brows rose. "William, why don't you have a seat? I need to check on something."

Arty gave me a pleading look as he crossed the office and stood with a hand on the handle of the door she'd indicated, while I backed up a step and sat in the only chair not behind the desk.

"Wish me luck," he mouthed.

I held up a thumb. "You've got this."

And through he went.

The girl disappeared through the door on her left, returning a moment later.

"Will, the major will see you in here."

I was no expert on the army, but living on campus with hundreds of soldiers, I was bound to pick up a few things. A major meeting with a raw recruit for intake—or whatever they called it—seemed like a bit of overkill, but I didn't really have a choice, so I rose and entered the door she was holding open.

"Come in, son." A lean man with thick spectacles stood and stretched out a hand. Unsure of proper protocol, I stepped forward and shook it. "You go by Will, right?"

I tried to keep the growing alarm from my face. "Yes, sir." "Good, very good. Have a seat." He motioned to a comfortable-looking leather couch across from his modest desk. "Would you like anything to drink?"

For the first time since we'd enlisted, nerves flared throughout my body, and a bead of sweat trickled down my forehead. "Uh, no, sir. I'm fine. Thank you though."

"That's fine." He smiled and nodded, then snatched a folder, rounded his desk, and sat on the opposite end of the couch. He riffled through a few papers in the folder, then handed one to me.

"This is your class schedule for second half."

I read:

*English A-1$^2$English Composition (Messrs. Gordon, Bailey, and McCreary)*

*History 55$^2$History of Russia (Associate. Professor Karpovich)*

*Economics 11b$^2$The Economics of Socialism (Dr. PM Sweezy)*

*Economics 62b2Industrial Organization and Control (Professor Mason)*

*American LiteratureGeneral Topics (Professor TBD)*

*Political Science 3$^2$General Topics (Professor TBD)*

*Anatomy 31$^2$General Topics (Professor TBD)*

*Government 4Elements of International Law (Associate Professor PS Wild)*

"Sir?"

"Yes, Will?""I didn't sign up for some of these courses. I'm not even sure Harvard teaches American literature. I've definitely never been in the building where they would."

He grinned. "They do now. Those courses were assigned to you based on your future participation in a select government program."

I looked from the paper to the major. "I'm sorry, sir. I'm lost. I enlisted in the army. Arty and I both did, to help ... I mean, to fight."

He leaned back. "And we appreciate that, son, but my job is to put people in the right place to make the greatest impact. I believe you will best help America in this new program."

I glanced back at the course list, hoping for some hint I'd missed.

"I'm sorry, but I can't tell you any more than that." He rose and returned to sit behind his desk.

I had a thousand questions, but my voice refused to work.

"I have two orders for you, and it's extremely important you follow each. Do you understand?"

"Yes, sir."

He held up a finger. "First, attend to your studies like your life depends on them. It very well may." He raised another finger. "Second, tell no one about this conversation or the program. Make no mention of your ... unusual courses. You signed up for everything on that list on your own. Those were your selections, and you are excited to have received each of them."

"Sir—"

"Do not—I repeat—do not speak a word about the program or meeting with a major to anyone. If asked, you met with a staff sergeant who deferred your service until after your graduation in June 1942. You were given an educational exception to both enlistment and the draft, something you did not ask for, but are happy you received. Not a word about me or the program. Got it?"

"Uh, sure. I mean, yes, sir. I don't even know what I would be telling them."

His lips formed a tight line. "Exactly. So there's no need to even bring up the program at all. Understand?"

"No, sir. I don't understand *any* of this."

"Excellent. Dismissed." And he pointed to the door.

I stood, reread my course assignments as if they might've changed while in my hands, then back to the major. His finger still pointed toward the door, though his attention now rested with papers on his desk. I really had been dismissed.

When I walked back into the reception area, Arty was seated in the lone chair, head in his hands.

"Arty, you okay?" I asked.

I barely recognized his eyes when he looked up. They weren't wet or ringed with red, but there was a coldness in them I'd never seen before.

"Fine. Can we just go?" He stood and left without waiting for a reply.

# Chapter Seven

# Will

Arty didn't walk back to the dorm. He stalked. I'd never seen him so angry.

"What did they say?"

He glared back at me. "I report in twenty days."

I nearly stumbled.

"That's ... what you wanted, isn't it?" I barely knew what to say. My best friend was headed to war. I suddenly felt as helpless as I had when I was told my parents had died. There was no turning back, no changing course. The future was fixed.

"Yeah, but no," he snapped, storming into our building and heading down the hall toward our room.

Helplessness became confusion.

"Arty, you're not making sense. Talk to me."

He wheeled and stabbed a finger in my chest. I was so startled at the gentle boy's ferocity that I nearly fell backward.

"I report to goddammed Loeb House."

"Loeb? Where President Conant lives?"

He nodded like it made sense, then turned and entered our room. I found him lying on his back on his bed.

"Arty, why would you report to Harvard's president? Did they say what you're assigned to do?" I sat on the foot of his bed and watched his eyes fix on the crack crawling across our ceiling.

"Conant promised the government that some of our professors would start doing research for the war. I've been assigned to help one of them."

I finally breathed again. "Arty, that's great! Why are you so upset?"

"Because I wanted to *fight* the fucking bastards!" he shouted.

"Yeah, but—"

"You don't get it. Hitler's walling off the Jews. He did it in Poland, and he'll do it everywhere he can. People are scared, Will. They're trying to get out before he starts killing them."

"Killing them? You think he'd do that? There's got to be millions of Jews in Europe."

"Yeah, and they're stuck there behind his damned walls. The things he's saying in his speeches . . . it's getting so much worse."

I didn't know what to say. Arty and I had talked about the war, and I'd even overheard his parents talking about relatives in Poland and France, but I hadn't realized how deep his fear ran, how deeply it ran with all his people.

He took a few calming breaths, then glanced up.

"On top of all that, I'm sick of everybody telling me what I *can't* do, assuming I'm weak or whatever. You're strong and athletic. Nobody ever doubts *you* can do anything. I'm just a scrawny nothing who isn't even good enough to shoot Nazis."

Damn. I hadn't seen any of this coming.

"Arty, you're the smartest guy I know. If they have you helping with some secret research, there's gotta be a reason. Hell, I couldn't do any of that."

He rolled his eyes.

"Don't do that. Don't sell yourself short." Something in his casual dismissal had pissed me off. "You're not just my best friend, you're the best person I know. If they assigned you to help a professor build bombs, then those are going to be the best damn bombs ever made. You'll probably kill more Nazis than anybody in uniform."

His eyes finally left the ceiling as he turned his head and stared at me.

"I hadn't thought about it that way."

"They might even name a bomb after you, at least let you paint your name on it before it gets dropped."

He tried to fight a grin, but I saw his shell cracking.

"Arty the bombardier. The bombster. Bomb man."

"Those are *terrible* names."

"The Fourth Musketeer!"

"God, you're an idiot." He laughed and threw his pillow at me then moved to the end of the bed and sat beside me. "Where are they sending you?"

I tensed.

Arty straightened, and his glare intensified. "What is it?"

My eyes refused to meet his.

"Will, what?"

"I ... uh ... they want me to—"

"Jesus Christ, just say it!"

A nervous laugh escaped. "Jesus Christ? Thought he wasn't your guy."

He smacked me with the pillow again. "Tell me or I'll get violent, and I'm bombastic now, remember?"

I groaned. "Did you just crack a joke? You're going to be unbearable now. I should've just let you sulk."

"No getting sidetracked. What's your assignment?"

"They want me to finish my degree."

"Wait, what?" He cocked his head. "Your *college* degree? At Harvard? As in just stay here and keep going to class at Harvard?"

I nodded, still unable to look at him. The lie wasn't really a lie yet, but I could feel it gnawing around the edges like a starved rat.

"When do you report?"

I hesitated. "After graduation."

"What? Like *graduation* graduation? The one a year and a half away?" His voice had risen an octave and was threatening the integrity of our windows.

I nodded.

He leapt to his feet and began pacing. I could practically see his mind spinning.

"What the actual fuck?"

Arty never cursed.

I wanted to laugh or tease him, do *anything* other than continue this conversation.

And I didn't want to lie, not to Arty.

"What are you going to be doing after graduation?"

I sucked in a breath. Here was the tricky part. I could've made up a story, but keeping those details straight for over a year seemed almost as daunting as donning a uniform. So, I decided to stick with the truth; at least, the truth I could tell him. "I'm not sure. It sounded like they were still figuring it out."

I could hear my watch ticking in the silence that followed. A minute, maybe a year passed before he spoke again.

"Why?"

And there it was. The question for which I had no answer. I didn't even have a good lie to tell for that one, to Arty or myself.

I met his gaze and shrugged.

"Why are they not putting you in uniform and shipping you off like everyone else? You're fit for service. Hell, you'd make a great soldier. Why are they keeping you in college?" He was thinking aloud more than asking me. That's how Arty puzzled things out, so I kept quiet and let him continue his mental gymnastics.

Then he gave me a look that said *I asked you a question.*

*Shit.*

"Honestly, I don't know. The m ... man ... didn't tell me."

I blew out a sigh. I'd almost violated my orders less than an hour after receiving them. It didn't matter that they made no sense. Orders were orders.

Arty never missed anything. His gaze morphed into a glare the second I stumbled, but he had the good grace not to ask why I'd faltered. That day would come, but I'd have time to prepare an answer.

I held up my hands in surrender. "That's all I know. I swear."

His gaze hardened and his lips pursed, but he still didn't speak.

"Do you have to wear a uniform?" I asked, desperate to shift the focus back to him.

He rolled his eyes again.

"Yes. I'll become a uniformed soldier. Though, if my guess is right, most of my time will probably be spent in a lab coat."

"That's pretty cool, right?" I was so close to sweating then. *Please don't notice.*

He crossed his arms. "It's obvious you're nervous. You're hiding something. I'll pick it out of you, but stop worrying. I get it. We're in the army now."

I nodded, but knew even that statement to be a lie. I wasn't in anything. Yet.

# Chapter Eight

# **Will**

H arvard was abuzz as the second half began. Even without the ROTC and army units running drills in the courtyard, the sidewalks were crammed with students strolling about. When the men in uniform were present, the grassy field felt oddly claustrophobic.

"Come on," Arty griped. "We can't be late on the first day of a term. You know how the professors are, and we have Gordon this morning."

I finished lacing my shoe and stood from the step of our residence hall. "So?"

"So? Talk to anybody who's sat through his lectures and you won't be dragging your butt. Besides, English comp is always packed. If we're late, we'll have to sit in the front row."

That was all the motivation I needed. The last thing either of us enjoyed was sitting in the crosshairs of a professor, especially one on a mission. I fell in beside him as we walked quickly across the yard.

For our next classes, Arty and I had split up. I scanned my sheet to find American Lit next in my day's rotation. That was one of the courses assigned to me by the major, though I couldn't understand why they cared if a soldier could quote Mark Twain.

"Huh," I said to myself as I read where the class was to be held. "The Geographical Institute? A science building for American Lit? That's weird."

Utterly perplexed and more than a little curious, I turned toward the northeastern corner of campus and began my trek to the farthest reach of Harvard. Ten minutes later, the warmth of the building seeped into my bones as I scanned room numbers on doors until I found the classroom. Ten other students, each wearing an army or navy uniform, sat with erect backs and eyes forward as a man in navy attire seated behind a large metal desk cleared his throat. I tried to slip in unnoticed, but the door groaned and eleven pairs of eyes turned toward me.

"Will, come in. Take a seat there." The man pointed to a seat in the front row. "That will be the last time you are late, correct?"

"Uh, yes, sir," I said as I made my way to the indicated chair.

The man cleared his throat again, stood, and rounded the desk to pace before us as he spoke. His voice was clear, his tone crisp and precise.

"Gentlemen, I am Lieutenant Willard. For anyone outside this room, we are discussing famous American authors. Each of you will be given a list of writers and their most famous works. The entirety of your American Literature course will involve memorizing those names and titles. Don't waste your time actually reading the books."

The men seated around me chuckled.

"What we do in this room is classified. Those of you in uniform understand what that means." His gaze snapped to me, a dagger stabbing through the air. "Will, let me make this simple. Share a word of this class outside the walls, and you will either be sent to the front or to jail. I really don't care which. Understand?"

I couldn't breathe, much less respond, so I nodded.

"Good." He turned and leaned against his desk in the only casual gesture I'd seen from the man. "For the rest of this term, you will learn everything there is to know about military radio communications. You will learn the arts of electronics detection and evasion, as well as become proficient in Morse code. When you leave this room for the final time, you will be able to tear apart and reassemble radios and transmitters of various sizes and configurations. We will spend some time discussing secret codes and code breaking, but only as an introduction to future training.

"I expect two things from each of you. First, be on time. You navy boys like to say, 'If you're on time, you're late,' and you're absolutely right. It might be the only thing the navy got right."

A chorus of groans was beaten down by a far louder catcall of "hoo-ha!"

Willard grinned as the good-natured inter-service rivalry rang against the classroom's wooden walls. I glanced about to find the army men smiling and giving each other fist bumps.

Two sailors sat a row behind me. I'd been in such a rush to take my seat that I hadn't really looked at my classmates. One of the navy guys was the same man I'd seen earlier in the week, with the group who'd asked for directions to this very building.

Thomas was in my class, the one that didn't officially exist.

The corners of his eyes turned up as they met mine. His gaze was so intense, so fixed, I knocked a pen off my desk. It rolled to a stop at his perfectly polished boot.

He cocked a brow, then reached down, retrieved the pen, and held it out for me.

"Thanks," I said, snatching the pen and turning back toward the front so he couldn't stare at me anymore.

As the lieutenant wrapped his lecture, I glanced at my schedule to find each of the special classes assigned to me were held in this same room. Most of the men stood and stretched, but a few of us used the intermission to find the restroom, which was at the end of the long hallway opposite our classroom. When I returned, Thomas was leaning against the wall just outside the door.

"Hey," he said as I approached.

"Hey.""You're Will, right?"

I nodded. "Yeah. Sorry, what was your name again?"

He smirked, as if not believing I'd forgotten his name. "Thomas Arthur Jacobs."

"Very fancy. Do you always go by three names?"

He chuckled. "Always. And yes, I am quite fancy."

A dimple formed as one side of his mouth twisted upward, just as it had the other day in the yard. Something unfamiliar inside my chest stirred, and I was suddenly self-conscious.

"Well, fancy man, we'd better get back inside."

"Right. Wouldn't want to be late *again*."

His damn smirk grew as I passed, and I could feel his eyes on me all the way to my seat. Everything in me wanted to look up, to catch him staring, to challenge him to back off. What was he staring at me for, anyway?

"Alright, men, get settled," a stocky man in army green said as he entered the room and dropped a folder onto the desk. There were so many silver bars on his sleeve I could barely count how many years he'd served in uniform. Short-cropped black hair was thinning above a long scar that ran from his scalp to his right eye, and his bulbous nose looked to have been broken at least a few times. As the man scanned the room, locking eyes with each of us in turn, I saw a focus ... no, a hardness in his eyes, like they were made of marble and would never yield.

When the last student returned, the teacher marched to the door, closed and locked it, then turned to face us as he strode back to the desk. Even the way he moved was mechanical, as though the gears inside his well-worn machine only ground so far.

"I'm Sergeant Major Colin Stafford. You men are stuck with me for this term, so get over it." A ripple of chuckles spread through the students who were more used to the humor of senior enlisted men than I was. "You got the classified speech from Willard. I won't repeat it. I hate repeating things. I only have one fucking rule: Learn shit the first time so we can keep moving forward, or this class will get fucking painful. Got it?"

Most of the men replied with a snappy, "Yes, Sarge," as two voices behind me barked, "Yes, Sergeant Major."

"Goddammit. Will you squids stop the sucking-up crap? I get that's what you do on a ship when you're bored and there are no women around, but not in this class. I'm Sarge. Period."

The army guys laughed as the navy boys corrected themselves.

"Better." He straightened and stood with both hands behind his back, like some heroic statue that should've been lording over the Harvard Square. "I am going to teach you everything I know about military cartography, terrain, and camouflage. For you squids, that's maps and shit."

Another round of chuckles told me all I needed to know about the army guys' opinion of Professor Hard-Ass and his deadpanned ribbing of the sailors.

"Learn what I teach and you might see the end of the war."

An hour later, as I was gathering my notes and stuffing them into my leather satchel, Thomas appeared by my desk.

"Lunch?"

I startled. "Uh, I've never brought a guest into our hall."

His damned dimple resurfaced. "They have us up here in Andover Hall. The staff won't mind one more."

"Andover? The seminary?"

He shrugged. "I've been here two days. From what I can tell, they're stuffing us anywhere there's room. So, lunch?"

This whole Thomas thing was weird. It was like he was trying to get to know me or something. There weren't many navy guys on campus, and, while the inter-service rivalry seemed like good fun, I caught an undercurrent of actual animosity in the teasing banter. Maybe the guy was just away from home and bored. Maybe he needed a friend. Either way, I was hungry and his dorm was a lot closer than mine.

"Andover better have good food. I'm starving."

# Chapter Nine

# Thomas

By the time we entered Andover Hall, the tiny room they'd repurposed with dining tables was packed. We made our way to the long table, where lunch was spread before us in a buffet line. Thanks to wartime rationing, sandwiches were thinner than normal, and hot vegetables were generally reserved for dinner, but the fare wasn't bad.

"Grab whatever you want. We can go across the hall into one of the offices. Nobody uses them anymore," I told Will.

He looked like a scared rabbit as he scanned the room and saw he was the only guy not in uniform. Plate and drink in hand, I waited by the door and watched as he made his way down the line.

Will was a few inches taller than me, probably six foot, maybe six one. His shoulders were broad and his chest filled out his shirt nicely. He was still wrapped in his heavy winter coat, but it was hard to miss how athletic he looked. His skin was smooth and lightly tanned, making his dusty blond hair, which he kept swept back, appear lighter than it actually was. As he turned, poured tea from a pitcher, then looked up to find me waiting, I realized it was his eyes that drew me in more than anything. I couldn't remember ever seeing eyes so clear and blue, like some endless summer sky on a perfect, cloudless day.

I don't know what it was about the guy that made my pulse race, but from that first accidental meeting, I'd known I wanted to find out. I hadn't been able to get him out of my mind, despite having no clue how I would find him without looking like some crazed stalker.

Then he walked into class—into *my* class—the one no one could know about. How did that happen? Who was this guy?

"Where to?"

I nearly dropped my plate.

"Oh, sorry, was kind of ... never mind. Come on, just across the hall."

Habit drove me to the chair facing the door. If I'd had to sit with my back to it, I never would've been able to eat without twitching. Will didn't seem to care, settling into the wooden office chair, then scooping up his sandwich with both hands.

"What year are you?" I asked, unsure how to open the conversation.

"Third. I'm a junior," he said through a mouthful of sandwich. "You?"

I grinned. "I'm a lieutenant in the US Navy, not a college student. No offense."

He looked offended. "Sorry. I just thought—"

"The department can't handle all the training needs as we're gearing up, so they're sending us to campuses all over. I'm surprised we're being taught by uniforms and not lab coats."

Will took a sip of tea, then sat back, thinking.

"How'd you end up in my, um, American Lit class?" I asked.

His stare was almost too intense for me to hold. "I'm not supposed to talk about that."

My eyes widened.

"Sorry." He sat forward and fiddled with his sandwich without taking another bite. "The whole thing is weird."

"Weird? How?"

He set his sandwich down and picked up his glass, then set that down.

"Can we talk about something else? Have you lived in Boston your whole life?"

Now it was my turn to set my drink down. "My accent that strong?"

He grunted. "You sound like you just got off a boat from the island of Massachusetts. I doubt a deaf guy would miss your accent. No offense."

He was sharp. Damn, I was in trouble.

"Yeah, grew up here. My folks and brother live across the river."

"You close?"

"Yeah, pretty close. My brother's the one you'd have to watch out for."

His brow rose.

"Billy's a great kid. He's just … too clever for his own good. How's that?"

He grinned. "I might've been described that way a time or two, you know, when I was a kid."

"Not now?"

He laughed. "Oh, Arty would use those exact words. Janie would use a lot worse."

"Arty and Janie? Are they the two you were with the other day?"

He nodded. "Arty's my roommate. Janie's like a sister. We've … been through a lot together."

"In two and a half years of college?"

His eyes fell. "Yeah."

I ate a few bites, waiting for an explanation that didn't come. His eyes drifted again, and I could see he was remembering something painful. Everything in me wanted to ask, to tell him it was okay to talk to me, that I would listen.

Instead, I asked, "You like it here?"

He jerked up. "Sorry, what? I kind of got lost."

"At Harvard. You like it here?"

"Oh, sure. It's a great college. The winter can get rough, but most of the people are great."

"Even with all us military running around?"

He grunted. "I'm still not sure we're used to that. The war's changing everything."

"You said a mouthful there." The last thing I wanted was for our lunch to turn into another war conversation. Our whole lives revolved around the damn thing. "So, your accent is fairly flat, probably Midwest, but not too far. Chicago? Maybe just outside?"

He whistled. "You're good. Wow."

"It's a gift." I shrugged. "You have family back there?"

He shook his head, and something crossed his face, like a dark sheet being pulled down.

"No, it's just me now."

I took a bite, waiting for him to say more, but he went quiet again, his eyes drifting to another distant point in the past. I couldn't help but think this guy had more layers than anyone I'd met in a while. It was frustrating to only get a glimpse, but it made me want to know more. Everything about Will made me want more.

"What do you think of our classes so far?" God, I sounded like a lost school kid desperate for friends.

He glanced up. "American Lit sounds ... interesting. I'm not sure about Professor Squid Hater yet."

I nearly spat my tea. "Squid Hater. That's great." I swallowed and coughed. "You don't like our little rivalry? It's only been going on since, well, the beginning of the armed forces, probably a thousand years before."

He grinned, and his eyes brightened ... and there went my pulse again.

"It's alright. I'm more used to athletes giving each other grief in the dressing room than all this, but I guess it's kind of the same."

"You should hear my brother and me. This is tame."

"Billy, right? How old is he? Are you guys close?" he asked.

"Yeah, always have been. It's funny. I thought leaving my parents would be tough when I got my commission, but saying goodbye to that little monster was the worst." I smiled thinking about him. "It's hard to believe, but he's sixteen now."

"So, just a few years apart?"

I laughed. "How old do you think I am?"

"I don't know, nineteen, maybe twenty? You look really young."

"If I had a dollar for every time ... Yes, I look young. I'll *always* look young. I'm twenty-three, turn twenty-four in a few months."

"Easy, didn't meant to hoist your anchor ... or whatever you navy boys say."

I laughed again. "Hoist my anchor? I don't know what that means sitting here in an office, but I'm pretty sure it's vulgar."

His face flushed, and his eyes widened. "Man, I'm sorry. I didn't mean—"

"Will, relax. I'm teasing." The look of horror in his eyes was priceless. "You definitely hoist my anchor."

That's when he dropped his fork. It bounced off the table onto the floor, but his saucer-wide eyes never left mine.

"We'd better get back. Next class starts in ten." I stood, bent to retrieve his fallen fork, tossed it onto the table beside his plate, then walked toward the doorway. With a grin still parting my lips, I glanced back and said, "Anchors away!"

# Chapter Ten

# **Will**

" **•••** become proficient in the German language. You will also learn about German culture, their government structure and function, their political machinery, and military apparatus. This will be your most intensive—and perhaps, most important—course before you enter your final field of work. For that reason, this course will continue for the next three terms," the navy commander leaning against the desk said.

All I heard was Thomas saying, "You definitely hoist my anchor."

What the hell did that even mean? And why would Thomas say something like that? His cocky little smirk made me think he might just always spout off like that, but something in his eyes told me otherwise. He hadn't asked the others to lunch. I hadn't really seen him talking with any of the other men.

What was I thinking? He'd been on campus two days. For all I knew, he was thrown together with a group of sailors and soldiers he'd never met, and he was like any other freshman who was new on campus and searching for connections. I'd been like that when I was new.

But he wasn't a freshman. He wasn't even in college.

The guy was three years older than me and a lieutenant in the United States Navy, for Christ's sake. That meant he'd probably been in the service for several years and wasn't some homesick kid who'd just left home for the first time.

I snuck a peek behind me.

The moment my head turned, his eyes locked onto mine like a raptor scenting its prey. My head snapped back to the commander.

*Dammit. Now he knows I was looking.*

Then my rational brain chimed in. *So what if I looked back? It's not like he's some girl who just kissed me in the park. He's a guy in my class, nothing more. Who cares if I look back to see ... whatever.*

"... of your work will require extreme stealth. You'll be tested every moment of the day by every person you meet. It will be critical ..."

Holy shit. *You will be tested*.

What if *he* was a test?

What if Thomas was assigned to see if I would tell the secrets I knew, to see if I could be trusted? Secrets seemed to be part of this thing I was doing. What if part of the audition or tryout or interview ... whatever the government called it ... was to send friendly people my way to see what I would talk about, to see if I would spill the beans?

I didn't really have any beans to spill, did I? There was so much I didn't know here. Hell, I didn't even know what I was doing, much less why, or why they picked me to do it, whatever *it* was.

I replayed everything for the hundredth time.

I didn't know any secrets. What we were studying might count as secrets. Everyone kept telling us we'd be shot or jailed if we spilled them, but anyone with half a brain could figure out the military wasn't here for lessons in creative writing. It's not like I could endanger national security or the war effort if someone found out I was learning to read maps or speak German.

"Herr Shaw?"

I untangled from my mental contortion to find the commander standing before my desk, arms crossed, a very displeased look on his face.

"Do you have any idea what I just said?"

I looked up. "You called my name, sir."

An amused murmur traveled through the room, and I could practically feel Thomas's smirk behind me.

"At least you understood something," the commander said. "Anyone else ..."

I tried to focus. This stuff was important. If the instructors were right, my life might literally depend on my proficiency in their topics, but I couldn't stop my mind from spinning. Worse, I couldn't figure out why I was so distracted by a simple lunch with a fellow student.

None of this made any sense.

An hour passed in a blur. I didn't learn a single word in a foreign tongue.

As I stood to leave, the commander stepped toward me and leaned in to whisper in my ear, his voice stern but not unkind. "Will, a lot is riding on you, son. Get some rest and come back ready to learn."

He pulled back and our eyes locked.

At no point had he called *anyone* by their first name. I'd been lucid enough to catch that. Something in his tone, but more in his gaze, told me he was communicating as plainly and clearly as he knew how.

*Holy shit, what have I gotten myself into?*

"Yes, sir. Sorry, sir. It won't happen again. Sir."

# Chapter Eleven

# Will

By the time I made it back to the southern end of campus and the comfort of my dorm room, the afternoon sun had already begun to retreat beneath the line of trees along Harvard's western border.

Arty had mentioned a late afternoon class, so I wasn't surprised when I returned to an empty suite. The latest edition of *The Crimson* lay spread across his bed. It was our first day of the new term, and I already had more homework than on any day in my prior two and a half years in college, but still couldn't bring myself to crack a book.

"Talk to me *Crimson*," I said to the wrinkled paper, flipping through her pages.

And so she did.

**LOWELL LIBRARY RAIDED AGAIN BY SNOOPER MAN**

*The mysterious Snooper Man, phantom Lowell House marauder, left his mark last night in the Bellboy library for the second time in a row, completely baffling a police force of tutors, yard police, and janitors which has been trying to unmask the culprit.*

*In his latest call, the vandal turned the portrait of ex-President Lowell upside down and switched several volumes about on the shelves. Following the incident, the library staff announced that a thorough check-up of the books would be made to see if any were missing. In addition, a new "foolproof" lock will be installed on the library door.*

*The yard police staff have as yet no definite suspects in mind, but they are pursuing the trail of the Snooper Man in relentless fashion. One tutor threatened dire punishment to the guilty one when finally apprehended, declaring, "By golly, we'll string him up by the thumb s."*[1]

**STUDENT COUNCIL GIVES $642 IN SCHOLARSHIPS**

---

1. The Harvard Crimson, January 10, 1941

*E Langdon Burwell '41, Treasurer of the Student Council, yesterday announced that $642 has been given to members of the college in the form of scholarships; this is an increase of two hundred dollars over the sum given last year ...*[2]

## 1776 AND ALL THAT

*Congressional hearings on Bill 1776 are repeating the omissions of the 1940 campaign: the real issues are not coming out into the light. The big, overwhelming factor that hangs over all the squabbling in Washington is the probability that a terrific crisis is heading this way fast—namely, invasion of England by Germany in the first half of 1941. What will America do in that crisis? Can anyone picture President Roosevelt, and those enthusiasts Henry Stimson and Frank Knox, sitting back cautiously at such a time? Perhaps they have nothing definite in mind. They say they have to wait and see how things develop. But it is essential that we get from them some indication of what they might or might not do, if we are to place such wide discretion in their hands.*

2. Ibid, January 27, 1941

*The Lend-Lease Bill gives them huge powers; the Amer-*
*ican people, by passing it, will turn over vital decisions*
*to these men, and will be responsible for what they do.*
*No matter how you look at it, this is a shackle on the*
*people; it is an advance commitment to decisions in*
*which we will have no part. There is no denying that*
*this is the only efficient way of doing some things. But a*
*lot—everything, in fact—depends upon the attitude of*
*the men who are going to exercise this power. It is up to*
*them to try to show fairly and openly what acts the people*
*may be shackling themselves to, what moves they will be*
*held responsible for, and, above all, why they should take*
*on these responsibilities.*

*When Mr. Stimson was asked by the House Committee*
*what he thought of a ban on sending US warships into*
*war zones, he said he thought it would be a "shackle" on*
*the American people. This is a favorite expression of his;*
*he uses it often. Here he uses it to gain executive power to*
*send battleships into war zones ...*[3]

"Well, that was uplifting," I said, tossing the paper back onto Arty's bed, ignoring articles about the Chinese ski team visiting the States and the results of intercollegiate basketball contests. It was at once troublesome and oddly reassuring that the college continued to act

---

3. Ibid, January 20, 1941

like a college, despite the growing preparations for America's involvement in Europe.

I glanced at the stack of textbooks begging to be opened. Images of Professor Hard-Ass Squid Hater snarling like a rabid lion offered motivation. His nickname grew each time I thought of him, as did the faces he made in my imagination. Still, I was uninspired. I'd been sitting on my ass all day. I was stiff, tired, and getting cranky, and there was only one solution when I fell into that state: good old-fashioned exercise.

Ever since the opening of the Hemenway Gymnasium last year, a group of guys met each afternoon to play basketball. I wasn't the fastest on the court, but, without a referee to blow his annoying whistle, I could muscle my way through most defenders. Win or lose, the games usually worked up a good sweat and cleared my mind. That was exactly what I needed.

After a quick change, I made my way back up to the north side of campus, where Hemenway was nestled among ancient trees on the northwestern edge by Massachusetts Avenue.

The boxy red-brick building was the newest on campus, a monument to ghastly modern architecture amid a forest of beautifully historic structures, one dating back to 1720. Despite being a utilitarian blot on the canvas that was Harvard, Hemenway was a fantastically modern gymnasium that had quickly become a favorite of the more athletic students.

The familiar echo of balls thudding and sneakers screaming greeted me as I strolled into the brightly lit building. I returned a greeting wave from a couple of the regulars, then sat on a bench to strip off my heavy coat and lace up my sneakers.

I wasn't really paying attention to the game as the herd thundered back and forth a few yards away. At least, not until a familiar voice called out, "Hey, anchor boy, didn't know you played ball."

I sucked in a breath and slowly lifted my head to find Thomas, sweat dripping down his forehead and neck, wearing a crimson wool jersey. Well-defined shoulders capped his corded arms.

I'd never noticed the sleeveless shirts we wore before, never paid attention to the arms protruding from them, despite being up close and personal to plenty of them over the years. Why did the muscular, dripping wings of this navy guy make my heart pump faster? I tried not to stare, but a bead of sweat trickled down his shoulder onto his bicep that had tensed perfectly as he gripped the ball in his hands.

"Oh, hey. Yeah, I, uh, guess I ... play some. I mean, I, uh, play ... a few times—"

"Jesus, did you hit your head? You're stammering." He laughed through labored breaths that made his rounded chest rise and fall beneath his jersey.

I looked down and sinched my laces tight, then rose. I would not let this cocky sailor get under my skin. "Let me grab my jersey and show you."

His brows rose with his grin. "You're on."

I grabbed a white jersey from the bin and took my place on the bench beside my new teammates, all of whom were regulars I knew well. As I scanned the boys in maroon, I only recognized a couple.

"Who are all these guys?" I asked.

"Army, mostly. One navy guy. All new this week," the player beside me said, not taking his eyes off the action.

I whistled. "They're fast."

"Yeah," he said. "Time to slow 'em down. We're in."

Three of us rose as the action stopped and subs were exchanged by both teams. Our captain told me to take their point guard, so I stepped up to the man in bounding the ball. I felt a player press into my back, setting up a screen.

"You're about to lose," Thomas's voice whispered, and his body pressed into mine.

The ball flew past my outstretched hands, and I tripped over my own feet, trying to turn without running into Thomas again. He winked down at me, then raced to the other end.

*Oh, this is on now.*

Crimson crushed white. Again and again. It was never close.

As my teammates' frustration grew with each defeat, so did the physical play. There were no referees, no faculty or staff. We were on our own out there, and we meant to make the new guys pay for showing us up on our own court. Blocked shots slammed balls and players to the ground, while well-set picks devolved into thrown elbows and extended hips, sending opponents sprawling or limping to the bench.

Play finally stopped when an army elbow found my jaw and sent me reeling with stars dancing in my sight. I didn't even remember my head smacking the hardwood or my nose getting hit, just the tickle and tang of blood dribbling to my tongue.

"... coming to."

I heard the shuffling of several sneakers around me as a few guys gathered.

"Will, can you hear me?"

Why was Thomas talking to me? Where was he? I could hear him, but couldn't see him anywhere.

Then I remembered to open my eyes.

God, that hurt. Everything hurt.

As my lids crept open, several versions of Thomas's face danced into view. I couldn't understand why he wouldn't stand still—and why there were three of him.

"He's coming around," Thomas said. To whom, I wasn't sure. The triplets were all I could see.

I reached a hand up to touch one of them, but I only felt empty air.

"Geez, he must've really hit his head," a deep voice said from above. It sounded like Professor Hard-Ass Crummy Squid Hater.

"I added a word," I mumbled, then laughed at my own cleverness.

Someone whistled. "He's scrambled. Should I go get somebody?"

The Thomases shook their heads. "No, I've got med training. I'll take care of him."

*Wow. Thomas will take care of me. That's nice of him. Nobody's taken care of me in a long time.*

"Alright, see you in the morning," the deep voice said, and I heard the squealing of sneakers fade into the distance.

"Thomas?" I asked.

A hand pressed gently against my shoulder. "Don't sit up. I'm right here."

"What happened? Where are we?"

The Thomases smiled.

"We're in the gym. You took a pretty good hit, then banged your head."

"Why are there three of you? I didn't know—"

His laugh was tinged with something ... nervousness? Concern? I couldn't tell.

"Just relax. You'll be alright. You just need a minute for your head to clear."

I couldn't think of anything else to do, so I let the warmth of his palm, still pressed into my shoulder, comfort my aching body.

*His palm is pressed to my shoulder. It feels so strong and warm. Wait—*

My eyes flew wide, and I tried to sit up, but the Thomases and the gym spun, and I groaned in pain.

His hand pressed down until I relented.

"Easy. Please don't do that again. You need to ..."

I drifted off, not hearing whatever it was he thought I needed. It sounded important; I wanted to know. I mean, if I needed it, it must've been important, but my body and mind revolted and darkness took me.

Sometime later, my eyes drifted open again. I turned my head quickly, and a wave of dizziness punished me for my imprudence.

Slowly, I glanced around.

The gym was dimly lit and quiet. No one dribbled or ran. In fact, there was no one in the place.

"He wakes."

I turned to find Thomas sitting beside me. He'd changed from his crimson jersey into a royal blue long-sleeve woolen shirt.

"What happened? How long have I been out?"

His lips pinched. "Maybe an hour or two. You were awake for a while, but drifted off. You took a pretty good hit."

"What time is it?"

He shrugged. "Maybe ten. We played through dinner. After you got hurt, everybody left. The military guys didn't want to get blamed for hurting a student in their first week here."

I started to sit up. Thomas shot forward, his arm snaking behind to support my back.

"Here, let me help you. The last time you tried this it didn't go so well." His smirk held a tad less cockiness than usual.

"Thanks," I said, as I finally sat upright. I gripped my temples, and reached for my jaw. His hand grabbed mine and pulled it away.

"You probably shouldn't touch that. It's gonna leave a pretty bad bruise and will be sore for a while."

"I get hit that hard?"

He nodded, and his smirk found all its cockiness again. "Yeah, the game got pretty rough after you guys lost the fourth time."

"Four? Shit."

"I seem to recall you wanting to teach me something about basketball? What was that?"

"Fuck you," I said, chuckling.

Then I realized he was still holding my hand, the one that had meant to touch my bruised chin. I pulled free and stared at my fingers, wondering why they hadn't retreated sooner.

Then, I'm not sure why, I looked up and met his gaze. He still leaned near, so close I could feel his breath, just barely. His eyes were so blue, so intense and deep. I stared and thought ... then shook myself free and looked away.

"Sorry, I got a little dizzy again," I said.

I could feel his gaze. Then he stood and offered me his hand. "We should get you back to your room. You need to put some ice on that chin and nose, then get some sleep."

Reluctantly, I took his hand again and let him pull me to my feet. The world spun, and I wobbled. His arm shot around me faster than I could fall.

"I've got you. Just lean into me. Let me take your weight."

I didn't know what to say.

I'd played sports my whole life, been hit a thousand times. I knew what this was supposed to feel like, what getting the life knocked out of you did, how the world whirled and your stomach churned; but this was unlike anything I'd experienced before.

Something in me felt so much more than dizzy, and I didn't know what it was or what to do about it. Thomas being so close, wrapping his arm around me and holding me upright, only made the vibrating in my chest grow.

*This is nuts. I just need rest. I took a hit and my eggs are fried—nothing a good night's sleep won't fix.*

Thomas tossed my arm around his shoulder, and we limped across Harvard to my dorm.

# Chapter Twelve

# **Thomas**

The heavy door to Will's dorm banged shut behind me as I stepped onto the cold, snow-dusted stone of the steps. The air sliced across the yard, biting my nose and ears on its way by. Its moan reminded me of childhood ghost stories and made me long for the comfort of my bed's covers. I was dreading the walk back to my housing at the northern end of Harvard.

Teeth begging to chatter, lips crusting, I couldn't keep a wide grin from my face.

As I watched my feet leave shallow marks in the ground's unblemished white cloak, I could almost feel Will's arm wrapped around my shoulder. His tangy post-workout musk lingered in my nostrils. I breathed him in—getting a lungful of bitter air for my reminiscence.

It was worth it.

As we'd laid there on the gym floor, I swear he'd held my hand far longer than was necessary. I was just keeping him from touching his bleeding chin, but he'd held on. I absently rubbed my palm, feeling his skin pressing against mine, and my heart fluttered at the thought.

I probably imagined all that. He was delirious from hitting his head, weak and woozy. He probably had no idea what he was doing, or even knew he was holding another guy's hand, much less mine. I was seeing what I wanted to see—and it was a wonderful sight.

*What is it about Will that drives me so crazy?* I wondered, as I made my way past Memorial Hall. My warm feelings were losing the battle with winter's cold, and I was beginning to shiver. Then I realized I'd draped my heavy coat around Will's shoulders as we'd left the gymnasium.

*I'm going to freeze tomorrow morning,* I thought, then smiled at the vision of Will wrapped in *my* coat.

I hadn't been able to get the guy out of my head since that first day we'd almost met in the yard. Then we ended up in the same classes, the classified ones with objectives that forced us to keep each other's most private secrets to ourselves. We shared that together. More than a simple sense of camaraderie, those classes forced us into proximity for nearly half of each day, and would continue to do so until we both graduated the program in a year and a half. I didn't know why the military gods had smiled on me in that decision, but I tipped my head back and reveled in the icy flakes that melted against my skin in thanks.

I didn't even know if Will was … like me. Hell, I barely knew the guy. We hadn't yet finished our first week of term, had only sat through a few classes together, and had lunch once. What knucklehead thinks about another guy all the time? The war between giddiness and caution in my chest felt like fireworks on a dreary day, exploding brightly then fizzling into a smoldering mess.

I was being ridiculous; reckless, even.

It didn't make any sense for me to even think about dating another man, if that's what it was called when two men had lunch or did things together. I wasn't sure there *was* a term for it. There certainly wasn't one used openly without inserting a curse or other slanderous phrase—and the possibility of criminal or psychological confinement.

If anyone even suspected my feelings, I'd end up in a mental hospital with a woman babbling about seeing her dead child and a man diddling his … Or, with a war going on, I might end up on the front lines, fodder for the enemy.

No, they wouldn't do that. Unit cohesion wouldn't allow a man with my "perverse tendencies" to serve with good, upstanding men.

I'd end up in jail.

What was I doing?

"Great mood killer, Thomas," I breathed through chattering teeth, frustrated to come down from the high of Will's touch so quickly.

Then he flashed into my mind again.

His dusty hair flopping across his forehead as he ran, sweat streaming down his arms. He wasn't bulky like he worked out with weights, but the muscles of his arms were well formed and tight. I may have squeezed his shoulders a time or two while trying to revive him. God, they felt good, like small grapefruits that hadn't yet ripened, firm and …

I shook that thought free and laughed at myself. Grapefruits?

I'd just passed the Bio Labs building and Andover was in view, and with it, warmth. My pace quickened at the thought of a stack of blankets and a soft pillow. The only thing that would be missing was Will nestled in my arms.

"You've got to stop," I muttered. "He's probably not even interested."

"You alright, Lieutenant?"

"Shit!" I shouted, nearly sprawling out as I slipped on an icy patch.

"Whoa. Easy, sir." A steadying hand clamped on my arm.

My head snapped around to find one of the army guys in our class, Sergeant … something, I couldn't remember. He was a beefy, farm-raised boy from Iowa, or some other square state with more corn than people.

"Thanks," I said, pulling my arm free and righting myself. "Scared the dickens out of me, Sergeant."

"Sorry, sir." His grin told me he was more amused than sorry.

"Well, thanks for the hand. Have a good night," I said, turning.

"Sir?" he called after me.

"What is it, Sergeant?"

"How long do we have?"

I turned back to him. The rugged face that stared back at me somehow looked small and weak, the mask of a man fallen away to reveal a frightened child. He was asking how long before we shipped out, before we faced the Nazis with the rest of the world. My heart lurched at the anxiety etched so plainly in his eyes. He'd likely been thinking about that question all night.

"Unless things go to shit, not until we finish our training here in '43."

He let out a boundless breath, and his lips quirked in a halfhearted smile. "Okay, that's good. Thanks."

Without another word, he turned and vanished into the chilly night. I stared after him a moment, then the cold hit my bones and I retreated indoors.

# Chapter Thirteen

# Will

Arty was an early-to-bed, early-to-rise kind of guy. That had taken a lot of getting used to our freshman year, considering I was eager to explore everything Harvard had to offer, including the late-night festivities, official and otherwise. Despite still feeling woozy, I could slip into our room, strip down, and climb into bed without disturbing him.

When I rose the next morning, he was sitting at his desk, studiously scribbling notes from one of three textbooks spread open before him. I had no idea how the kid did it. He was the smartest guy I'd ever met.

"Morning," I mumbled, causing my swollen lower lip to throb.

"You get run over by a truck last night?" he asked without turning.

"Something like that." I sat upright. "Wow, that hurts."

He looked back and was by my side in a flash. "Take it slow. I'll get some ice."

I scooched on my butt so my back could lean against the wall. "No worries about me moving fast. I'll just wait here."

He gave me a tight grin and raced out the door.

Five, maybe ten minutes later, Arty returned with a wad of ice wrapped in a dish towel.

"Sorry that took so long. The kitchen couldn't understand why I wanted a bag of ice."

I grunted as he pressed the ice to my chin and lip. "Hold that there."

"I have news," he said, sitting at the foot of the bed, his eyes coming to life as though seeing a puppy for the first time. "I met a girl."

"Really?"

"Yeah." His hair flopped as he nodded. I'd never seen him grin so wide. "She's in this new program I'm part of. You know, the one I can't tell you about. They actually let a girl in. Can you believe it?"

I shrugged with my brows since my shoulders ached. "Huh."

"She's brilliant, Will. Smarter than any of us. And she's so pretty. She's got this long red hair the color of old copper wire that runs almost all the way down her back. It's like this bloody river of beauty."

"Ew. You might want to rethink your description before trying to woo her."

"Really? It's such a pretty color." He paused and cocked his head. "Anyway. She's got these eyes—"

"I would hope so."

"Shut up." He waved a hand. "Her eyes are so blue, like, really, Will, crazy blue. God, they could light up this whole building, they're so electric."

He was gushing. Actually gushing. I was worried my bed might get gush on it.

"And her skin is so pale. I don't think she's ever been out in the sun. It's like she's one of those Asian dolls, so perfect and smooth and pure."

"Smooth? You felt her skin?"

"No!" He looked like I'd punched him in the gut. "Of course not! What kind of gentleman do you think I am?"

"The smooth-skin-loving kind, apparently."

He groused. "If you weren't hurt, I'd throw something."

I gave him another brow shrug. "Stinks for you."

"Anyway!" he huffed. "The best part ... wait for it ... she's a Jew!"

I kept waiting for the best part.

"Will! Don't you get it?"

"Uh, not really. I mean, woohoo. Go Jews."

"I'm so going to hit you when you recover from getting hit." He stood and began darting about our tiny room, like some pent-up dog whose energy had nowhere to go. "She's *Jewish*, Will. That means my parents won't hate her. She'd even be acceptable."

He couldn't see my mouth form an O. God, that hurt.

"They would never be so forward as to say I couldn't date a Gentile—my dad is a politician, after all—but if I did, they would find a million reasons she wasn't good enough for me. With another Jew, she's practically in the family already!"

He was close to shouting that last part. I'd never seen him so worked up.

"Does this copper-headed goddess have a name?"

"Oh yeah. It's as pretty as she is."

He stared out the window with a giddy grin on his face.

"Well?"

"Oh, sorry. Elizabeth."

"Like the Queen?"

He rolled his eyes. "No, dummy. It means 'God is my oath' in Hebrew. Isn't that amazing?"

I wasn't sure anyone had ever told me the meaning of a girl's name before, much less how amazing it was.

"Uh, sure, really amazing."

He tossed the rumpled covers at my legs.

"You should ask her to the dance this weekend."

He froze. All color drained from his face, as if I'd wiped him with a rag dripping with turpentine.

"You have talked to her, right?"

"Well, not technically," he said, slumping back onto the bed beside me.

"Arty, seriously? You're in the same class or program or whatever, and you haven't talked to her?"

I didn't think his face could fall any further, but it did.

"She's just so pretty and smart and—"

"Arthur Wendel Ableman." I leaned forward despite the thrumming in my head. "You are every bit as smart as, well, anybody else. And you might not be all pretty like she is, but you're not bad ... for a guy ... and a smart guy at that, I guess."

His eyes slowly rose. "Really?"

"I'm not the best judge here, but sure. You're swell." How had this conversation become so painful? "Arty, you're the kindest, most amazing friend I've ever had, really. Just talk to her. I promise she'll see what Janie and I love so much about you."

He held my gaze a moment, and I thought he might cry. Or wilt. Or crawl under the covers at my feet.

Jesus.

"Thanks, Will," he said, sucking in a raspy breath, then nodding, more to himself than to me. "I'm going to talk to her today, introduce myself, maybe even shake her hand."

"Um, Arty—"

"What? Too much? Should I kiss her hand? No, that's terrible. What?"

I shook my head and chuckled. "Just talk to her, okay?"

He nodded, and I swore I could actually see twelve permutations of a conversation battling for supremacy in his head.

# Chapter Fourteen

# **Thomas**

"Why do mornings hate me?" I mumbled as I puckered my dry lips in a failed attempt to moisten them. The sun had yet to rise, which should've been the first clue that people should stay in bed, but the military rarely listened to sound logic. Morning calisthenics were part of life in uniform, a part I hated with every fiber of my being. Come to think of it, morning *anything* was pretty bad.

I pushed myself off my mattress and scratched my itchy scalp. It would have to wait to get washed until the workout was done. My cap would take care of any rebellion in its ranks. I threw on a T-shirt and shorts, then layered myself into the navy's finest tracksuit before heading outside. Despite my woolen shield, the morning was a bitter mistress, sinking her icy fangs into every bit of exposed skin.

"This is really not fun," I grumbled.

"Suck it up, buttercup." Two army guys passed me on either side, jogging toward the yard with golden retriever grins and lolling tongues, as if a morning run in arctic conditions was something to relish.

I shook my head and fell in behind them. The army–navy ribbing had gone on since the services were founded and would likely outlive us all. Friendly competition drove us to be better, to outgrow and outsmart our peers. It also wore thin at times, as evidenced last night in our basketball game.

That thought sent my mind right back to Will, and I wondered if he struggled to wake up in the mornings too. Did his hair stand in ever-licked swirls after a night of restless sleep? He probably woke perfectly ready to conquer the day. He just had that look.

Then I remembered the bloody lip and banged-up chin from the night before and wondered how he was feeling. His lip was probably swollen and his chin blue. That made me want to see him, to check his injuries and offer support, to rub salve to ease his aches. Hell, I wanted to brush his hair back again, like I'd done while he was passed out.

I'd been so lost in my morning fog that I ran right into the back of one of the army guys.

"Hey!" he cried out, as he stumbled forward, then down to his knees.

"Oh, shit, sorry." I shot forward and helped him up. "I wasn't watching when you stopped. Sorry."

He brushed himself off and shot me a steely glare. "Fuckin' navy fag."

My eyes widened. "Hey, I'm sorry. I didn't mean—"

Another pair of soldiers stepped up. One growled, "Somebody find a fag? I heard they're all over this campus. Regular haven for 'em."

"Heard that too. Gotta be on guard or they'll get ya." The guy I'd knocked down laughed, then shook his head. "No pansies out here, just this clumsy squid. That's almost the same thing though, right?"

"Damn right!" The trio laughed, and I felt my blood beginning to boil, though I couldn't decide which slur burned me more.

"Problem here, boys?" The voice of Baker Raymond, the senior-ranking navy officer in our cohort, snapped everyone's head around.

"Sir, no, sir. We were just joking around," one of the army guys said.

Baker eyed them, then glanced to me. His eyes narrowed.

"Fine. You three, join the grunts over there." He pointed to the far rank of soldiers. "I need a word with the lieutenant."

"Yes, sir," they said, looking relieved to be joining their brethren.

When they were out of earshot, Baker turned to me. "What the fuck was that?"

I shrugged. "I got lost in thought and bumped into one of them. They decided to start talking shit."

"About you?"

I shook my head. "Nah. They were just being assholes."

He stared a moment longer, then nodded once and began stretching.

Baker had been my best friend for more than a year, ever since I'd been assigned to the Office of Naval Intelligence. He was sharp, witty, and saw through people better than anyone I knew. There was no doubt in my mind he knew exactly what those guys had been talking about—and how they'd meant the slurs to smear all over my tracksuit—but he kept his observations to himself.

Most of us looked up to Baker, both figuratively and literally. At six-five, he towered above most, but it was his raptor's gaze and stern countenance that gave most men pause. I hadn't seen any boys since meeting Baker, but I wondered what he knew or suspected. I never dated girls or talked about them. Other guys were obsessed with talking about women. I was so sick of looking at photos or sketches of girlfriends—or potential girlfriends—or girls with potential—or girls with tits, because no man had ever seen tits before; but it was part of the ritual to gawk and moan like you wanted to jump them every time a guy shared his newest prospect.

Had Baker picked up on any of it? Did he notice I took a back seat in those conversations? Did he suspect? The idea of losing his friendship, of losing his trust, was almost more than I wanted to contemplate.

"Fall in!" A stern voice boomed from the front of the yard. A moment later, we were formed up and jogging our way around campus.

I'd almost escaped the rabbit hole of misery, but my mind replayed the men's taunts again and again throughout our run. After several years in uniform, you'd think I would've been used to hearing men banter like that, but it still made my skin crawl. I wanted to stand up to them, to tell them guys were just guys, no matter who they liked, but I knew that would've been a fool's errand. They wouldn't have heard a word. They sure wouldn't have believed me or agreed at all. And if they ever found out I leaned that way, I'd be drummed out of the navy, or worse—definitely worse. Some guys got beat up, while others got their neck stretched. It didn't matter that those same guys would likely find comfort in the arms of another man once they were a thousand miles from any willing woman, or so I'd heard. They were on home soil and had to show their brothers they were real men, as if loving another man somehow stole one's manhood.

And the whole thing made me think about Will again. Dammit.

What if he really was ... or if there was a chance ... if we could ...

I couldn't be thinking like that. I *had* to stop.

Staying with him last night put me perilously close to a raging fire, and if I kept going back, I would definitely get burned. It wasn't just my future or safety at play, it was Will's. Even if he wasn't like me, others would think he was by association. We hadn't known each other long, but I couldn't bear the thought of him getting hurt because of something I said or did.

How was I ever supposed to be happy? Was that even possible?

By the time we stumbled to a halt in the yard, my legs were almost as weary as my mind—and the day had just begun.

# Chapter Fifteen

# Will

**THE MOVIEGOER**

*When Stirling Hayden and his body arrived in Hollywood, many skeptics said that the mere fact that he was a nautical fellow, and very good-looking, did not necessarily imply that he would make a good actor. These skeptics were answered by the realists, who said that the mere fact that he might not be a good actor did not necessarily imply that he would be a failure in Hollywood. Now, both of these arguments were based on rational grounds, but the realist school of thought failed to take one factor into consideration: just how bad Mr. Hayden's acting actually was. It is not bad in the conventional Hollywood sense; it sinks. And consequently Mr. Hayden, handsome or no, body or no, is a failure .*

*. .*

YARDLING BASKETBALL TEAM LOSES TO
EXETER FOR SEASON'S FIRST DEFEAT


*Feeling the sting of defeat for the first time in four starts,*
*the Freshman basketball team dropped a close game to*
*Exeter Saturday afternoon at Exeter by a score of 52–50*
*...* [1]


**CHEEK TO CHEEK**


*Faculty cooperation has given the house dance com-*
*mittees a much-needed shot in the arm. Accepting the*
*committees' proposal, it has overcome the restrictions of*
*rising labor costs and a limited budget which threat-*
*ened to confine the undergraduates to only one big fall*
*dance. The main problem was the relatively high cost*
*of preparing the dining halls for the dances; the la-*
*bor shortage and the increased number of tables and*
*chairs made the cost prohibitive for the university. But*
*the dance committees' offer to set up as well as clear*
*out the dining hall furniture has been matched by the*
*university, which has agreed to rearrange the eating*

---

1. The Harvard Crimson, January 12, 1942

*hours on the day after and so facilitate the setting-up. Together they form a workable solution to a ticklish and unnecessary problem.*

*War nerves and acceleration pressure make school parties vital as the best possible way to blow off the lid. Yet without this faculty reasonableness, the future dancing of the red-blooded Harvard man would have to be squeezed into the anemic form of common-room record dances. The last time the university made this gracious gesture, excessive breakage and undergraduates welching on promises forced it to draw back. Another failure and it won't be repeated.*[2]

D ances weren't mere traditions at Harvard, they were life.
        Prior to the war, houses hosted dances nearly every weekend. As the nation tightened its belt, so did the Crimson horde, though we would sooner go into the utter darkness of night than give up our weekend frolics in their entirety.

The first fling of the season was hosted by the women of Briggs Hall on the Radcliffe campus. Women had only recently been allowed to attend classes on the Harvard campus proper, but most still lived

---

2. Ibid, January 12, 1942

across Massachusetts Avenue on the Radcliffe property. Given the expanding number of men, particularly men in the service, the annual Briggs Jig[3] was more popular than ever.

"I can't believe she said yes!" Arty bounced around our room so fast I thought he might hurt himself. "She actually said yes."

"That's great. I'm proud of you, bud."

"What am I going to wear, Will? I've never been to a dance with a girl before. I mean, I've been to plenty of dances, but never walked in with a girl on my arm—not that she's going to actually hold my arm. I mean, she can if she wants to. I think it would be really swell, and I might throw up."

"That would be bad for the coloring of her dress," I said through chuckles.

"Right. No throwing up. Maybe I should write this stuff down." He turned toward his desk and began riffling through pages for a blank sheet of paper.

"If you need to write that one down, we're in real trouble."

He froze, then turned so slowly I thought something might've been wrong. "You're right. I should know that. Holy cow, Will."

For a split second, he let me believe he was serious, then a ball cap sailed over my head and into the wall.

I ducked and held up my hands.

"You deserve that, jerk."

"I'm looking out for your date's best interest. How's that being a jerk?"

"First, she's not my date."

I sat up. "Why not? You asked her out, and you're taking her to a dance. That sounds like a date to me."

---

3. This one's fictional. Sorry, lads and lasses. Casey made this up.

"Darn it. Maybe ... God, Will, are you this nervous before a date? I've never seen you nervous, ever." He thought a moment. "Come to think of it, I've never seen you go on a date. Hanging out with Janie and me doesn't count."

I grunted. "You can say that again."

Another cap sailed by.

"We're perfectly acceptable hanger-outers, thank you very much."

"True," I agreed. "But you're not dates, and certainly not at the same time. I mean, really, Arty, would you want me to bring someone else with us if you and I went out?"

His mouth fell open. "You want to go out with me? On a date?"

"No, absolutely not. I'm not Jewish enough for you, remember?" I smirked.

"Why am I listening to you? Nothing you're saying is helping me get ready for tonight. What are you wearing?"

"I don't know. Probably my charcoal suit, maybe with a crimson tie. You know, sport a little school pride while shaking my booty."

He nodded thoughtfully. "That's good. But what if she wears something that doesn't match crimson?"

"We're at Harvard. Everything goes with crimson."

"Right," he said, turning back to comb through his wardrobe for the tenth time.

---

Janie was standing just inside the lobby when I arrived. Her hair was pinned up in a fashion I was sure had a French or Italian name I'd never be able to remember. She wore a gown of shimmering emerald that drank in the light around it. She was stunning.

"Whoa, Janie. You look hot to trot!"

Her laugh filled the entry and warmed me down to my toes. Then she twirled to make her dress billow, and all heads turned.

A second later, her hands were busy fiddling with my tie. "You look handsome too, but this tie is a wreck. What blind man did this for you?"

I grunted and raised a hand. "Guilty. Guess I was in a rush."

"Have you seen Arty yet?"

I shook my head, careful not to interrupt her efforts. "Not yet. He was going to meet Elizabeth at her house and escort her across campus."

She let out an "Aww" as her eyes rolled back slightly.

"He was so nervous all day. I tried to get him to drink some whiskey for courage, but he wouldn't even consider it, said he wanted to be perfectly clear when he saw her again."

"I'm so happy for him. Have you met Elizabeth?"

I couldn't hold back a laugh. "Arty just met her this week. Well, just talked to her. It took him two days to work up the guts to introduce himself and talk about something other than classwork."

She grinned. "Our little boy is growing up."

She smoothed the knot, stepped back to examine it, then nodded. "Perfect. Now you're ready to find your own happiness."

I grinned. "Who said I'm not happy?"

Her arms crossed so quickly I almost stepped back at the motion.

"William, don't you dare sass me. I know you better than you know yourself, and you're lonely. I can see it in your eyes. Don't hide in the corner all night when there are perfectly lovely girls who would die for a dance with my spiffy best friend."

I kept the grin on my face, despite my gut clenching. The thought of asking a girl to dance made me more nervous than Arty had been in extending his hand to one, if that was even a thing. Being nervous wasn't like me either, certainly not where people were concerned. I'd never been shy or afraid to make the acquaintance of anyone, but something about asking a girl to dance or stroll—or even just chat—felt awkward, like it wasn't something I was supposed to do.

Not that there was anything wrong with it.

I knew better.

I just didn't feel ... I don't know ... like I wanted to do any of those things. I wasn't sure. I just hadn't tried in so long that ... Maybe *that* was it. I was just out of practice and I needed to try again, to get back on the horse. Not that I would be mounting anyone, certainly not at the dance. God, why was this so hard?

Maybe, just maybe, if the right girl were there and I gave it a real shot, I'd enjoy a whirl around the dance floor and a moonlit stroll afterward.

"I promise."

She cocked her head. "You promise what?"

I raised my hand like in a courtroom drama. "I, William John Shaw, do solemnly promise to try my best to meet a girl tonight. If I find one I like, I'll ask her to dance."

"And?" She raised an expectant and perfectly plucked brow.

"I will bring said girl to be reviewed by the lady of the ball, Miss Janie Lynn Woodson."

Her pearlescent smile lit up the dim lobby as she clapped her fingertips and hopped excitedly. "Excellent!"

It was time to turn the blinding light away from me. "What about you? Any fish on your hook?"

"Ew." She slapped my arm playfully. "That's a terrible way to talk about men—and *me*! Besides, they're more sausages than fish."

We shared a laugh for only a second before she pointed and practically leapt away from me. "Oh, there's Ty Goodwin. He's just dreamy. He's my fish ... I mean sausage. Mine!"

Before I could blink, she was gone, and I was left standing alone in the lobby.

I stood there, unmoving, watching students enter the hall. Something had compelled me to stay in this spot, and the idea of observing, of standing and letting things happen around me, I just lost myself in it.

"Will." My roommate's familiar voice turned my head toward the door.

Arty, dressed in his finest black suit with sky blue pinstripes, strode into the lobby as if he were royalty ascending a throne. The girl on his arm stole all the oxygen from the room. I could feel others who'd been focused on their dates or finding the punch bowl turn and stare. I'd thought Arty's descriptions to have been fanciful, puppy-love renderings of a dopey girl who was more likely bucktoothed and befreckled.

She was none of that. She was stunning.

Lustrous auburn hair wound in artistic swirls atop her head, then down her back in a waterfall of color that flowed as she walked. Her eyes were alive against the sapphire of her gown, but her smile ... When she turned and smiled, it felt as if the entire world stopped and gravitated toward her.

Arty was a lost puppy, gazing up like she'd cast a spell and captured his soul.

"This is Elizabeth. She's in my, um, special class."

She laughed, and I swear I heard bells somewhere.

"Oh, Arty, you make us sound slow or something. We're scientists."

The way she gripped his arm and nuzzled up to him struck me. This gorgeous creature was as enamored with Arty—our Arty—as he was with her.

My jaw hung open, and I couldn't stop staring.

"Come on. We're going to dance."

They vanished through the doors that led to the dining-hall-turned-dance-floor.

Arty was going to dance.

Again, my brain refused to register what was happening. The smartest yet least coordinated person I'd ever known was leading his movie-star date—who appeared completely besotted by him—onto a dance floor. Had the world turned completely upside down?

Unable to resist their gravitational pull, I followed the joyful sounds of brass instruments into the hall. I'd only been in this house once before, and remembered the place was dimly lit, almost like some gothic painting where the artist ran out of yellow and white, leaving everything looking like the skies might open up at any moment. That night, as I strode through the double-door entry, brilliant light accompanied snappy swing music, creating a festive, vibrant atmosphere I hadn't thought possible in the place. Everywhere I looked, girls in gowns spun and hopped around guys in sharp suits. The walls were lined with guys and gals waiting their turn on the floor, while dozens of couples tried to keep up with the music's quickening pace.

As had become the case throughout Harvard, about half the men present served, and were dressed in either the muddy green of the army or the midnight blue of the navy's dress uniform.

Everyone looked so happy.

Had I not known the reason for all the military folk, the whole night would've felt like some fairytale affair. War be damned, we were having a ball.

I heard a familiar laugh and turned to find Janie spinning, nearly out of control, held by the hand of a member of the Harvard baseball team. His smile was almost as wide as hers as he twirled her about then pulled her into his chest. Leave it to Janie to snag a senior letterman.

I scanned the floor, finally locating Arty and Elizabeth; well, I located Elizabeth. She was dancing like she'd been born to it, while Arty wriggled like a worm on a hook about to be tossed into a catfish pond. The two couldn't have been less alike, and yet their smiles were exact replicas of the ones I'd just seen on Janie and her date's faces.

Topsy-turvy. That was the technical term for what the world had become.

Then something caught my eye near a long table filled with snacks and drinks. Two men in deep blue with golden buttons and glittering thread at their wrists stood watching the party. One of them looked up, as if sensing my gaze, and our eyes met from across the dance floor.

Thomas smiled and inclined his head, and I thought the room might've spun faster than Janie's dance. I tried to look away, to put dancers between us so I might remain hidden, but the song ended and the dancers fled so others might take their place. I clawed at my tie, loosening it, because breathing had become an Olympic sport I wasn't trained for. Heat flooded my neck and face, and the darn room wouldn't stay still.

What was happening? None of this was new: the evening out, the dance, the music. I'd only had one cup of punch, which I was sure had been spiked with some cheap brand of rum or brandy, but only one cup. That wasn't enough to make a whole house spin. Why had seeing Thomas sent my whole system into shock? No matter how much I tried to slow my breathing, I couldn't bring my racing heart under control.

It didn't make any sense.

I turned and fled for the safety of the steps and the cold of the courtyard.

As I stared at the snow, pacing across the slick landing without a care for my footing, my brain decided sprints were in order.

Thomas was my friend. He'd helped me when I was hurt. He was kind and thoughtful—and one of the few people who knew about my secret classes.

Why had I run from a simple gaze? All he'd done was acknowledge my presence, as anyone with good grace would do, especially in a social setting like a dance.

It didn't make any sense for me to run, but something deep inside knew I couldn't stay. I couldn't stand there beneath his gaze, feeling the weight of his stare. I didn't even know why his stare had weight.

That was ridiculous.

And staring back at him was ... I didn't know what ... a Herculean effort, and it suddenly terrified me.

Worse, I'd stepped away to escape, but his face, his eyes, his smile, they filled my mind, even while standing beneath the stars outside the hall. I'd bolted to be free of his gaze but found it everywhere.

"I needed air too."

I nearly fell off the steps onto my face. Thomas's hand gripping my arm was the only thing that saved me.

"Good God, Thomas! You scared me to death." I made to brush his hand away, but it lingered—and for some ungodly reason, I let it. My eyes drifted to his hand, then, slowly, I turned to find his smile wide and his eyes warm.

"Glad you're here. Baker's already danced with a half-dozen girls. I got tired of holding up the wall on my own."

Holding up the wall? He was a handsome fella. Any number of girls would've tripped over themselves to dance with him. Why was he stuck in the shadows while others had fun? That was a silly thing to say. Then again, I was standing outside in the snow and cold while the music played. Who was I to judge?

He finally released my arm, and my hand found its way up, as if searching for his missing grip.

"Yeah, I get it. Janie and Arty are having a blast."

"But you're not?" he asked.

I shrugged. "It's okay, I guess. Dances haven't ever been my thing. I just come so Janie will leave me alone. There's no winning an argument with her when she's set her mind, *especially* about the social calendar."

"She sounds like a good friend."

"The best—just don't tell her I said that."

He grinned again, and something in my chest expanded. I reached up and rubbed it, unsure how to handle the foreign sensation.

"Want to take a walk, get away from the music for a few?"

My head was starting to ache from all the noise, and the cold air felt good against my skin. Janie would kill me for skipping out on our promise, but maybe a walk was just what I needed to get in the mood.

"Sure. Sounds good."

# Chapter Sixteen

# Thomas

I'm not sure what came over me, asking Will to take a stroll like that. Nobody would think twice about two students walking across campus, even a pair dressed as formally as we were, but we'd both left friends at the dance, friends who would wonder where we'd gone. Our only salvation was that our friends didn't know each other, so there wouldn't be any comparing of notes or parsing things out.

"You hate dances that much?" I asked as we ambled along the sidewalk, leaving shallow prints in the fresh snow.

"Huh?"

"The dance. You just ... I don't know. You looked miserable, like a scared kitten that wanted to run."

His gaze darted toward me, then back to the snow. "Dances are okay, I guess."

I waited for him to say more, but he didn't. His voice was off, more tentative than normal, like he was tiptoeing around something.

"You feel alright? How's your chin?" The bruising on his chin hadn't quite matched the color of some of the girls' dresses, but it was close, and his lip was still swollen.

"Fine. I feel fine." He reached up and touched his chin. "Guess I'm still a little sore, especially my lip."

We walked in silence for a moment. I wasn't sure how to fill the void, what to ask or say. There were few times when my mouth wouldn't get ahead of my brain, but for some reason, my words wouldn't work. I glanced at Will. His hair had fallen from its perfectly slicked place to flop across the right side of his face. The moon chose that moment to peek from behind the clouds. I stared as his jaw resolved from darkness into a beautifully squared essence of manhood.

He looked over, and I forced my head to snap forward again.

"What do you do in the navy?" he asked suddenly.

"Uh, what? My job?""Yeah. We're in all these classes. You know, like American Lit?" He said the name like it was a movie title. "Are you part of some special unit or something? I don't know a lot about the navy."

I hesitated. "I can't really talk about it."

He stopped walking. "Really?"

I looked over and shrugged, as if that said everything.

"I've known a bunch of army guys since this whole mess started. One works in logistics, another in intelligence, a few more do strategic planning. At least, I think that's what they call it. Nobody's ever said they can't talk about what they do. Not here, at Harvard."

I didn't know what to say to that. Technically, I wasn't even supposed to confirm I worked in the Office of Naval Intelligence, much less talk about my specific work. Will had to know I did something in the covert world, given our classes, but still ...

"You're not a spy, are you? Out there in a dark coat and hat, sneaking around, snapping photos of naked diplomats and such?"

I half coughed, half laughed. "Naked diplomats?"

"I probably watch too many movies," he said.

I latched on to that preserver. "Really? Which ones? Seen any good ones lately?"

We'd walked between a pair of buildings and were about to cross Appian Way. The brick and stone edifice of Christ Church, one of the oldest buildings around, stared down at us. Its blocky form looked more like a medieval guard tower than a religious building, especially in the moonlight. Will stared up at it, hesitating before answering. I hoped he was lost in thought about all the movies he'd seen and not wondering about my two-step around his questions.

"I like the thrillers a lot more than dramas or comedies. *Confessions of a Nazi Spy* was pretty good."

"Didn't that come out in '39?"

"Yeah, sounds right. It was a couple years ago." He blew on his hands as he rubbed them together, then stuffed them back into his pockets as we started walking again. "That Alfred Hitchcock one, what was it called?"

"*Foreign Correspondent*?"

"Yeah, that was it. Didn't it get an Oscar?"

"I think it was nominated, but I'm not sure it won. I really don't follow that sort—"

"Oh, me either," he said quickly. "I just remember a lot of talk 'cause I'd seen that one."

"Sure. Makes sense." I pretended to look at a particularly old grave marker, but was really staring at Will's jaw again. "What will you do? I mean, after school?"

He grunted. "Hell if I know. They won't tell me what I'm training for. Maybe I'll end up being the spy instead of you. Or, if you really are one, maybe we'll get to snoop around together. That'd be a hoot, wouldn't it?"

I knew he was picturing us in one of his spy movies, sneaking about and exposing the enemy, but I couldn't help seeing the pair of us sitting in a café, sipping coffee and reading a paper, or strolling down a cobblestone street hand in hand. I looked down, searching for his hand, longing to take it in my own, but his were still tucked inside the warmth of his pockets.

"I'd like that," slipped out of my mouth, in a small, almost reverent voice.

He turned and stared with one brow slightly furrowed, as if he was trying to puzzle my meaning.

"Well, that's pretty out there, but maybe we could help each other get through these classes. You navy guys stick together, or could you study with a regular bloke?"

My heart thumped so hard I swear he could hear it beating, but he just turned back to examine other stones inside the gated yard.

"You mean, like a study partner?""Yeah," he said. "Arty, Janie, and I study together all the time, but they can't help with our, um—" He glanced around, as if we might have been followed. It was the cutest thing he'd done all night. "You know, our *special* classes, like anatomy. All those terms, it's like learning a whole different language."

I barked a laugh. "Guess it is like that," I said, because it was *literally* learning a new language. "Yeah, sure. Study partners. Sounds good."

"Great. We can figure out when and where tomorrow. We just started and I already feel like I'm falling behind. They keep talking about how our lives ... I mean, how *so much* depends on us learning all this. It's just a lot, you know?"

"Yeah, it is, but I'll help you. You'll be okay."

The moon was behind him, so I couldn't see his face, but I thought he smiled.

That settled, Will gave the headstone one last appraisal and we strolled on.

As we passed the church's graveyard on our left and the Cambridge School to our right, campus appeared across the street. I wondered how long we'd walk before Will decided he needed to head back to the dance.

"God, I don't want to go back," he said, as if reading my thoughts.

"Really?"

He stared up at the almost-full moon. "I really should though. Arty will want me to talk to Elizabeth some. I've never seen him so excited."

"He's a good friend, isn't he?"

"Arty? Yeah, he's the best, like the brother I never had. Funny how that happens, isn't it?"

"What?"

"How somebody so different from you can find a way in and become so important. Where else but Harvard could a dopey science kid end up being my best friend?" He chuckled. "But I couldn't imagine any of this without him."

I watched his gaze drift into the night, then finally surrendered. "Guess we should get you back, then."

We turned without crossing Mass. Ave., wove back past the churches and through the houses of Radcliffe. On our walk toward campus, our conversation never faltered, but as we headed back to the dance, we didn't speak a word. It was an odd thing though. Not for a second did I feel a need to fill that silence, and I don't think Will did either. It felt good walking together, lost in thought, enjoying the night air and starless night.

Will climbed the steps, but turned before gripping the door handle. He turned back and smiled my way. "Thanks for the walk. You're pretty good company, ya know?"

The goofy grin that parted my lips must've been a sight. Will's eyes lit up and his own smile widened, then he opened the door and vanished into the hall.

I stared at the double doors, my grin frozen in place.

I couldn't move, or didn't want to move, I wasn't sure which. I wanted to feel that helpless, hopeful happiness until the sun came up. Cold be damned.

"Where'd you go?"

I nearly jumped out of my shoes. The sidewalk was slick with ice, no longer covered in snow, and I stumbled and landed on my butt. A hand shot out before me, offering a lift from the ground. I followed up the arm to find Baker staring, a brow cocked in amusement ... and something else I couldn't pin down.

Then I remembered nearly scaring the life out of Will on exactly that spot earlier in the evening and laughter tumbled out of me. Baker's eyes widened.

"Did you hit your head or what? Looked more like a backside plant from here."

I grabbed his hand and let him pull me to my feet. "No, just ... you reminded me of something funny. That's all."

"So, where'd you go? I was looking for you all over."

"Oh, just out for a walk. It was kinda stuffy in there."

He eyed me in a way I knew meant he wasn't buying any of it.

"With that guy?"

"What?" My heart did that leaping, pounding thing again, and my mouth suddenly went dry. "What guy?"

His voice lowered. "The civilian in our classes. Will something."

I stared, unmoving. Baker had been dancing when I'd left. There was no way he saw me chase after Will. He couldn't have—

"I saw you leave all of a sudden, so I came out to see if you were alright. You two were almost to the edge of Radcliffe when I spotted you."

Shit, he *had* seen us.

Baker was a lieutenant commander, the senior officer among the navy men in our program. He might've been my best friend, but he was married to the navy. If he thought ... if he even suspected ...

"Look," his voice became a whisper. "Be careful, okay? You're my guy, Thomas. You always will be, but I can't protect you from some things ... if you understand my meaning."

I tried to speak. I really tried. For the second time that night, words failed me.

"I see how you look at him. He gives you the same looks, even though he tries to hide them. And if I can see it, other people will too. You have too much to do after all this to ... never mind. Just be careful, okay?"

He patted my shoulder, then turned and hopped up the steps.

"I want another dance. There's a girl in here who's knockin' my socks off, and if I'm lucky, she'll do more than that later." He winked and disappeared, just like Will had, leaving me once again staring at the closed double doors.

# Chapter Seventeen

# Will

I'd always been good at school. Good grades came almost as easily as learning, but maybe that's how it was supposed to work.

My freshman year at Harvard had been a rude awakening. The professors taught at a lightning pace, assigning homework that required far more time than the few hours we spent in class, and the tests—sweet Jesus, they loved tests and quizzes. When my folks died, one might've thought the staff would've taken pity on the poor boy who was now alone in the world, but one would've been mistaken. There were no exceptions or carve-outs for grieving orphans. The work kept coming, and I had to keep up or drown under its weight.

Looking back, the overwhelming nature of freshman studies likely saved me from folding in on myself during the darkest days of my life. Perhaps they knew I needed to stay busy. Would they have been that kind? That thoughtful? Probably not. They swamped everyone with work, and I was no exception. Either way, I was oddly grateful for it; at least, I was grateful in retrospect. At the time, I was miserable.

The amount of work involved in this new term made my freshman year look like a stroll in the park. Janie thought Arty and I were just bellyaching, as she hadn't noticed an increase in workload from her instructors. We, however, were taking special classes we couldn't discuss with anyone, not even each other, and those teachers were determined to hammer our raw ore into sharp, finely honed edges. In order to accomplish that worthy task, they pushed us to the outer edges of our limits, heaping on more homework and more detailed exams than I'd known could exist in one term. While ordinary students—the few who remained on campus—enjoyed extracurricular activities in the evenings, we were held up in libraries and study rooms, buried under tomes of knowledge both ancient and modern.

We fell into the rhythm of a college routine in the weeks that followed the dance, like mice running in their wheel so quickly they forget to eat or sleep. Most nights, as I flopped into bed, my brain hurt. It wasn't so much a headache. No, it felt more like someone slapping me every time I tried to think again. I learned not to think in bed. It stung.

I'm not sure I would've survived that term's academic rigor without Thomas.

Political Science, otherwise known as All Things German, was our last class of each day, ending in the early afternoon. We walked across Massachusetts Avenue, back onto the campus proper, to barricade ourselves in a study room in my house. I never wondered why we didn't study in Andover, where he was housed and where our classes were held. Walking back to my dorm just became automatic, a ritual I never thought to question.

Thomas already spoke fluent German, though his delivery was still heavily burdened by his Bostonian accent. He helped me learn the language, while I made fun of his horrid accent to make him sound more natural.

Who was I kidding? It was fun to tease him. German already required an unnatural amount of phlegm. Add the upturned nose of a smart-ass Boston native, and you got a ridiculously funny—and equally hard to follow—version of the Arian tongue.

During those first few weeks, I was also surprised to learn he spoke French and Russian. I'd never been around any Russian speakers, so I couldn't vouch for his accent, but his French was even worse than his German. I was pretty sure he'd get shot if he ever did anything more than order from a menu.

Our radio and communications studies came easily to me. My brain was wired a bit like a radio, all parallel circuits and such. It just made sense. The clandestine nature of cloaking and detection, as well as the more recent innovations in miniaturization, came quickly to me.

Thomas was not blessed with parallel circuits.

I came to wonder if some of his circuits met at all when it came to mechanical things. We must've taken our sample radio apart and reassembled it a hundred times, and he still left parts out—and not a screw here or there, but the important ones, like the power pack that made the whole thing work.

But the bane of our existence was Sergeant Major Stafford and his cartography course. You'd think any idiot could read a map, see how the lines scrunched together or spread apart, and just know what the land would look like. Oh, no. It couldn't possibly be that simple. Throw in weather, changes since the map was made, elements of camouflage, and a hundred other variables, and there was *never* a consistently right answer to any question.

Studying with Thomas was easy. It felt comfortable. Despite the amount of work I knew faced us, I found myself looking forward to our study sessions throughout the day. Something about just being with him made me feel, I don't know, relaxed.

I'd just returned to my room and laid down on the bed. Insomnia had been my constant companion for years, but had abandoned me when this term began. Most nights, I fell asleep with my nose still in a book, something I'd never done before.

"Will!" Arty's voice followed the banging of the door as it flew open and slammed against the stopper. "Oh, sorry. Didn't know you were asleep. You feeling okay? It's just eight thirty."

I sat up on my side and propped up on an elbow.

"It's okay. I just laid down. What's up?"

He didn't ask twice, darting across the room to land beside me on the bed.

"I think I love her."

I laughed and sat upright. "Whoa. Easy. Start over from the beginning of ... whatever this is."

He was practically vibrating with excitement. His cheeks were flushed, and I could feel waves of heat coming off his skin, despite just walking in from the cold.

"I think Elizabeth is the one, Will. I really do. She's the most incredible woman in all the world. I mean, in the whole damn world."

Arty and Elizabeth had become a regular item, eating lunch together most days and going out for ice cream or a Coke several evenings each week. On the rare occasion when we were both in the room and not asleep, he babbled incessantly about her hair or eyes or something she'd said, the way she laughed or the way she made him laugh. It was like listening to a kid who'd just had his first kiss under the bleachers. I couldn't help but smile every time he brought up her name. In a world going mad, it was nice to see a bit of pure happiness.

I grinned. "Okay, I'll bite. Why? Did something happen?"

"No, nothing happened. I mean, well, everything happened. So yes. I guess. I don't know." He sucked in a breath. "She's just so perfect, Will, and I feel like my insides are going to tumble out every time I see her."

"Uh, Arty, that's gross. Don't ever tell her that, okay?"

He scowled. "Right. Good call. Anyway, she's amazing and smart and ... God, Will, have you *seen* her? She could be in pictures. How does a guy like me end up with a girl like that?"

I chuckled. "I would say I've wondered the same thing, but Arty, you're a great guy. You deserve the best. Don't you know that?"

He brushed my praise aside. "Whatever. Will, I can't even describe how it feels. I mean, something stupid like holding hands makes my heart race and my mind go numb. It's like everything in me overloads and I can't breathe or think. All I can do is feel ... and *everything* feels amazing."

"Okay," I said slowly. "That all sounds grand, but isn't it a little early to think she's the one? That's a pretty big leap."

"Whatever. I don't care about being careful anymore. She makes me want to leap and jump and scream, all at the same time, and that's hard to do in the snow." His laughter was infectious. Before I could respond, he hopped to his feet, tossed the books he'd been carrying on his desk, and raced to the door. "We're going for ice cream. See you later if you're up."

The head-spinning visit ended as quickly as it had begun, leaving me once again on my bed in the dark. Only this time, my brain decided it wanted to engage.

Despite feeling exhausted, thoughts whirled about, and images of Thomas fluttered to life in my mind's eye. The look in Arty's eyes when he described Elizabeth reminded me of him. I'd see it sometimes when we studied. I'd be buried in a book and feel his gaze, only to find him staring when I looked up. I hadn't thought much about it before, but Arty's passion just now was so similar to ...

Then Arty's words about how her touch felt. He'd said holding hands made his heart race and his mind go numb. I thought back to when Thomas had put his hand on my chest and held me down, that night I'd been hurt in the gym. I could feel the pressure against me, his warmth. I didn't understand why, but his grasp had calmed and comforted me. Pain laced through my chin and the back of my head, but feeling his palm pressing into my shoulder somehow made me forget my throbbing aches, if only for a moment.

It was so odd.

I remembered his eyes. They were so vivid in my mind, so deep and brown, with the tiniest flecks of gold dancing at the edges. I thought he was studying my chin and busted lip, but replaying the moment, there was something else, something almost *hidden* in his gaze.

I remembered holding his hand a moment too long when he'd kept me from touching my chin. His grip was strong, and I could almost feel the smoothness of his skin.

In the time I'd known him, that might've been the longest he'd gone without smirking.

Then his half-grin appeared before me, and I found myself grinning.

My heart had raced.

My mind had gone numb.

I bolted upright, and the dorm room spun as a wave of something akin to nausea flooded through me. I didn't have to vomit, but my stomach roiled, and my head swam. Heat battered my senses.

Arty had said her touch made his heart race and his mind …

"Oh shit."

---

I'd been cooped up in the small study room on the first floor of my house for more than an hour. My stomach finally settled after two mugs of hot tea and a plate of warm mashed potatoes from the dining hall. Rations were beginning to take effect across the country and, while Harvard often lived in its own privileged bubble, our choice in menu items had recently diminished to support the war effort. Thankfully, drab potatoes were exactly what my troubled stomach needed.

Professor Karpovich, my instructor in the history of Russia, had warned of an upcoming pop quiz. That seemed to go against the general idea of a pop quiz, giving warning and all, but it was much appreciated all the same. I'd finally focused my wandering mind on Catherine the Great and her alleged proclivity toward horses when two sharp raps sounded.

My pulse immediately flipped into double time.

The door opened and Thomas peered in, a smile parting his lips when our eyes met.

"Hey," he said, stepping inside and closing the door behind him. "You ready for some *Germanistik*?"

I glanced at my pocket watch sitting beside a stack of books and my tea mug. He was timelier than my aged timepiece.

"Yeah, sure," I said, glancing back toward the sketch of Catherine in my textbook.

His feet shuffled closer.

The smack of something heavy vibrated the table. I guessed he'd dropped his books.

A chair scraped against the floor, then stilled, then scraped a few times as he got comfortable.

Then nothing.

Silence stretched so long I looked up to see if he'd left.

He was sitting directly across from me, his hands folded on top of each other on the table, and his eyes fixed ... on me.

"What's wrong, Will?"

I glanced down, then back up quickly. "Nothing. I'm fine, really. Just fine. Why would you say that?"

"Well, for one, you're stammering. You aren't always the most eloquent fellow, but you rarely stammer." His smirk appeared. "Two, you only just looked up at me, and, as quickly as you looked up, you stuck your nose back down in that book that I know you're not reading because your eyes never moved across the page."

"I was studying—"

"The picture of a long-dead Russian empress and her, um, horse?" There was a chuckle in his voice.

"Yes, as a matter of fact, that's the lesson, I mean, topic or subject ... thing."

"The *thing*?" His whole face smirked, though I wasn't sure how.

"You know, the thing we'll be tested on. We have a test ... I mean, exam, or ... pop quiz. Yeah, a pop quiz."

"And you know a *pop* quiz is coming because ...?"

"Professor Karpovich told us it was coming soon. So, I decided to study, you know, to be ready."

He unfolded his hands and rested his elbows on the table, leaning forward. "You're a good boy, Will. A good little student."

"Oh, fuck off," I said, more sharply than intended.

His brow raised. "Somebody has their unmentionables in a bunch."

I crossed my arms in the most mature gesture possible, not pouty at all. "I am a man. My underclothes are most mentionable, thank you very much."

He laughed. "Oh, forgive me, sir. Should I mention them, then?"

My face flushed, and I swear his grin widened.

"Can we just get it on ... I mean, get on with it?"

He laughed as he rose and made his way to the chair beside me, sliding his stack of books as he walked around the table. I shrank away, but didn't scoot my chair.

"Easy, soldier. We only have one German language book. I'm just coming around so we can share."

Right. He was right. We always shared when we studied German. Why was I so anxious? So hot? Why was I sweating?

"*Das ist besser*," he said, settling beside me as he reached to open his book. His breath wafted by, and I could smell coffee and some sort of sweet confection. It was heady. Then fire or lightning or ice or an army of tiny ants with sharp, pointed boots marched up my arm as his arm brushed mine. We both wore long-sleeve shirts, so it's not like our skin touched, but I felt it all the same.

I squirmed and couldn't get comfortable.

"Is there anything you want to talk about, Will? You seem really, I don't know, off."

My eyes fell to my hands, then roamed to my lap, then to my book—everywhere but up to him.

"You know you can tell me anything, right? We're in all the classes for keeping secrets. I can keep yours too."

Oh God. Oh God. Oh God.

I didn't even know what my own secret meant. Hell, a day ago I hadn't even recognized I had a secret. Even then, I wasn't sure it was real, whether I really felt all those things, what Arty had said about Elizabeth ... and how Thomas ...

Breathing was so hard. I reached up and tugged at my collar. It was rounded and loose, but I could feel it pressing into my neck. The room felt so hot, and that bubbling and churning in my stomach returned even stronger than before my calming potato elixir.

Thomas's hand gently rested on my arm, and the unholy blazes of hell shot through me. I startled, nearly leaping to my feet, but my chair banged into the wall behind us and held me fast in place.

"Easy, Will. It's just me. Breathe." His voice was so calm, so easy and warm and ... I could taste it ... I mean, feel it against my skin. I wanted to feel it so badly. It was warm and sweet and—

"Will," he whispered, and I felt him only inches away.

I kept my head down, but darted my eyes toward him as best I could.

He was so close.

"You can talk to me. I don't know how, we've only known each other for such a short time, but you feel like a best friend. Like *more* than a best friend."

That did *not* help.

I mean, it felt like my heart had bounced off a mountain and was soaring over a river screaming "Wee!" all the way. I guess, in that way, it felt amazing.

But he was not helping me ground myself and shake this feeling that I wanted to—

His fingers found my face and turned my head toward him.

My world began to spin again.

"Will, I trust you."

And he pressed his lips into mine.

# Chapter Eighteen

# Thomas

My hand cupped his cheek as our lips remained fixed. I could feel him trying to decide, to pull back or press forward. The last thing I wanted was to scare him away, so I didn't move, like sitting in a tree stand watching a deer amble by with perked ears as it sniffed the air. One hint and it would dart away.

He didn't dart away.

But he didn't press into me either.

I finally pulled back and looked into his frightened, nearly trembling eyes. His face had been so red, so full of color and heat, but was now nearly as pale as the snow outside. I wanted to comfort him, to tell him it was alright, that everything would be fine, but I was almost as overcome in that moment as he was. My heart was a rabbit with massive feet, thumping so hard my chest rattled, but I felt a joy rolling through me, waves of it, that I couldn't remember knowing before. Looking at Will, that joy flowered and grew. Right there, in that room, it flourished, and I thought I might jump out of my skin and holler to the world.

"I've wanted to do that since the day we met," I breathed, not trusting my full voice to speak.

He blinked, and somehow, his eyes widened further.

My hand still rested on his cheek. I couldn't let go. I didn't want to.

"Thomas ... I ... I'm not ..."

He slowly pulled back and my hand fell away. He reached up and touched his cheek as though searching for it. His gaze, so erratic only moments earlier, still hadn't left mine.

"I've never ..." he tried again. "I mean, I don't like, um, boys, I guess."

I couldn't help myself, and a nervous chuckle escaped. "Boys?"

His face flushed again, scarlet chasing away ashen fear.

"You know what I mean."

I took his hand in mine and gently rubbed small circles on the back of it with my thumb. "I do ... like boys, I mean. I've known it for a while now, since joining the navy."

His brows scrunched. "Really? I thought the navy wouldn't take ... men like you."

It hurt how he said that. I tried not to let it show. What were "men like me" supposed to be like? I was strong and smart, loyal, committed to my country as much as anyone. I was serving, by my own choice, not some lottery that forced me into a uniform. I was ready to do my duty and give my life, if that's what it took, to see an end to the evil that was Hitler. I was a good man, and I knew it.

That's what men like me were. It burned me that anyone would think otherwise, or even consider my service less than anyone else's.

"I didn't mean anything by that, Thomas," he said, and I felt his fingers close on mine. My heart stopped dead still. "You're such a good man. I know that. It's just ... all this ... I mean, this is wrong, isn't it?"

I drew in a deep breath, then blew it out. This conversation was so painful, and it always went downhill fast.

"If you are religious, sure. Christians, Jews, whoever, they all think the same about ... us." He flinched when I said "us," but I pressed on. "The law isn't on our side either. Doctors think we're sick or cock-eyed, however they say it, and most folks just think faggots are bad business."

Will blanched and yanked his hand away.

"You shouldn't use that word, not even here, in private. What if someone heard you?" he whispered, his gaze darting back toward the door as though it would open at any moment and the police would barge in.

"Sorry," I muttered.

He hadn't pulled away, other than his hand, and was staring back at me. I took that as a good sign and sat back to let him think. My heart ached to watch him struggle with his feelings. I remembered how hard it had been for me when I began wondering about myself.

He ran a hand through his hair, then pressed both palms to his eyes. As if reading my thoughts, he asked, "How long have you known? I mean, about yourself, kissing guys and all."

Will wasn't innocent. I'd learned that over the past month or so. He'd grown up in a privileged family, but had a mischievous streak I was sure had landed him in trouble more than a time or two. He'd hinted at some of his past, but the memory of his parents—of the loss of his parents—brought revelations from his youth to a halt each time.

In that moment though, there was an air of innocence about him I hadn't seen before. It was as if he'd opened his eyes for the first time, and what he saw was so foreign, so unreal, that he hardly knew how to process what he was seeing, much less understand it.

But he'd opened the door by asking about my experience, and I resolved to answer. I decided to trust Will, even more than I already did, and that was, apparently, a hell of a lot more than my training taught me to trust anyone, especially someone I'd known for a little over a month.

I scratched my scalp, almost mirroring him.

"Guess I was fifteen, maybe sixteen. There was a guy in school, Maxwell. We were on the basketball team together. I don't think he ever knew how sweet I was on him, but his smile could make my toes curl."

"You knew right away? Just like that?"

I let out a sardonic laugh. "Lord, no. First time I thought about him as more than a friend or teammate, it scared the dickens out of me. I knew I was gonna get locked up or sent away to a sanatorium. My parents would've killed me. Not literally, they aren't like that, but they wouldn't have taken it well. At least, that's all I could think at the time."

"So, what happened. I mean, with Maxwell. What did you do?"

I stared into the tabletop, wishing its grains would stop swirling in my eyes.

"Nothing. I did nothing."

Will leaned forward, his brows bunched again. "If you didn't do anything, how do you know—?"

"How do I know I'm a homosexual?"

He flinched again. It was crazy how much power these words held. They might as well have been darts or knives, piercing our skin when spoken.

"I've never had a girlfriend," I said.

"That doesn't mean anything. Neither have I." Will crossed his arms like he'd just proven a point.

I grinned and raised one brow, then watched his arms uncross as his face fell in recognition.

"That, in itself, didn't mean anything. Maybe I was shy, or didn't find a girl who excited me? Who knows?" I leaned forward and looked into his eyes. "But I *knew*, Will. I just knew."

"But how?" his voice pleaded more than asked.

I thought a moment. "Because, when I saw him, my heart raced, and I thought the sun shone just a bit brighter. When he laughed, I could feel it in my soul. When we weren't together, he was all I could think about. Hell, I dreamed about him, Will. I actually dreamed of his face. Who does that?"

"Huh. You had it bad, I guess," he muttered.

"You think?" I laughed. "My best friend at the time was calling on this girl, prettiest thing in our class, and he talked about how she made him feel. It was all the same, Will, the exact same. I don't know how any of this works, or why we like who we like, but I know those feelings. I know how they make me happy, how they make me want ... more. They're real, and they're not bad like people think. They're just not."

I hadn't meant to get so ... passionate. My voice had risen and I was punching my heart at the end. It felt like moisture had formed in my eyes, and I wiped it away.

Will just stared.

After an eternal moment in which my mind imagined Will running out of the room, or calling for the house master, or yelling "faggot" at the top of his lungs, he asked the last thing I dreamed would whisper across his lips.

"And ... you feel those things ... about me?"

# Chapter Nineteen

# **Will**

That might've been the stupidest question in the history of stupid questions. I couldn't have sounded more pathetic if I'd tried. Was I really so desperate to be liked, if that's even what Thomas was saying? I mean, I knew what he was saying—or I thought I did.

Thomas didn't flinch. His mouth didn't even quirk into a smug grin.

He just leaned forward, took both my hands in his, and stared into my eyes. I'd never known anyone to say so much with just a gaze.

"You drive me crazy, Will."

"In a good way?" God, stupidity kept falling out of my mouth.

He chuckled. "In the best way. I'm mad about you."

"Really?"

He nodded and squeezed my hands. "I think about you all the time."

I looked down at our hands.

He waited.

A thousand thoughts whirled, but when I opened my mouth, nothing came out. I couldn't speak. I could barely slow my brain enough to think.

When my chest clenched, I freed my hands from his, stood, and moved so the table was between us.

Thomas watched in silence as I paced.

I looked over to find his face no longer passive. The confidence I'd seen earlier had vanished, replaced by something far more tentative. He was waiting for me to say something, but I didn't trust words to work without betraying me.

What finally came out stunned us both. "Are you hungry?"

He cocked his head, like a puppet whose strings had been yanked too hard.

I almost laughed.

He stood and smiled. "Let's get some dinner."

I wasn't sure what I expected, but running into Arty and Janie in the dining hall wasn't it. Before I'd even seen them, Janie leapt to her feet, waved like a drowning swimmer at a passing boat, and yelled my name loud enough to echo off the paneled walls. I wanted to crawl under a table, not go sit with them.

But, with the spotlight—and every eye in the place—firmly on Thomas and me, we strode over and sat like we'd intended to dine with them all along.

"Hey," I said, desperate to keep my voice from wobbling—or from throwing up all over the floor.

Arty held up a broccoli floret he'd speared with his fork in greeting.

Janie narrowed her eyes, the same eyes that darted from me to Thomas, then back.

"Hello, William," she said deliberately. My heart sank. She only called me by my full name when she was angry or suspicious. "And who is this handsome gentleman?"

Thomas did that half-stand thing to show respect to the lady addressing him and bobbed his head. "I'm Thomas—Lieutenant Thomas Jacobs, ma'am. You must be Janie. Will talks about you all the time. You're even prettier than he said."

Janie batted her lashes and smiled broadly. "Oh, Thomas, stop that." She looked at me sideways, but spoke to him. "He really said I was pretty?"

"Oh, he did. I think his exact words were—"

"Look, they have chicken tonight. We get real meat for a change." I pointed to a passing porter whose tray was filled with freshly served plates.

"Be right there, sir," the porter said, nodding my way.

When I looked back, the three of them were staring at me. To be fair, Thomas was smirking. Janie and Arty were staring. One of Arty's cheeks was pooched out like a chipmunk from the broccoli he'd just shoved in, and his fork floated in midair, as though his hand didn't know how to return it to his plate.

"What? I like chicken."

"Of course you do," Janie said, her eyes shifting to Thomas. "How do you two know each other? Will hasn't mentioned you before."

I was breaking into a sweat, but Thomas didn't flinch. As he leaned across the table for the pitcher of water, he said, "We have several classes together. Will's been helping me with political science. It's not really my thing."

Janie's brows shot up, and her gaze fixed back on me.

"You have been helping someone with political science? *You?*"

I nodded. "Sure. Yeah. Why not me?"

"Because you hate politics. I didn't even know you were taking poli sci." She'd set her utensils down and was fully engrossed in her interrogation. I glanced to Arty, hoping for a subject change or some other lifeline, but he just chewed and stared.

Thomas leaned across and whispered, "It's just called political science. It's really a secret military training we can't talk about."

There was a heartbeat of silence, then Janie burst out laughing. Students seated at nearby tables turned to see what was so funny.

"Janie, keep it down," I said, trying to keep my voice calm.

"Or what? You'll arrest me? Or maybe shoot me right here with your miniature pistol? Oh, I know, you'll stab me with a push pin laced with poison that you made from that bouquet over there. That's how you'd do it, isn't it?"

"Janie, please!"

"Oh, come on, Will, you know I love you dearly, but the idea is rather funny. Even you must admit that." She finally calmed herself, then leaned over to brush her shoulder against Arty's. "Will Shaw, Secret Agent Man. That's so rich!"

She dabbed her eyes with her napkin.

I looked at Thomas, but his damn smirk was all I got in return.

As the porter served Thomas and me, someone near the door began shouting for everyone to settle and listen. He turned the radio's volume up as high as it would go.

*"... replay of his address to the United Kingdom via radio earlier today.*

[Announcer's voice replaced by that of British Prime Minister Winston Churchill]

*"I speak to you all under the shadow of a heavy and far-reaching military defeat. It is a British and Imperial defeat. Singapore has fallen. This, therefore, is one of those moments when the British race and nation can show their quality and their genius. This is one of those moments when it can draw from the heart of misfortune the vital impulses of victory. We must remember that we are no longer alone ...*

*"Here is the moment to display the calm and poise combined with grim determination which not so long ago brought us out of the very jaws of death. Here is another occasion to show—as so often in our long history—that we can meet reverses with dignity and renewed accessions of strength.* "[1]

"Dear God," Arty muttered.

"There were more than a hundred thousand men stationed on that island a month ago." All warmth had drained from Thomas's voice.

"How—?" Arty asked.

"Bombardment. The Japs have been hitting the island hard, and, from what I've heard, the British weren't as ready for an assault as they claimed."

---

1. Excerpt from transcript of radio address by British Prime Minister Winston Churchill on February 15, 1942

Janie's eyes shot up. "How do you know that?"He met her gaze with steel. "It's been all over the news; the bombardment, I mean. The radio's always on up at Andover, being a house for military guys."

Janie eyed him. "I suppose that makes sense."

"You can't get away from the war in that place. It's one reason I like coming down here to study with Will."

I didn't think anyone else noticed, but I swore her eyes narrowed; but if she was thinking anything, she didn't let on.

"The Germans own Europe. Now the Japanese have parts of China and are taking islands all over the Pacific. How are we supposed to survive this?" A rare crack showed in Janie's perfectly maintained shell, but, as quickly as it appeared, it vanished. "Well, that's what you boys are here for, I guess. You'll keep us all safe, won't you, Thomas?"

He didn't smile or smirk. His face was stone.

"Every man in uniform will give our lives for yours, Janie—for all of yours."

He stood and turned to me.

"I should get back to Andover. Let's talk more tomorrow."

# Chapter Twenty

# **Will**

Arty and Janie stared without speaking long after Thomas left. My brain couldn't decide whether to focus on the Singapore news or obsess over the host of unresolved questions raised by the study session—and the kiss.

Janie finally set her glass down, leaned toward me, and whispered, "Thomas is very handsome, don't you think?"

I blanched. "Sure, I guess. I mean, I never really thought about it. He's just a guy in my class. That's all."

Her maniacal brow shot up. "Huh."

I crossed my arms. "Huh? Huh, what? What does that mean?"

"I have a mountain of homework," Arty said, standing. He patted my shoulder and chuckled as he walked by. "You're on your own, General Custer."

I shot to my feet, banging my knee on the underside of the table. "Ow. Wait up. I need to get going too, to study ... and stuff."

"We're not done talking, William Shaw," Janie's most matronly tone warned.

"Yeah, sure, fine. Talk soon, okay?"

I practically elbowed Arty out of the way as I fled the dining hall. He called out, but I didn't wait for him, just headed to the study room to gather my books. I'd barely escaped Janie's all-seeing eye, the last thing I wanted was a grilling by my roommate.

The study room was blessedly empty. I closed the door behind me and leaned against it. My head throbbed and my heart ached. How had things gotten so complicated? I hadn't asked for any of this. I certainly hadn't asked to be kissed, especially not by a man.

Part of me wanted to be disgusted. The very idea of two men kissing was universally reviled. No part of decent society accepted such perversion. Even the law banned deviant activity, of which kissing a man was most definitely the top of that slippery slope.

How could I have let Thomas do that?

Thomas.

He was ... a homosexual.

I slumped to the floor as that thought sank in.

Thomas had always seemed so normal. He didn't sway when he walked, or lisp, or anything those people did. And he was strong and athletic, more so than most of the guys in our classes. Never in a million years would I have guessed he ...

"He's in the navy, for God's sake," I muttered, as though service shielded every man from unnatural thoughts.

Unable to wallow on the floor any longer, I pushed myself up and stepped to the table. Thomas and I had left without straightening up, our books open and splayed across the table top. They were now neatly stacked, with a folded note sitting atop the pile.

I picked up the note and read:

*Will,*

*Thanks for the study session and dinner. Sorry it got weird.*

*If it makes you feel any better, I was probably just as nervous as you were about the whole thing.*

*Keep your chin up. Seriously, keep it up. No more falling. It took me forever to get you to stop bleeding all over the place.*

*Talk soon.*

*T*

Despite everything, I laughed, certain Thomas had smirked as he wrote that last bit.

I folded the note and shoved it in my pocket, then grabbed my books and headed upstairs. Arty was sitting at his desk with his nose buried in the fattest textbook I'd ever seen. He slammed it shut and shoved it aside as I entered.

"Does that book have pictures, or do you actually have to read the whole thing?"

He laughed nervously, like his mother had just caught him hitting his little brother.

"Yeah, pictures. That's a good one."

I shook my head. Sometimes Arty was just weird.

"Sorry," he said. "It's for one of the classes I can't talk about. You know, the ones in the president's building about science and stuff."

"Science and stuff?"

He nodded. "There's a lot of technical terms, but that about covers it."

"Thanks for dumbing it down for me."

He smiled weakly. "So, Janie was riding you pretty hard down there. You okay?"

Shit. Here we go.

"Yeah, I'm good."

I dropped my books onto my desk and fell onto my bed.

He moved to sit on his bed facing me. "You know we're friends, right?"

I rolled onto my side to look at him. "We're not friends; you're my brother, Arty. You're family."

"I think so too. Yeah, definitely." His smile was genuine again. "So, brothers tell each other stuff."

"Again with stuff? Do I have to go all sciency with you? It's not really my area."

He chuckled. "No, no science. Just … Will …"

He fumbled with his fingers, then words shot out of his mouth like a ball from a cannon: "Are you in love with that Thomas guy?"

I stared, dumbfounded, then sat upright. "Arty—"

"Will, please don't tell me he's just a friend or a guy in your class. We've lived together for two and a half years, and you've never mentioned a girl—*any* girl—not even once."

"Will, I just—"

"You're a good-looking guy. Girls are always trying to catch your eye, but you never seem to notice." He stood and began pacing between our beds. It looked like he was avoiding my gaze at all costs. "I thought maybe you were just sheltered or clueless. I mean, *I'm* clueless. Seriously. If either of us should be scared to talk to a girl, it's your dopey best friend, right?"

I wanted to argue, but my voice wouldn't work. I was sure my heart had stopped beating.

"Deep down, I knew better. I'm pretty sure I've always known better. You were an athlete back home, probably popular. Girls would've been all over you then, but you've never talked about any of them either."

Terror seized my throat as Arty sat beside me and gripped my forearm with a bony hand.

"Is it true?"

"What difference does it make?" I snapped. "It's not like two men could ever go out or be together or whatever. He'd get kicked out of the navy, and we'd end up in jail—or worse, some asylum. Even *your* people would take us outside the city walls and stone us."

He chuckled. "I'm pretty sure stonings ended a few centuries ago."

"Right. They'd probably bring them back, just for us."

I couldn't look up. If his eyes held an ounce of the cruel judgment I suspected, it would crush me. I couldn't take that, not from Arty.

"Arty, it doesn't matter how I feel or what I might want. The world—people—just won't let me have any of it. Plenty of folk would sooner see me die in the war than live a life with another man."

"So, it's true?"

He waited quietly, his hand never leaving my arm.

I looked up and spoke in a small, broken voice. "I don't know. Maybe."

"Which part? That you like men, or that you like Thomas?"

"Dammit, Arty, I don't know, alright. I don't know."

I hadn't meant to yell. Arty didn't deserve my anger, but feelings I couldn't identify, much less understand, were clawing to escape, and I had no clue how to handle them.

I flopped back and stared at the ceiling.

Arty followed suit, lying on his side facing me, placing one hand on my chest. He'd made that gesture a thousand times, and I knew it to be one of pure brotherly love, but in that moment, his hand felt like a thousand-pound stone.

"Arty, I … I've never thought about another guy … *that* way. I swear."

"Really? Not even a little?"

"No. I mean, I had plenty of friends I liked hanging out with, but that's normal, right?"

"Sure." He hesitated, then asked, "What's he like? Tell me about him."

Laughter from a group of students outside in the yard filled the silence of the moment. I was glad for the chance to think.

"His name is Thomas Jacobs. He's a lieutenant in the navy. I really don't know what he does, because he's all secretive about it. I guess we all have our secrets these days." I gave Arty a tight smile. "He's sarcastic and funny. And smart. He plays it down, but Jesus, he's really smart. Oh, and he's athletic too. You should see him on the court. And he has medical training; not like a doctor or anything, but more than the basics. He helped me when I got knocked out the other week."

"You told me." I caught a grin on Arty's face.

"Oh, sorry." I put my hands behind my head and continued examining the ceiling tiles. Arty lifted his hand to let me shift, then returned it to my chest. He'll never know how much that meant, how comforting—no, how *reassuring*—that was.

"And you like spending time with him?"

"Well, yeah. I mean, I've always liked spending time with him. He's a really good guy, and he's helped me get through some classes I probably would've failed out of."

"You would *never* fail a class, Will." His voice was wry. "That's it? You enjoy spending time with him because he's smart and helpful?"

"Sounds pretty lame when you say it like that."

"Why do you think this is more than friendship?" I blew out a breath. "God, Arty. That's all *your* fault."

"My fault?" He sat up. "Please tell me how it's my fault you're sweet on a boy."

"I'm not sweet—" His frown cut me off. "Okay, maybe I'm a little ... whatever."

He cocked a brow.

"Fine. It's *your* fault because of how you talked about Elizabeth after the dance."

He laughed. "I can't wait to hear this. Go on."

"You went on and on about how her hand touching yours made your world spin, and how you could feel the warmth of her breath in your chest, and when she smiled the whole room got all bright. I hadn't thought about it before, but Thomas smiled at me from across the dance hall, and I remember how the room got hot and bright all of a sudden, and I just thought, if that's how it felt with you and Elizabeth, then this must be the same with Thomas and me. It's the same, isn't it?"

"Sure sounds like it." His grin widened. "What is it about Thomas? Why's he special enough to make you realize … to make you feel all this?"

I closed my eyes and saw Thomas's smile. A familiar warmth bloomed in my chest, and for the first time, I surrendered to its embrace.

"He puts on this air of being tough or whatever, but he really cares."

"About you?"

My voice caught. "I meant in general. He cares about people and the country. Stuff like that."

"But you think he cares about you too?"

"Uh … well … yeah. I think so. He said something like that today."

"Do you care about him?"

There it was: the question I'd been avoiding. I'd never been afraid of a question before, but one had never held so much power. It sounded so simple and innocent, but there was more meaning in those few words than anything I'd ever been asked.

The answer would change my life forever.

"I guess I do."

# Chapter Twenty-One

# **Thomas**

I walked into our radios and codes class to find Will already seated in his front row chair, reading diligently. I started to take the long way to my seat, the route that would've taken me by the instructor's desk and past Will, but nerves got the better of me. A few of the other students were also seated, and the last thing I wanted was to make Will uncomfortable in front of others. He didn't look up as I snaked my way through the chairs to my spot behind him.

As I set my books down, I noticed one lone paperback on my desk. Red print across the top read, *Rand McNally: BOSTON Guide*. An illustration of familiar trees, roads, and buildings consumed the rest of the cover.

Curious, I peeled off my winter coat and laid it on the chair to my left, then sat and examined the book. Nothing on the outside offered any hint of where it came from or who might've left it behind. It appeared to be new, with an unbroken spine and unblemished cover. I opened it and was about to thumb through the pages when a piece of folded paper fluttered out. I caught it before it could fall to the floor, then unfolded it to reveal neat block lettering in black ink that read:

*Thought you might show me around your hometown sometime. It would be nice to get away from campus, just us. Maybe we can pick up where our study session ended?*

*W*

My heart nearly leapt out of my chest.

I'd spent most of the previous night tossing and turning, unable to sleep. I hadn't walked into that room intending to kiss him. Hell, the thought didn't cross my mind until I was leaning forward, but that one kiss had confirmed everything my heart had been telling me: I was nuts about Will.

He let our lips linger—and that had upended everything he thought he knew.

It changed how he viewed me, and I was terrified of what that meant. Would he be revolted, like so many others? Would he be too frightened by what others would think to give us a chance? Would he say something that might derail everything I'd worked so hard for?

He had the power to destroy my career. I'd given it to him with that one kiss.

It had also changed how he viewed himself—at least, I thought that was probably the case. I remembered my own struggles with accepting who I was, who I was attracted to, and how the world saw people like me. It was never easy, and I was sure Will was beginning to battle those doubts and fears.

He hadn't leaned into the kiss, but he hadn't pulled back either. He could've stood or pushed me away. He could've run out the door.

He could've done so many things, but he did the one thing I'd hoped for above all else.

He stayed.

His eyes weren't filled with fear, but it was there, beneath it all. He hadn't seen the kiss coming and had no idea how to handle everything it implied.

I wanted to wrap him in my arms and tell him everything would be alright, but how could I say that? Society wouldn't accept him now, and, with war raging across the globe, the world was going to hell. Nothing was alright, and might never be again.

Somehow, in the midst of so much turmoil, his kiss was perfect.

I folded the note and stuffed it in my pocket so it couldn't fall out of the book again. As I stared at the city guide, I couldn't wipe the boyish grin from my face.

In his own, very Will way, he was staying ... again.

# Chapter Twenty-Two

# Will

Arty and I stood on the steps outside of Janie's house, pacing in the chilly air.

"Is she ever on time?" Arty grumbled.

"How long have we known her, Arty? Did you really just ask me that?"

He grunted and blew hot breath into his cupped hands.

"And why aren't we waiting inside, in the *warm* lobby?" he asked.

"Because I'm right here and ready to go," Janie's voice sang from the opening door. She stepped out and spun so we could fully appreciate our date for the evening. "Sorry I'm late, boys. It takes so long to make things just right for you two."

"We sincerely appreciate the effort, m'lady," I said, extending a hand and bowing at the waist.

She giggled, took my hand, and descended the stairs like royalty greeting her subjects.

"It is so good to be seen by one's people."

Arty rolled his eyes. "It's so good to finally see you so we can get out of this damn cold. Can we go now?"

Janie turned toward me. "Elizabeth needs to get him in a better mood."

I laughed and nodded.

Arty looked back. "She does just fine. She doesn't make a guy freeze his manhood off."

Janie dropped my hand and flitted up to Arty, wrapping her arms around him. "Aww, Arty Bug, is your wittle worm cold and swivvled?"

I nearly doubled over laughing at her baby talk. Arty hated it when she called him Arty Bug, and his expressions were hysterical.

He shook off her arms and fast-walked until he was far ahead of us.

Janie took my arm and giggled at her own cleverness, then lowered her voice, "So, how's Thomas?"

I nearly stumbled. "Thomas? Um, he's fine, I guess."

She eyed me sideways, the grin never leaving her lips. "William John Shaw, it's time you and I had a talk."

I groaned. "Come on, ma. Not now. Can we not just have a fun night?"

"I'm your older and far prettier sister, *never* your mother." She cocked her head, then said, "You are rather pretty though. I never really noticed before."

"Thanks, I think, but I prefer handsome or rugged, maybe snappy when I'm wearing a suit. Pretty sounds so—"

"So appropriate, I think," she finished my sentence in a very different way that I'd intended. "I like Thomas."

I couldn't help but peek at her. She was positively glowing with ... something annoying.

"Do you want me to set you up? He's single."

She tutted. "Not from what I hear."

I stopped walking and turned, all humor drained from my voice. "What have you heard? And who from?"

She shook her head like I was a child asking silly questions. "Will, no one has told me anything. That was a turn of phrase."

I turned and started walking again. Arty was nearly to the street. "Fine, but why would you say—"

"You haven't denied it."

"What?"

"That you like Thomas—and I don't mean as a study buddy or basketball teammate or friend. You *like* him, and from what I've seen, he's head over heels for you."

Nearly a week had passed since Thomas and I encountered Janie and Arty in the dining hall. Our afternoon study sessions had continued without further incident. We'd played basketball a couple nights, thankfully without injury. There had been no further social interaction, no talk of touring Boston or any other city. We'd simply acted like the friends we were. I knew all that would change. I wanted it to, but there had been nothing to set off anyone's alarm bells since that lunch.

Janie's sixth sense was unearthly.

With no safe route of escape, I mumbled, "I really like him, Janie. I mean, I still don't get it, the whole liking boys thing. It's so new and ... nothing I've ever experienced before ... but Thomas is great."

I peeked over to find her beaming again.

"I knew it!" Her voice rose, and Arty turned back and raised his arms, urging us to catch up. "Sorry," she whispered. "I don't think he heard us."

I glanced around. "There's nobody nearby, but we should keep it down. Arty's okay. He already knows."

Now she stopped walking, and her hands flew to her hips.

"How long has he known while I sat by with my hand over my mouth?"

Shit. I was on thin ice now.

"Sorry. I didn't ... I'm still figuring out how I feel about it all. I didn't tell him. He asked me about it."

"How'd that go? Given his background, I've been worried he might not take well to the idea."

"I hadn't even had time to think about that when he brought it up. He's great. Same ole Arty. Nothing changed at all."

"Huh," she said. "That's a relief."

"And you? You're ... okay with this? With me, still?"

She stopped walking again and wheeled me to face her, gripping my shoulders.

"William Shaw, how *dare* you ask me that. I have stood by you through your darkest hours. Now, when you're finally seeing a glimmer of light, you think I would abandon you? Do you think our friendship means so little to me?"

I staggered back. "Janie, I'm sorry. I just—"

"You just what? Took me for one of those self-righteous prudes who would toss you aside if I found out ... everything?" She looked around, then lowered her voice. "I love you, Will, no matter what. Don't you ever doubt that again. Do you understand me? I will take these shoes off and—"

I laughed and held up my palms. "I give. No shoe beating, please."

She smirked and took my arm, moving us forward once more.

"You should invite Thomas to join us for bowling."

My brow furrowed. "But that's our time, the three of us."

She shrugged, as if I'd said something ridiculous. "Now there's four. We can play teams, unless you want to do every-man-for-himself and compete against your beau."

"He's not my beau," I protested through a giggle of my own. "Yet."

She elbowed me, and her smile lit up the dark night.

"I'm just so excited for you, Will. If anyone on this campus deserves to find happiness, it's you."

I thought back to my freshman year. The torrent of emotions that year at the loss of my parents was set with the backdrop of the Germans invading their neighbors. The whole nation's emotions were on edge. No one knew whether to be angry or scared, probably both, and my own sadness was a shroud over everything.

Spending time with Thomas, that kiss, was the first truly unburdened moment of happiness I could remember in years. I was shocked and terrified in the moment, but also elated in ways my heart had never known.

I reached over and kissed her on the cheek, earning widened eyes and a questioning brow.

"Yeah, maybe I do. Thanks, Janie."

# Chapter Twenty-Three

# **Thomas**

Will and I ate lunch together at Andover every day after he left me that note. Most of the other students in our special military classes also ate there, so we were never without others at our table.

As the term progressed, so did our studies, and time for basketball or other activities fell by the wayside. For most, the escalation of homework and testing was cause to groan. For Will and me, it was the ideal excuse to spend hours together each evening.

I quickly learned that Will was as stubbornly focused as he was diligent. It was amazing to see him lower his guard as soon as the door closed behind us. It was like having my own private Will that no one in the world got to see but me. Each evening began with our arms tangled and lips locked. He was passionate, somehow gentle and firm at the same time, and his touch lit a fire in my chest that spread to places I'd not felt stir in a long while; but a few kisses into a perfectly planned make-out session, he'd put a hand on my chest and push me back, insisting we turn our attention to German or one of our other courses of study.

March arrived before spring was even a hint on the wind, and Harvard remained a bitter icebox punctuated by flurries. Despite the cold—and our need to study every waking moment of every day—Will allowed a few hours of respite for his requested tour of Boston. I was so excited to spend time together off-campus that I'd barely slept the night before.

At five-something in the morning, I gave up on rest and made my way down to the dining hall, where I was not surprised to see a couple dozen military guys eating before their morning workout.

Bleary-eyed porters brought me breakfast and much-needed coffee.

"Is *The Crimson* out yet?" I asked as a thin porter with a balding pate filled my cup. The smell of the freshly brewed beans was heaven.

"Just arrived," he said, pointing to a stack of papers on the table by the door where the radio sat. A moment later, he returned and handed me a copy, along with a plate of eggs and fried potatoes. Sadly, bacon wasn't on the ration list that day.

## STUDENTS' COOPERATION CALLED FOR IN BLACKOUT

*For the first time since hostilities broke out in 1939, war conditions will hit home at Harvard tonight when, with the sounding of the public sirens, Cambridge blacks out its lights from 10–10:30.*

*Never before in the history of the college has a blackout been attempted, but yesterday university officials ex-*

*pressed confidence that tonight's drill, though without precedent, would be a complete success.*[1]

## Business as Usual

*The slogan for the blackout seems to be "business as usual." In a final statement to the residents of Cambridge, Major Ralph W. Robart, chief air raid warden, asked that "everyone carry on life and business as near usual as is possible during the blackout."*

*"The public," he added, "has only two duties during the practice: the first is to keep off the street; the second is to show no lights and leave none burning in unoccupied homes, apartments, or parked automobiles."*[2]

## No Hindering

---

1. The Harvard Crimson, March 5, 1942

2. Ibid, April 16, 1942

*Supplementing Major Robart's statements were several dictums issued by Dean Hanford and Aldrich Durant, chief warden of the Harvard District, calling for co-operation from the student body and adding that any student found seriously hindering the blackout "may have his connection with the university dishonorably severed."*

*The duties of the hundreds of air raid wardens de-tailed to patrol Cambridge's streets this evening will be twofold. First, they are charged with the responsibility of preventing panic, and second, they are to see that all lights are extinguished as promptly as possible. In connection with the latter task, it was announced that smoking or lighting matches outdoors during the black-out is expressly forbidden.*

*Preparing for tonight's drill, Leverett House held its own practice blackout yesterday evening from 10–10:15. The blackout was pronounced successful, all lights having been extinguished by two minutes after ten.[3]*

---

3. Ibid, July 15, 1942

"Well, isn't that fun?" I grumbled into a forkful of eggs, then tossed the paper onto the table.

"Not much of a reader this morning?" a voice asked from behind. I startled so badly the eggs fell back onto the plate as the fork clattered against the china.

Will rounded and sat beside me. "Whoa, bit jumpy?"

His grin was almost as adorable as his mussed-up hair. It looked like he'd tried to quell a serious bout of bedhead, but failed miserably.

"Hey," I said, glancing around for familiar faces. "What are you doing up this early? And at Andover?"

He shrugged. "Couldn't sleep, so I decided to take a run around campus. A little birdy told me I'd find you here."

He wiggled his brows like some over-acting comedian in the picture shows.

The porter appeared and took Will's order, then drifted away.

"Who is this little bird?"

"Sources and methods, my friend. I could never divulge—"

"What do you know about sources and methods?" I asked, likely a tad too keenly.

He sat back and crossed his arms. "I know many things. I've been to the movies."

I laughed and rolled my eyes, privately letting out a relieved sigh. Baker was the only person on campus who knew what I did for the navy, specifically for the Office of Naval Intelligence. No one *could* know, not even Will. For a moment, I'd thought—

"You're so anxious this morning." His smirk grew. "It's almost as though you have something important planned today."

"If only there were someone I wanted to share it with," I said dramatically.

"If only." His eyes quirked into a grin of their own, and my heart did a somersault.

He glanced at *The Crimson* I'd just tossed down and raised a brow. "Something in there cheese you off?"

It took me a second to register his horrific British accent, then a chuckle escaped. "Yeah, blackout drills on campus cheese me right up."

"*Off*. It's cheese *off*, not up. Don't you navy boys know anything?"

"We're taking German, not British English, or whatever you'd call that."

He glowered with mock indignance. "They're our closest ally. You should learn to communicate with them."

I groaned and downed the last of my coffee. "And how would you say that in German?"

He scrunched up his nose and thought, then asked, "*Spasti*?"

"You calling me a dumbass this early in the morning?" I said through a laugh.

"*Fotze*?"

His face was the picture of ignorant innocence.

"Shh. Keep it down," I said, glancing at the tables around to see if anyone nearby recognized the German curses. "You just called me a motherf—"

"Oh, crap! Thomas, I'm sorry."

"We have a lot more work to do on your German," I said, biting back laughter. I leaned in and lowered my voice. "We'll get you there, my *Schnuckel schnecke*."

Like a child sounding out a reading lesson, his brow furrowed, and I could see Will's mind spinning through his limited vocabulary.

"Little ... something. I don't know *Schnecke*," he whispered back.

"The literal translation would be something like 'bite-sized nibble snail,' but think of it like 'cuddle bunny' or 'sweet thing' in English."

"Nibble snail? I'm sorry, I'm still stuck on the part where you called me your nibble snail. That might be the most disgusting thing anyone's ever called me—and I've been called a lot of things."

"It's supposed to be sweet, actually." I laughed and nodded. "It's a German thing. A term of endearment, like a pet name."

"Dear God, it's only been a few weeks since ... well, you know ... and you're giving me a pet name that leaves a snot trail? That's ghastly ... and kind of cute. I think."

"It's both." I stood. "And trust me, you leave a trail everywhere you go."

He rose and followed me out the door.

"I'm not sure how to take that, especially since I'm stuck with you all day."

I grinned over my shoulder. "Guess we'll find out ... how you take it, I mean."

Will nearly ran into the doorframe.

# Chapter Twenty-Four

# **Will**

"**R**eady to sweat?" Thomas asked as we strode out of the dining hall into a stunning sunrise that kissed the school's historic buildings with a thousand shades of light.

Throughout the 1941–42 terms, exercise became a volatile issue on campus. Harvard vacillated between inviting students to participate with their military brothers in morning and afternoon exercise sessions and requiring said participation. Thankfully, common sense finally prevailed and the sessions had become optional once more. The result of this intellectual battle over physical prowess was that a certain number of civilian students continued to enjoy morning calisthenics or runs. The days of only seeing men in drab green or khaki doing jumping jacks or running about in formation were over.

We jogged south across Mass. Ave. to find one group already lined up in ranks, walking through a stretching routine. A student with tight-cropped black hair and a bulging neck and arms was barking at another group in the yard's corner nearest us.

An hour later, despite the morning chill, we were both sweating and leaning over. Nobody knew the "push to your limits" approach to exercise like the military.

"Shower and meet back at Andover?" I asked through heavy breaths as we walked to the edge of the yard away from the others.

"Together?"

Thomas's eyes were filled with mischief.

"Well, yeah. We can't exactly meet back there separately."

His grin widened. "I was talking about showering."

My head swiveled so fast, I nearly splayed across the sidewalk.

"Thomas," I whispered urgently. "There are students everywhere!"

He shrugged. "I don't want to shower with *them*, but if you're into—"

"Holy moly. Please stop."

"So that's a 'no' to scrubbing my back?"

I shook my head and turned toward my house. "I'll see you in a half-hour or so. Try to behave until then."

I walked into Andover House to find Thomas sitting alone on an uncomfortable-looking couch in the lobby. One guy in army dress passed on his way out, but the entrance was otherwise quiet.

He was reading *The Crimson* again and didn't notice when I entered.

"If I walk in and see you reading one more time, I might start thinking you're smart or something."

Thomas's smug grin emerged as the sound of newspaper rustling filled the room. He folded it twice, dramatic in his diligence, then flung the sacred broadsheet at my chest. I did a jump-back-duck-and-cover dance move, but wasn't fast or dexterous enough to avoid a direct hit.

"Assault! I've been assaulted. Help!" I cried.

Thomas laughed as he stood. "This is the main military barracks on campus. You won't find help here. Assaulting is what we do, especially grunts like the guy who just walked out."

He *had* seen me enter.

A corner of his mouth twisted. "You think I don't see everything?"

"Are you some kind of freakish spy?" I scoffed.

His grin flattened, and he shook his head. I knew we were in the same classes training for something special, but I hadn't worked out exactly what it might be—or if everyone in the classes would end up in the same program. No one talked about it. Ever. The word "spy" had practically sent Thomas into a tizzy.

"Come on, we have a full day," he said, closing the door on a subject I hadn't intended to open. "Our car should be waiting."

"Our car?"

"Yep," was all he said as he practically raced me to the main street.

We stopped before an electric blue Packard with whitewall tires that gleamed in the morning sunlight.

I whistled. "How—?"

"I don't talk about my folks much, but they're kind of loaded." He leaned in to whisper in my ear. "We have certain ... privileges."

He stepped back as the driver raced around, opened the back door and gave an awkward dip of his head. "Mr. Jacobs, good to see you again."

"Thanks, James," he said, then turned back and winked at me before climbing in.

I glanced at the driver, but he was staring at some distant point and refused to make eye contact.

Catching a taxi or even a private car wouldn't have raised an eyebrow a year ago, but with the national gas ration and the governor's order restricting taxi services so long as we remained at war, *no one* enjoyed those luxuries. I'd expected us to take a trolly or bus—or spend most of the day hiking in the not-yet-spring air.

Was Thomas some kind of American royalty I didn't know about?

My parents had been well off, leaving me a small fortune when they passed, but this went beyond wealth. Thomas's family had privilege that came from something greater than money.

"A private car with a driver? Seriously?" I said as I climbed into the back seat beside him and the door closed behind me.

"What?" He painted on his most innocent face. "He'll take us to our starting point, then meet us for our last stop before bringing us back to campus. We'll walk most of the day."

I couldn't stop staring at him. "Still, a car and driver, one you know by name?"

"My dad is ..." He eyed the front seat as James settled in and slammed his door. "I'll tell you about him later, okay?"

Like all Harvard students, I'd visited Boston many times, usually to enjoy the night life or simply escape the intensity of the college's curriculum. I recognized buildings and landmarks as we whizzed past. We drove for nearly a half-hour before James stopped the car at the front door of the Old North Church. Thomas didn't even glance my way, just hopped out when his door opened. I scooched across the back seat and followed, then watched as James folded his lanky frame back into the sapphire sedan and pulled away.

Turning toward the historic place of worship, I said, "I've lived across the river from this place for two and a half years and have never visited most of the historic sites."

"Really?" Thomas sounded surprised.

"Yeah. Arty, Janie, and I come here sometimes, more to hang out at the Commons or eat at Quincy. Janie loves that place. The few other times I've wandered into town were with some of the basketball guys who wanted a drink in a bar not covered in crimson banners, and it's hard to sightsee after the sun's set." I placed a hand on the brick of the church, running my fingers across the rugged surface as if to feel history itself. The classic Georgian architecture wasn't especially striking, red bricks stacked atop each other in blocky, squared-off walls. The only interesting feature was the steeple, which rose high above the surrounding buildings for many blocks. I squinted up to see smaller replicas of the primary steeple adorning each corner of the three-tiered structure.

"That spot up there"—Thomas pointed to the center tier of the steeple where windows gazed across Boston—"that's where the lanterns were hung when the British troops landed."

"You mean the ones that triggered Paul Revere's ride?"

He nodded. "One if by land, two if by sea ... that whole thing started up there."

I whistled. "I knew all this was here, but seeing it up close is like stories coming to life."

He watched a moment as I stared up at America's revolutionary past, then gripped my shoulder and pointed across from the church. "That's the new Paul Revere statue. It's only a couple years old; 1940, I think."

Atop a tall stone base was the man himself riding a horse, cast in bronze wearing a colonial cloak and hat.

"Nice." We walked to the statue and stared in silence. I could almost hear the clanking of the horse's shoes against the cobblestones and the shouts of alarm from its rider. "Guess I haven't been here more than twice since Pearl Harbor, now that I think about it," I said, more to myself than to Thomas.

"Feels good to get out, doesn't it?"

"That's for sure." I nodded. "So, what's the plan? You haven't told me anything about what we're doing today."

He grinned, his lips twisted somewhere between pride, amusement, and outright conspiracy, I wasn't sure which.

"Since you haven't seen the sights, I thought we'd take in some of the historic landmarks. You might dread German classes, but you light up anytime stories of the past come up."

He'd been paying attention to what I liked in class?

My chest swelled and I couldn't suppress a smile. "I love history, always have, but I was kind of hoping to learn more about you and your family. This is your hometown, after all."

He returned my smile, and I swear, the sun shone a little brighter. "We have all day for you to ask anything you want. Besides, our last stop is ... personal to me. I think you'll learn more than you want to then."

The wryness I'd seen a moment earlier had vanished, replaced by something deeper, and he struggled to hold my gaze as he spoke. I got the impression he was nervous about that last stop. I wanted to ask a dozen questions, but decided to let him take the lead. If something was important to him, I wanted to give him room to share it in his own time and way.

I might actually learn more about him by *how* he shared things than *what* he shared.

That thought stuck, and I found myself studying his every move, searching for bits or clues that revealed more of Thomas than he intended. I'd never been so curious about anyone, so intrigued. Everything about him made me want to know more. He was a puzzle I desperately wanted to solve; but, somewhere in the back of my mind, I suspected there would always be parts of him unfolding, surprising me.

The promise of that thrilled me more than I could've expected. It was like pollen to a bee, an instinctual craving that *needed*—

"If you're done touching the building in ways that make it uncomfortable, we'll get this show started."

We strolled a few blocks to stand before a wooden house nestled in between taller brick buildings. Its horizontal planks were painted a drab green that made the army's uniform appear colorful and bright. The three-story structure was crowned by a lean-to roof covered in dark shingles even more drab than the paint. The only truly interesting features of the home were upside-down finials that hung from the corners of each floor, looking like teardrops shed by the sad structure.

"That's Paul Revere's house," Thomas said.

The building was suddenly fascinating and beautiful.

"The original roof wasn't tall like that. They remodeled it to fit with the style of the area in the middle of the 1800s. Revere owned the place from around 1770 until 1800. He had a kitchen put in, adding that chimney sometime around 1795. Since then, it's changed hands and been remodeled several times, mostly as a retail shop. The one thing that never changed too much was the outside face."

"How do you know all this?" I said, more amazed at Thomas's recall of random historical facts than the actual building standing before us.

"My hometown, remember?"

He turned, as if that explained everything perfectly.

The sun hadn't quite hit her zenith, but she was close. We walked another few blocks before Thomas turned and asked, "Hungry?"

"Always."

"Quincy's just ahead. Let's grab something there."

Grinning, he bumped into my shoulder, nudging me in the direction of one of the city's oldest marketplaces. It was strange. When we'd first set out, I'd felt the flutter of anxiousness welling deep in my gut.

We'd spent a lot of time together over the past month or so on campus, but something about leaving the cocoon of our college life felt more significant than our other strolls. Plus, I'd never been anywhere with another guy—at least, not one who made my insides roil.

Yet, here we were, shoulder to shoulder, strolling along North Street in the middle of Boston. To anyone watching, we were a pair of college students enjoying the last moments of our carefree youth; although, given the war and everything that went with it, I wasn't sure how young one had to be before carefree actually applied.

Glancing over at Thomas, my chest swelled again, filling with the excitement of newness and possibility, the fear of being discovered, and the unexpected longing to grasp his hand and walk even closer. How could a person feel all those things at once? It was like wrestling a dolphin with bare hands—assuming people wrestled dolphins.

I grinned at the silliness of my inner dialogue's imagery.

"Wanna share?" Thomas said. I hadn't noticed him watching me.

"Oh, uh, sorry. I was just ... never mind. It was silly."

"I like silly, obviously." He gestured from my head to my feet.

"First you call me a slug. Now you call me silly? Is this supposed to be endearing?"

He raised a scolding finger. "First of all, I never called you a slug. You are my little nibble snail. That's a very different type of snot-trail-leaving creature. Slugs are disgusting and dissolve in salt. Snails are adorable and taste wonderful when well seasoned."

"You want to salt me now?" I mocked.

"Nope. Eat you."

I tripped over my own feet and nearly ran into a light pole.

"Maybe I should call you Grace instead," he jibed.

"You're going to be the death of me, Thomas Jacobs."

He leaned in and pressed his shoulder against mine. "Not until I eat you first, William Shaw."

God, his lips were so close. I could taste his breath, smell the sweetness of the hazelnut cream he'd put in his coffee. I wanted to run my tongue over his and taste it for real. I wanted to . . .

"You know you drive me crazy, right?" he growled.

*One foot in front of the other. Just walk. Focus on not tripping.*

"I've dreamed about all the things we're going to do together. They were messy, sticky dreams, Will. So incredibly hot." He licked his lips, then rasped, "I want you naked, Will. I want to grab your arms and hold you down, to feel your heat against mine, to lick your neck and bite your—"

"Oh, look, there's the market," I squealed, and pointed like an excited five-year-old spotting a circus. When he looked, I took off at a half-jog, if only to avoid hearing exactly what he wanted to bite. I couldn't take it, not yet, and definitely not in the middle of the street.

I already wanted to lace our fingers as we walked and stare into his eyes until the sun set. Now he's talking tongues and teeth! I'd never been a prude, but sweet Maria and all things holy, he was talking about the two of us doing all the things men and women did. I mean, I knew men did them too, in their own way. I guess I knew. I'd never really thought about it, but, hypothetically, I understood that somewhere … oh, hell, I didn't know *anything*, and here Thomas was saying he wanted to toss me like a worn-out rug.

I couldn't decide if I was more terrified or aroused. Every part of me had stiffened as he spoke, and the more he rumbled like a lion preparing to pounce, and the more his breath washed over me, filling me with his scent and taste, the stiffer I got.

What was this man doing to me?

We reached the first of the stalls that lined South Market Street, where vendors sold everything from ripe fruits to freshly butchered meats. Some items had become precious thanks to wartime rations, but the market still thrived as hundreds of locals milled about.

Several of the stalls beneath tan canopies offered prepared meals, much like a fair or carnival. Small areas of outdoor seating offered shoppers a respite, though the cold of the day kept most moving.

Thomas insisted on getting our lunch. He argued that he'd been the one to ask me on the journey, so it was his treat. I only began to worry when he also insisted he pick our meals, then directed me with a policeman's palm toward an empty table.

While he waited at the stall, I sat back and enjoyed a rare moment of people-watching. Couples strolled with locked arms. Mothers chased children while fathers bartered with vendors. A few held youngsters aloft on their shoulders. Everyone appeared at ease, as though nothing was wrong in the world—at least, not in their world.

As numb as we'd become to seeing uniformed soldiers and sailors, it was still somewhat jarring to see men in green and blue everywhere. I tried to remember a time when the only men in uniform were policemen, but that seemed like a time lost to the past almost as distant as Paul Revere and his famous midnight ride. Could we ever turn the clock back? Would the world ever be normal again?

"You're gonna love this." Thomas appeared, balancing two trays filled with food and drinks. "I got a little of everything, so we can just share. I wanted you to get to try it all. Oh, and since it's cold, I got you a big hot chocolate."

He beamed like he'd just bought me a diamond ring.

His smile and easy gaze made my heart flutter.

"How'd you know I love hot chocolate? And don't say you've been watching me drink. I can't remember the last time I had one."

He grinned, then leaned in and whispered, "You haven't learned about sources and methods yet. Lesson number one: Never share them."

Self-satisfaction dripped off him as he sat back and began arranging the food. I marveled at the warmth flooding through me as I watched him perform such simple acts. He glanced up and quirked a brow.

"What? You're grinning like you just stole a kid's candy."

I barked a laugh. "That's terrible. I would never ... well, there was this one time—"

"Why were you grinning?" He wasn't going to let that go.

"I ... I don't know." I ran a hand through my hair. Half of it flopped back into my face, unwilling to stay slicked back. "I guess I just ... I'm just happy."

He held my gaze, then the warmest, most genuine light filled his eyes. "That's all I ever want, Will. That's all I need."

"But I want you—"

"I'm happier than I've ever been. Hell, I didn't know a guy could even feel like this. Just seeing you walk into Andover makes me turn all dreamy."

I waited for a man and woman to stroll by. The last thing we needed was to be overheard talking about our feelings. That almost sobered me. Almost.

"Really? *I* make you feel that way?" I asked. I knew it was true. Any idiot could see how he looked at me. That was what was so endearing—and frightening. *Anyone* could see, if only they looked.

"You know you do, you big slug." He winked. "Now here, try this. They're deviled eggs, but not like any you've ever had."

An hour later, armed with fresh hot chocolate and overstuffed bellies, we continued our tour. The red bricks, blue-tiled roof, and golden adornments atop Old State House, Boston's longest-serving public building, gleamed like beacons of freedom in the sunlight.

"The original building on this site was called the Town House. It was basically built out of wooden twigs in 1657 and burned in the fire of 1711. This replacement was made of sturdier stuff in 1712. At one point, the British kicked the assembly out to use the building as a barracks. Eventually, the soldiers left and the main floor was converted into a merchant's exchange, complete with warehouses in the basement. The Royal Governor of Massachusetts set up his council chamber on one side of the second floor, while the Massachusetts Supreme Court and Suffolk County courts took over the other.

"Since then, it's served as the Massachusetts State House, the Boston City Hall, and was even used to hide a few famous abolitionist newsmen during the mid-1800s. It was rented out for commercial use until 1881 when the Bostonian Society was formed to preserve its historic importance against the tide of progress sweeping through the city."

I couldn't stop staring at Thomas. Halfway into his spiel, I'd stopped listening to his words. How did he know so much about everything? And how could he be so handsome talking about it? I watched his lips move and imagined myself reaching up and pressing a fingertip against them, gently rubbing around them until his mouth opened, then leaning up to press my own lips to his. I could almost taste the sugar on his tongue ...

Wait, that was my own hot chocolate. I'd taken a sip while staring mindlessly, and now he stood there, staring back at me.

"You okay?" he asked.

"Oh, yeah, sure. Sorry. I'm good. Old building. Really great and pretty. It has good lips ... I mean, bones ... or bricks. It has great bricks ... and stuff."

"Bricks and stuff?" He nearly doubled over. "You didn't hear a word I said, did you?"

My eyes lowered. "My mind might've wandered a bit."

He shook his head. The skin around his eyes crinkled in the most adorable way when he smiled that big.

I wanted to kiss those wrinkles too.

"Alright. I see how this is," he said, checking his pocket watch. "Let's hit the last couple sites. James should have the car waiting by the time we get to the last one."

As we strolled by the King's Chapel and its accompanying burying ground, Thomas rattled off a list of names of famous people buried beneath aged stones. The only one to really catch my ear was Mary Chilton, believed to be the first woman to step off the Mayflower. The rest were a blur of religious leaders of the day, most of whom played some role in America's rebellion against their British overlords of the day.

We walked past the tall, steepled church on the left, and I was surprised when Thomas remained silent. He'd been such an active tour guide that I expected a dozen random facts to tumble out of his mouth with every building we passed.

When we rounded the next corner and the Massachusetts State House loomed like some domed cathedral to colonial Americana, I could almost feel Thomas vibrating with excitement.

"Some older residents of Boston still call this the New State House, despite its completion date in January of 1798. It cost a grand total of one hundred thirty-three thousand dollars to construct, and that was five times more than the allocated budget. Politicians were furious at the overrun."

I stared at the tall windows with their rounded tops, and the lofty columns on the portico, my mind drifting back to a simpler time when states and nations were forming. I wondered what it would've been like to stand on those steps and witness the first government to serve the people from inside its grand halls. Again, that same gust of historical fervor I'd felt at the Old North Church roared to life in my imagination.

"The dome was gilded with gold leaf until Hitler decided to march across Europe. They painted it to avoid reflections during blackouts, and to make it harder to spot if the city was ever bombed. If we'd come here a year ago, you would've seen it reflecting the sun in every direction. Now, it's just a gray blur atop a stately old mansion."

I snorted. "It's just gray paint. When the war's over, I'm sure it'll be glittering again." Then the weight of his words truly sank in and my voice lowered. "It's hard to think of Boston taking bombs like London did. We've always been so far away, like the oceans were moats made to protect us from everyone else. When did the world get so small?"

He smiled, but it was the thin one that meant his mind was elsewhere. I'd seen it before in class. It didn't come close to his eyes.

"It's been small for a while. Most people are lucky enough not to know it."

I didn't know how to respond to a statement that complex. I wasn't even sure I understood all its layers. With every conversation, Thomas was proving to be more of an enigma than I'd imagined.

"Come on, one last sight before we meet James."

He gripped my elbow and guided me forward. His touch held none of his earlier aggression or hunger, but its pressure through my coat sent an unexpected reassurance and comfort through me.

I glanced up, and his eyes finally smiled again.

## Chapter Twenty-Five

# Thomas

Watching Will experience my hometown through fresh eyes was one of the most delightful things I'd witnessed in years. I'd always loved history—almost as much as I loved the navy—but I'd worried the heavy dose of the past I had planned for today might become monotonous to him. Most guys our age cared more about the bars and athletic fields of Boston than the monuments to America's founding.

To my surprise, every feature of every building fascinated him. He reached out and touched each one, as though absorbing their meaning and significance into himself. There was a reverence in the way he treated our little tour, and not because we were on a date (if that's what two men going out could be called in 1942). Will genuinely respected history, and his childlike curiosity and passion for learning inspired me.

The whole day felt like taking a kid on his first visit to a zoo, watching his eyes go wide at the lions, and struggling to explain why giraffes had long necks. The sense of wonder in his eyes each time we rounded a corner and a new landmark appeared thrilled me even more than I'd expected.

Will thrilled me more too. I knew I was falling for him. I figured that out the first week after we met. He'd proven himself to be kind, generous, funny, and so many other things that made my heart race. Now, watching him stare up at the State House, more layers of this man unfurled before me, and I couldn't help but stare. He was beautiful on the outside, with a strong jaw and eyes that bore into my soul, but the man I was coming to know outmatched any possible physical feature.

His wit was sharp, but in a playful, innocent way. He made me laugh more than anyone I'd ever known, and his heart was bigger than all of Boston. Above all, he was genuine and true. There was no falseness to Will, only a good man trying his best to do right by his friends and the world around him. I spent so much time peering through masks that I had come to crave the simple honesty he shrugged off as common decency.

"I'm ready," he said, turning toward me. "Where to next?"

He stepped up next to me and let our hands brush. A wave of dizziness washed over me, and I wanted to grab his hand and never let it go. Instead, I pointed across Beacon Street to our next destination.

"The Commons?" he asked, his head tilting.

"Yep. James will be parked near the corner of Charles and Beacon. We have to walk through the park to get to him."

Will's bottom lip vanished as he moistened it. God, I wanted to …

"Sounds good," he said, taking off across the street. "Race you."

He was halfway across the street before the image of his lips left my mind and my feet began to respond. He stepped onto the park's lawn and slowed to a halt, raising both fists in victory. I was still bewildered by my daydream and blundered into him. We hit the grass and rolled, a tangle of arms and legs.

Our bodies were entwined, me on top of him.

Our eyes met.

Our lips were *so* close.

His breath warmed my cheeks.

It felt like the whole world had frozen in time, and only we could move.

"You boys alright? That looked like quite the tumble."

I looked up to find a middle-aged police officer some twenty paces away, racing toward us with a concerned look on his face. Will squirmed out from under me and struggled to his feet. I lost my balance and landed on my rear.

"We're good, officer," Will said, waving. "My friend's just a bit clumsy."

The policeman grinned and tipped his cap. "Looks like you won the race, son. Congratulations."

Will laughed, reaching a hand out to haul me to my feet. "Thanks. Do I get a prize that doesn't involve a bruise?"

"Wrong race for prizes. You boys have a nice day." The officer chuckled and kept walking.

"I've got your prize," I growled in Will's ear.

He spun and shoved my chest with both hands, knocking me back on my rump.

"Hey!"

He cocked a brow and leaned over. "Maybe I am *your* prize."

I think my insides melted—all of them, everything inside my skin. It just turned to jelly or pudding or mush of some kind. The fire in Will's eyes seared into me, and I thought I might never be able to stand. He offered his hand again, but this time, his fingers teased my palm before he helped me up. I thought I might die right there.

"You're killing me, snail."

"That's nibble snail to you, thank you very much."

In that moment, staring up into his eyes, the last of my defenses shattered, and I fell completely, hopelessly, shamelessly in love with Will Shaw.

———

We approached a circular pond whose surface rippled in the breeze. In another month, a fountain at its center would shoot water three times a man's height, and dozens of children would run within its watery sheets.

"You brought me to the Frog Pond?" Will asked, a bemused smirk teasing his lips.

"Yes, Great Nibbler of the Snail Clan."

He laughed and rolled his eyes. "I'll ignore your desecration of my conchological name, but only this one time. Slander me further, and we shall duel." He pantomimed pointing a sword at me.

"I don't know which is worse: you making up a scientific classification for a nickname, or threatening me with eighteenth-century revenge."

"Again, you offend me, sir. Conchology is a proper area of study. Ask anyone serious about the understanding and preservation of mollusks."

"Dear God, what have I created?" I slapped my hand to my forehead. "Back to the pond. Anyone who's spent any time in Boston has visited the Commons and seen this pond, but few know its history or how it earned its name."

The dubious look on his face nearly made me laugh again. "Body of water plus tadpoles equals frogs. What am I missing?"

"First, the pond has no frogs today. Look around. Listen closely. Nada frogacious."

"Frogacious isn't a word."

"Can I tell my story, or do you want to take a swim? I'm not above shoving you in."

He took a step back and held up his palms, but his grin widened to almost painful proportions.

"As I was saying, there are no frogs today, but there used to be. In fact, the Charles River ran much closer to the Commons in the 1700s. There's actually an account written in 1910 describing colonial and French sailors celebrating the surrender of Cornwallis during the Revolutionary War with an, and I quote, 'amphibian repast.' In the nineteenth century, locals would fish here for hornpout—what we call bullhead catfish."

Will's mouth was open, but he didn't speak.

"As Boston grew and society became polite, there was debate about changing the name to something more genteel, like Crescent Pond or Quincy Lake, but those were rejected in favor of the beloved moniker given a hundred years earlier."

"How the hell do you ... *why* do you know any of this?" Will's eyes looked like they were about to pop out of their sockets. "All day, you've been spouting facts like you lived through the Revolution. Tiny bits about this building or that trail. I figured it must've been a Boston school thing, or maybe you had a cruel tutor who made you memorize random facts. Then we come here, and you know the etymology of the catfish? Seriously?"

I grinned. "I only know what they called catfish back then, not the true etymology, but I'm sure we could look that up when we get back to Harvard, if you're interested."

"I'm going to throw you in now. Hold your breath."

Before I could dodge, he stepped forward, arms outstretched, and gripped the lapels of my coat.

"Boys, you aren't thinking of a swim on a cold day like this, are you?"

Our heads snapped up to find that same policeman grinning and tapping his foot.

Will released my lapels and made a show of smoothing them out, then patted my chest and stepped back. "No, sir. Just joshing."

"Alright. That's fine, just fine."

"That guy's creepy, sneaking up on folks like that," Will muttered.

I chuckled. "Enough conchology. Let's go find James."

We strolled around the pond toward Charles Street, and the body of a blue car resolved in the distance. "Looks like our ride awaits."

"Has James been with your family long?"

I'd wondered when Will would start asking questions about my family.

"All my life. He was in the room when I was born, and practically raised me with my mom while my father traveled. He's still like the uncle or father I never had, even though I still have one."

Will's gaze became distant, and his face fell.

"Aw, shit, Will. I'm sorry. I didn't meant to remind you—"

"It's okay. I want to know about your family, really. It just brings up memories. That's all."

We were nearly at the car, so I turned and stopped him with a hand on his arm, then leaned in and whispered, "James knows about me; I mean, that I like men."

Will nearly fell backward. "Really?"

I nodded. "He's the only one. My mother and father wouldn't … they wouldn't be okay with it. James has always been alone, but he … gets us."

Understanding dawned on Will's face, and I could see his mind spinning with more questions.

"We can talk about it later. Let's get to our next stop. This is the one I've been wanting to show you all day. It was my favorite place in the world growing up. I promise, no frog jokes."

"And no besmirching the snail?"

I shoved him toward the car. "No, Great Slug. Your slimy honor will remain intact."

James was waiting with the door open, a knowing grin plastered across his face.

"Master Jacobs. Good to see you again, sir." Then he looked Will dead in the eye. "And you, Master Shaw. It's nice seeing someone put a smile on that young man's face."

"Uh, thanks, James." Will flinched, glancing back at me with a questioning, almost desperate gaze.

I nodded and let my own smile widen. "Told you. My parents might be clueless, but James sees everything."

James checked out Will's butt as he climbed in the car. I cleared my throat loudly.

"Well done, sir," he said, raising one brow as he turned back toward me. "Very well done."

I winked and joined Will in the back seat.

As I settled into my seat, Will surprised me, reaching over and taking my hand in his. I'd held another man's hand before, but never in the back seat of our family's car. My heart knew how much I'd fallen, but my mind still wondered if Will felt the same, if he was falling or if this was some exploration for him, some experience he would move on from when I was no longer novel or interesting.

I'd learned to cage fear, to keep it at bay so I could do what was difficult. Sharing moments with Will somehow unleashed that beast, and the thought of losing him threatened to overwhelm me. Confidence was never something I lacked; and yet, as we sat in the back of the car, I didn't know if I should simply ask how he felt or ... would that be too much? Would that scare him away? Would he think I wanted more than he could offer?

I did want more. I wanted *everything*.

We'd only known each other a few months, and my waking dreams were filled of our future together, of our lives together. Hell, my sleeping dreams were far more vivid, but equally clear.

I wanted Will Shaw to be mine.

I couldn't imagine a more exhilarating thought—or a more terrifying one.

There wasn't a place in America that accepted us, at least not one I knew of. We were shunned in temples and churches, scorned by elders of communities as mentally defective deviants. Even the law forbade our very existence. Being with another man was hard enough; add the war and whatever our respective assignments would be, wherever they might take us, and the whole thing might prove impossible.

The more I thought, the shallower my breaths became. The car felt stuffy, and the walls began closing in.

*Dear God, what's happening to me?*

Will, watching me wrestle my inner demons, squeezed my hand.

I could barely meet his eyes.

His gaze drifted to our interlaced fingers, and he gently traced the lines on the back of my hand. His touch sent shivers up my arm. His strength flowed into me, bracing my chest and lungs, steadying my mind.

"Where are we going now?" he asked.

I drew in a deep breath, and a voice I barely recognized whispered, "To my favorite place in Boston. I used to hide there when I was a kid. It was my safe place when the world felt like it was closing in around me and I just wanted to hide."

His caress ceased as he placed his hand atop mine, encasing me in his warmth.

There were no words for that moment. I wondered if he knew how he moved me. I hoped he did.

The car rolled to a stop. James threw it into park and hopped out, then opened my door. I squeezed Will's hand and stepped out. He scooted across the seat and climbed after me.

# Chapter Twenty-Six

# **Will**

We strode toward the entrance to a large park. An ocean of trees spread before us, a canvas of dense green and skeletal brown limbs. Spring had yet to wrest control from winter, and many of the trees that would soon flower stood barren and without bud.

"The Arnold Arboretum?" I read the sign aloud.

Thomas turned, and I saw that the mischievous grin I'd come to like so much had returned. "Come on. We have the place to ourselves."

A lone guard, almost as old as the trees towering above the entrance, strained to stand as we approached. "Mr. Jacobs? Is that really you?"

The man squinted and held up a hand to shield the sun. As we neared, the man's eyes brightened and a smile formed. "Young Thomas, welcome back. Sweet Jesus, you've gone and grown up on me now. Look at you."

"Young Thomas?" I whispered, eager to finally get a little payback for all the nicknames I'd accumulated, though this one lacked the zest I'd hoped for.

He ignored me and plowed into the old man, lifting his spindly legs off the ground.

"Yes, Mr. Grace, I'm back, and I'm finally big enough to pick you up, for a change."

The old man laughed and slapped his shoulder playfully.

"I hope you don't mind the last-minute disturbance."

"Mind? Never. We've closed down just for you, young master. You've got near two hundred acres to yourself. Hope it's enough."

Thomas stepped back and scratched his chin thoughtfully, then nodded. "I suppose it'll have to do."

Mr. Grace chuckled and shook his head then peered over Thomas's shoulder at me.

"I hope you don't mind. I brought a friend this time."

"Really? You have friends now?" The guard's brows rose with the curl of his lips. "In all the years you've been coming here, I've never seen anyone with you. Just a lonely boy and a lot of trees."

Thomas stepped aside so Mr. Grace could see me better. "This is Will. He's a fellow student at the college. I've been showing him the sights today, making a proper Bostonian out of him."

"Nice to meet you, Mr. Will," he said, saluting with two fingers to the brim of his battered cap. "Going anywhere in particular? They even sent the staff home for your visit, so there's nobody to show you around."

Thomas nodded. "I was taking him to meet the Old Timer."

Mr. Grace beamed. "Good choice. Very good."

"We'd best get going. I want to get in and out before the sun sets." Thomas clapped him on the shoulder once more. "Thanks again, Mr. Grace."

We stepped through the gate and heard a loud clank as Mr. Grace closed and locked it behind us. If I'd had a hundred questions about Thomas before we arrived, a thousand more now swirled in my head. Who got a whole park to shut down just so he could visit? I'd known he came from money—everyone at Harvard did—but there's a difference between rich and wealthy. I was starting to think there might be a third tier, one so wealthy I hadn't known it existed before that day.

We rounded a bend in the path and the peaceful quiet of the man-made forest enveloped us. Thomas slowed and took my hand, entwining our fingers as we'd done in the car. With his other hand, he brushed my hair back and leaned in. His lips were warm and soft as they pressed into mine. I lost track of time as we stood there, unmoving, our lips and hands together.

It was a perfect moment.

When he pulled back and our lips parted, I had to fight the urge to lean in and steal them back.

"I've wanted to do that all day." I shuddered at the rasp in his voice.

"Me too."

He pressed his forehead against mine for only a second, then raised my hand to his lips and kissed it. "Let's go meet the old man. I think you're going to like him."

The path rose and fell, winding in and out of trees of every shape and color. I knew we were walking in the heart of a major American city, but couldn't hear anything beyond the wind in the trees or an occasional call from a winter-hardy bird.

"I think this might be the most peaceful place on earth," I said, staring at a lazy river as we strode past.

"This place was founded in 1873. The city and Harvard entered a joint venture a few years later to allow for better fundraising. The arboretum is part of the Emerald Necklace, a seven-mile stretch of parks and parkways designed by Frederick Law Olmsted and Charles Sprague Sargent, the arboretum's first director."

Silence hung in the air as we walked.

"How do you know all this stuff? All day, it's been like listening to a professor."

He turned. "Sorry—"

"No, I didn't mean ... I didn't mean that in a bad way. I've loved it. It's just that ... it's a lot of information. It's ... impressive."

I'd never seen him so thrown off. His cheeks actually colored.

"Guess I've always been curious and liked learning things. I was alone a lot as a kid, so books and places like this were where I found myself. I guess some of it stuck."

I grunted. "I guess. I'm scared to say *anything* for fear you'll remember it in twenty years."

He grinned. "Are you saying you want to be with me for twenty years?"

I bumped him with my shoulder. "Shut up, you. Take me to this old man of yours."

"We're almost there. See those rocks?" He pointed about fifty paces up the path. "He's just on the other side." We climbed over a mound of gray stone to reveal what looked like a knotty old stump standing nearly to my shoulders. Ancient knots where limbs had once protruded looked like boils on the rugged bark. One thin branch rose from the stump high above our heads. Its own limbs, spreading in all directions, were laden with brilliant pink petals.

There were no other trees within fifty feet. The tree stood alone.

"Will, this is the Old Timer." Then he turned to the tree, bowed at the waist, and said, "*Konnichiha roujin.*"

"Did you just greet the tree?"

"He is the oldest tree in the arboretum. He deserves respect." He laid a hand on the trunk, as if caressing a lover. "Isn't he beautiful?"

I finally looked at the tree—really looked. It was almost like looking at a truly ancient wizard from some children's fable. His back was bent, yet unbroken. His head crowned with a glorious shroud. There was majesty in his withered pose.

"He really is," I said, cupping a thin branch of faded crimson tears.

"This is one place I'd come when I was little. I sat over there, leaned against the rock, and stared at this tree. I always thought of this as my private hideaway, somewhere other people didn't know existed. When I was twelve, maybe thirteen, I learned the staff kept visitors away when I was down here. So much for my secret hiding place."

I tried to picture a young Thomas pressed against the stone. What would drive a boy to hide and stare at a tree? He was right. It was stunning, but still ...

I'd been so lost in thought that I hadn't seen him step closer. His arms found their way around me, and he pulled me into him. His eyes found mine, and I could swear he looked suddenly nervous.

"Will, I brought you here because ... I wanted to ... Will ... " He looked away, gathering his thoughts, then returned to me. "We've only known each other a few months, and we've spent a lot of time together, but still ... it would be crazy to think ... for either of us ... I mean ... shit ... Will, I wake up in the morning, and you're the first thought in my mind. When I go to class, I look for you, even in the classes we don't share. I see your smile when I close my eyes; and when I go to sleep, you're always with me. I see you—no, I *feel* you—next to me. I've never felt like this for anyone, and it scares me to death, but I can't stand a day without us being together."

"Thomas—"

"I brought you here because this place is special to me in ways I could never explain. Standing here, under this tree, it's ... it's important to me." He wet his lips. "I'm absolutely crazy about you, Will. I didn't come to Harvard looking for anything, and I know you weren't even looking at men that way ... or at all ... I don't know. It's just ...

hell, we're both joining the damn war next year, and there's no telling where they'll send us. It's nuts to think anything, but I don't care. I don't know how long we have. I want to spend every moment I have left with you."

There was moisture at the edges of his eyes, and his lips trembled as he spoke. I could almost feel his heart racing as he held me.

A flutter of pink drifted from the tree, as petals landed on our shoulders. Even the Old Timer wept at our moment.

"Thomas, I think I love you."

I wasn't sure where the hell that came from. It certainly hadn't been in my brain as I stared into his eyes. Had those damned petals poisoned me? I tried to reel them back in, but words were funny things. Once spoken, they bore a life of their own.

"I love you too. God, I love you so much it hurts."

His hold on me tightened, and his mouth covered mine. Gone was the gentle caress from before. He was all passion and fire. Every longing he'd had for me was poured into that kiss, and my whole body roused at his touch.

I moaned as his hands found their way beneath my shirt, the rough skin of his hands teasing my back, kneading my muscles, then winding their way to my stomach.

"Thomas—"

He didn't let me speak.

I unbuttoned his coat and untucked his shirt. He flinched as my hands touched his sides. "Damn, your hands are cold."

I grinned and pressed them into his back, earning another flinch. "Warm them up for me, will you?"

"Yes, sir."

The sun had nearly set as we lay against the stone, holding each other, staring up at the aged tree. Thomas ran tender fingers through my hair, as I nuzzled my head into the crook of his neck.

I'd never felt so at peace.

"Thomas, can I ask you something?"

"Alright."

"Tell me about your family."

He didn't answer for a long moment. Then, "What would you like to know?"

I pushed back to face him. "You know my family was well off, right?"

He nodded. "You inherited everything."

"Right. So, I don't care that you come from money. I get it. But Thomas, you have a car and driver in the middle of a war when gas is rationed more than meat. Oh, and the driver calls you 'Master Jacobs,' which is pretty old-school wealthy, almost *regal*. Now, we come to this massive park that you apparently asked to be closed down just for our visit, and they did it without so much as blinking."

He smirked. "That wasn't a question."

"Who *are* you?"

He didn't sit up, but I could see his sardonic grin growing. The fucker was enjoying this.

"I'm Thomas Jacobs, the man who's crazy about you. Isn't that enough?"

"No!" I caught myself. "Yes, it's enough. It's *everything*, and I *love* you, asshole, but all this is ... it's a lot, Thomas."

He sat up slowly, faced me, and took both my hands. When his eyes met mine, he held my gaze so long I wasn't sure he would ever speak.

Then he said, "My name is Thomas Arthur Jacobs—"

"I know that—"

"Du Pont."

# Chapter Twenty-Seven

# **Will**

I stared at Thomas, unable to process the name I'd just heard. The du Ponts were one of the wealthiest families in the world.

"Thomas ... du Pont? As in *the* du Ponts? The ones in Delaware?"

He nodded slowly. "Phillipe Irénée du Pont is my father."

"The military hardware guy?"

He shrugged thoughtfully. "Military hardware is a crude term. My great-great-grandfather brought our family to America, where we discovered an opening in a very profitable market: supplying gunpowder to the US government. Over the years, our business interests have ... evolved. My father operates the businesses that still focus on matters of armament and war."

I barely heard him after he named his father. He spoke so casually.

"But ... your last name is Jacobs. Even James called you Master Jacobs."

He allowed a shallow grin. "When I joined the navy, we decided to withhold my true last name. The admirals feared it would paint a target on me, even within our own service. No one, including the professors and students at Harvard, knows who I truly am. Except President Conant. And now you."

"Thanks, I guess. Golly, that's a lot to tell a guy. But you can trust me."

"I know." He smiled and brushed the hair back from my face.

As unbelievable as this was, it explained so much. Thomas carried himself differently than other students—than anyone I knew, really. He wasn't arrogant or rude, but his *presence* commanded attention without him putting forth the slightest effort. When he walked into a room, you felt something change in the air. It was hard to describe. I had thought he'd been blessed with an extra dose of charisma, which was probably true, but his upbringing in the household of American royalty prepared him for things I couldn't imagine, and truly rounded out the picture of the man sitting before me.

He'd talked about how his father was always gone, traveling for work. I'd assumed he was a salesman or something normal that stole time from his family. A few times he'd mentioned his mother being distant, and that he'd had a closer relationship with others in their household. I assumed he'd meant a nanny or au pair, but now, images of an army of servants in white gloves and tails sprung to mind, with James chasing after the precocious little Thomas all over their insanely large mansion. My rational mind knew that was all a fiction, that I was projecting whatever I was taught to think of the super-rich, but—

"My family lives here in Boston; well, on the outskirts. We have a few hundred acres you might drive by thinking are little more than abandoned farmland. The estate's buildings are far from view of the road. My father enjoys his privacy."

"Buildings? Your *estate* has buildings, *plural*?"

"Let me think. It's hard to remember them all sometimes." His playful, shit-eating smirk consumed the corner of his mouth. "There's the main house where we live—well, lived, I'm not there anymore, obviously—the servants' residence, the stables and paddock, the carport, the pool house, the bird sanctuary, the greenhouse, and a few small hunting lodges on the northern, eastern, and southern edges of the forest—but those are little more than log cabins where kills can be prepared for butchering. The forested land isn't technically ours, though by arrangement with the National Park Service, we maintain it as part of our holdings. The gardens aren't technically buildings, but I suppose they should count for something, as well as the pond and its dock. The pond is large enough to paddle around on. You would love it."

My word. He was really a du Pont. *My* Thomas was—

"James has been with us forever. Everything I told you about him is true. He's like a father, brother, and uncle, all rolled into one. Several of the other staff are also more family to me than my father or mother ever were. A few of them wouldn't take to me having a man on my arm, but a couple would love anyone who made me happy. I hope you can meet them someday."

I felt like my brain was taking inventory, and the number of products or shelves or whatever were outpacing its ability to recon.

"And your brother?"

"He's alright. By the time he was old enough to bother me, I was a teenager, and my tutors had me busy ten or eleven hours a day. We were never very close."

"Wait. Ten hours? You studied for ten hours a day as a kid?"

He shrugged again, as though this whole thing was the most normal situation in the world. "I suppose homework added another couple of hours. By the time I was sixteen, I could carry on conversations in French, German, and broken Russian. There's no way my father could've known Hitler would try to conquer the world, but I'm grateful for all of it now. It should be useful soon."

"Dear God."

"See why this place became so special to me? It was my escape from ... everything."

He stared a moment, letting me mull over this information, waiting for some reaction or response. I just stared at the Old Timer and let my brain struggle. I wasn't sure thoughts were really forming. It was just spinning.

He leaned forward and took my hand. "Will, I'm still me. Nothing's changed. I'm just Thomas."

I wanted to believe him. My whole being begged to believe him, but—

"Talk to me, *please*. Tell me this doesn't change how you feel . . . about me." His voice no longer held the confidence I'd come to love, and his gaze wavered under my scrutiny.

His doubt stabbed at my heart.

"Thomas, I meant what I said before. I love you. Full stop. You could be the King of England, and I would still love you."

He smirked. "But I'd live *so* far away."

"Idiot." I jerked my hand back and shoved his chest.

It felt good to laugh.

"This might take me a little getting used to though. I mean, it's a lot to take in."

He reclaimed my hand and stared into my soul. "All the time I have in this life is yours. Take it."

# Chapter Twenty-Eight

# Thomas

"**M**r. du Pont," Will said, as though trying to taste the words, to see if the name was savory or sweet—or utterly revolting on the tongue.

Trusting Will with my name and all it implied left me feeling more naked and exposed than when James and I had first spoken about my attraction to boys. I'd been so terrified back then. James was everything: a faux father, an older brother, a trusted friend. The thought of dimming the affection that shone so brightly in his eyes tore at my heart in ways I couldn't fathom.

Lying there, beneath the ancient tree that had become so special to me, desperate to hold Will's gaze and not wither like a plant beneath a scorching sun, those same fears surged to the fore. The anguish and ache of an incalculable loss, however different this time around, made breathing an impossible torture.

Still, I waited.

He stared up for a long moment, then a curl formed across his lips, and he rolled onto his side to face me. His hand unclasped from mine and rose to gently brush through my hair. My whole body shivered at his touch, as I held my breath.

His eyes shifted, drifting from mine to some distant place, but his fingers continued stroking my hair. "Ever since my freshman year, the whole world has felt like it's spinning out of control. I mean, when my parents ... That was so hard, Thomas. It still is." He drew in a breath. "Arty and Janie became everything. They wrapped me in their arms and held me for dear life, like I might float away if they loosened their grip for even a minute. I don't think I could've ... I don't know."

I watched as a thousand emotions danced across his face. The urge to reach out, to pull him to me, to hold him and ease his pain, flooded through me.

Still, I waited.

"Then Pearl Harbor happened, and the world spun again. Maybe it just sped up. I don't know." He let out an uncomfortable chuckle. "Everything changed. And I get it, everything changed for everybody, but for me ... it wasn't like I had a direction anyway. I was still just going through the motions, doing what I was supposed to do at Harvard. I didn't know what I wanted anymore."

His fingers stilled, then his hand cupped my cheek. "Then I met you."

My breath hitched, unable to exhale until he spoke again.

His eyes found mine once more. "I think my world spun harder when you walked into my life than at any time before."

"Really?" I breathed out.

"You changed everything again." He nodded, and his palm pressed more firmly against my skin. "I think I fell in love with you that first day in the yard. I just didn't know it."

I couldn't stop the smile that bloomed, filling my soul with light.

"Thomas, I can't stop thinking about you. I haven't stopped thinking about you since that first day we met. When I see you walk into a room, everyone else fades into the background. It's like they're not there. All I see is you. I've never felt that about anyone, and it scared me at first." He grunted a laugh. "Hell, it *still* terrifies me. Men aren't supposed to … you know."

I nodded, but couldn't speak.

"But after everything, I just can't bring myself to care anymore."

I cocked a brow, unsure how to read that. He grinned and leaned forward, pressing his forehead to mine. My body screamed at the sensation.

"I don't care what anyone thinks, Thomas. I don't care what might happen. We're going to war anyway. What are they going to do, lock us up before they send us to fight? I lost everything I loved when my parents died, and, in my darkest hours, I wondered if I would ever know love that pure and deep again. Then you walked into the yard."

My eyes watered, but I dared not move.

"I know, from my heart to my toes, that I love you, Thomas du Pont. I don't care that you are American royalty. I mean, it's pretty neat and all, but that name isn't who you are. It's just the family you were born into. The man I've come to know, to love, is so much more than just a name."

Will was talking more about his feelings than at any time since I'd known him. He was opening up and every part of him was pouring out. I wanted to wait, to hear whatever he would say next. I really did.

But sunlight was bursting from my pores, and I couldn't hold it back any longer.

I reached up, grabbed his face with both hands, and pulled his lips into mine.

Whatever he was going to say would have to wait.

For those over 18 who enjoy spice, visit https://dl.bookfunnel.co m/r6p5zlw5t9for a scene that doesn't fade to black!

# Chapter Twenty-Nine

# **Thomas**

**"FRANCE FOREVER" CONDEMNS LAVAL**

*Harvard Unit will Bolster French Spirit, Aid DeGaulle*

*Emphasizing how much the activities of Free France will contribute to the morale of the French people, George H Gerard '43, president of the Harvard Unit of France Forever, declared soon after Laval's reinstatement that the unit would immediately resume its work of publicizing the truth about conditions in France.*

*"The Vichy government has been set up as a tool to deceive the people as to how deep in slavery they really*

*are—it neither can nor wants to resist Germany. Even unoccupied France is now under the control of Hitler, and all the people are completely oppressed.*

*"The beginning of full collaboration by the Laval regime will make all French people bitterly turn away from Vichy and hopefully turn toward the United Nations for help. From this time forward, Vichy no longer represents France."*

*Future plans have been mapped by the committee of the unit. All members will cooperate in the resumption of activities, which will include movies to raise funds for ambulances, a broadcast forum, a letter to General DeGaulle in London, and the furthering of efforts to establish units in other colleges all over the country.*

In the weeks that followed our visit to the arboretum, what had begun beneath the petals of the Old Timer flowered into more than I could have ever dreamed. We met every morning to run with the troops and the few students who continued the routine, then ate breakfast together, either at his house or Andover. We did the same with lunch and dinner, alternating between our respective dining halls based on the quality of the day's menu. We studied, played basketball, or simply sat around my dorm room and chatted in the few hours that remained.

If Will hadn't had a roommate and I hadn't lived in military barracks, I doubt we would've slept apart. The idea of him next to me all night filled my heart, and I wondered what it would feel like to wake to his head on my chest, with his breath teasing my skin as he slept.

Arty and Janie accepted me into their fold without so much as a questioning glance. Baker took to Will like a little brother, wrestling playfully in the yard and staining his pants green.

The five of us ate together as often as not. Janie walked with her arm latched onto mine, giving many the impression we were courting. As much as I hated the falsity of that farce, it served us well.

No one questioned us. Not even once.

It was Monday, the third one in April, and Will sat in his usual place, studying from his stack of ever-present books. Our classmates were settled, and Lieutenant Willard was clearing his throat as I raced through the door and took my seat.

"Good of you to join us, Mr. Jacobs," Willard said, peering over the top of his glasses at me.

Willard stood, a file in his hand. "I don't have to tell you how the war is going. You hear it on the radio just like we do—and we expect each of you to stay informed. Some of the programs here at Harvard, and in other colleges around the country, are altering the schedules for their courses of study. Likewise, Commander Jeffers, Sergeant Major Stafford, and I have received orders to accelerate the pace of your training.

"This will impact you in several ways. First, unless you receive specific orders to the contrary, everyone in this room will remain on campus throughout the summer. Our classes will break for commencement week, but that's it."

A round of groans passed through the class, and a few of the guys whispered about trips they'd have to cancel. No one was happy.

"Second," the lieutenant continued, "your workload in these classes will increase substantially over the summer. You will not enroll in any regular Harvard classes during that term. Your fall and spring term classes will also be assigned, so there's no need to enroll on your own.

"Finally, some of you will complete your training in May and be given immediate assignments within your respective services. I know you were all expecting another year here, but Uncle Sam has had to adapt, and so will you.

"I don't have a list of who's impacted by that last bit yet, so don't ask. As soon as we can share it, we will. Questions?"

Nobody moved.

The jovial mood that had reigned before class started was now about as sullen as it could get, with each man surely wondering if his time at Harvard was now measured in weeks rather than months or years.

"Good." Willard nodded, as if everything was settled. He stepped forward and began handing out sheets from his folder. "These are street maps of Paris, Berlin, London, Washington, DC, and Amsterdam. In one week, you will be expected to navigate easily through Paris using those maps. In one month, your maps will be taken away, and you should be able to navigate from any point, to any point, without assistance. Over the course of the summer, we will repeat the exercise until you have mastered each of those maps. All of your studies are important, but this exercise may save your life more than any other. Treat it as such. Understood?"

A chorus of, "Yes, sir," answered.

"Good." He glanced at a clock on the wall. "You have forty minutes of this class remaining, plus your other two. They are canceled today. Use these hours to begin memorizing these maps. Each of your instructors will quiz you on this daily. Oh, and I shouldn't have to remind you, but the very existence of these maps is classified. They don't leave Andover. Got it?"

"Yes, sir," we barked again, as he turned and strode out the door.

Will and I sat on the floor of my dorm room staring blankly at ancient lines that moved in no discernible pattern.

"What's an *arrondissement*?" he asked, sounding out each syllable like a kid struggling with *aluminum* or some other tongue-tangling word.

"An *arrondissement*," I said, in perfectly accented provincial French, earning an appreciative brow raise, "is a section of town. Think of them like administrative districts for dividing up local government's areas of responsibility."

We stared another moment in silence.

"Why are we doing this, Thomas?"

When I looked up, he'd tossed his map aside. "What do you mean? It's part of our class assignment."

"I know that." He glared out the tops of his eyeballs like I'd said the dumbest thing ever. "But why? What's this all for? I still don't know what they want me to do after all this studying is over; and now, that might be a lot sooner than we'd thought."

He leaned back against my bed and tossed his head back to rest on the mattress, staring up at the ceiling. I hardly knew how to answer him. I hadn't been told exactly where I would be sent or what I'd be doing, and I certainly hadn't been told anything about his future work. The government didn't work that way, sharing information with people who weren't directly involved in a mission.

I realized, in that moment, that the whole concept of secret work was new to Will. He might've read about it in a book or seen it in a film, but writers and Hollywood often missed the mark when creating their stories. The work we did was far different from the sensationalized ones that sold books or movie tickets.

I tried to remember when I was new with the ONI. I barely knew what the letters stood for, much less what they did. My first assignment was deciphering maps and helping identify objects from blurry aerial photos. Identifying German ships, tiny dots of gray on a vast field of blue, was painstaking and often impossible. I hated that work, but it was important for keeping our fleet safe in future engagement.

My time sitting behind a desk would be over soon. Baker had told me as much. German U-boats were wreaking havoc on shipping lanes and convoys, so the ONI[1] was expanding its mission to include gathering intelligence on their capabilities and missions. I would be the tip of the spear in that effort, a job that would put me in the crosshairs of every Nazi assigned to sail or protect those ships.

When I'd first learned of my future mission, I was excited. I'd never dreamed of working in the field as a secret agent. Like Will, my closest interaction with that world had been on a Saturday night in a theater. I was about to step into those films, to become those characters in real life.

Looking at Will, my excitement morphed into something else, something akin to terror, but at a deeper, more primal level. I didn't

---

1. Office of Naval Intelligence, one of the primary US intelligence services in the first half of the 20th century

know what they had in mind for Will, but if he was in this program, he was being groomed for the field. He would be the tip of another spear, facing the business end of other rifles, putting his life in perpetual danger. The idea of Will being in danger chilled me to my core.

The rustling of him sitting up and leaning forward stirred me.

"What is it? You turned pale all of a sudden."

My mouth was so dry. I swallowed hard. "I don't know what they're training you for," I croaked out.

"Can you tell me anything about what you're going to do?"

I met his gaze. There was curiosity, and a tinge of something darker in his eyes.

"I really can't. I'm sorry." I lowered my head, unable to watch the disappointment and frustration creep into his features. "Just ... make me a promise, okay?"

"What?"

"Learn this stuff really well, especially the classes that come next. These aren't some hypothetical math classes designed to help you think better. This stuff will either save your life or get you killed."

A hundred heartbeats thrummed in my ears before he spoke again. "So, you think they're sending me over there for real?"

I looked up and could feel the moisture forming in my eyes. "I honestly don't know."

# Chapter Thirty

# Thomas

**Commencement Program**

*World War II heightened the pomp and seriousness of the traditional commencement ceremonies this morning in the Sever Quadrangle as Harvard's first War Class JH twenty-five years received their degrees and prepared to step into their place in the fight for freedom.*

*The safely 300-year-old ritual, solemnizing the awards of nearly 2,000 degrees, opened with the colorful formal academic procession when the Governor and Lieutenant Governor of the Commonwealth, the mayors of Boston and Cambridge, and other public officials, officers of the army and navy, dignitaries of the church, and*

*candidates for degrees, alumni, and special guests, in
cap and gown or other formal attire, solemnly marched
into Sever Quadrangle.*

*At nine o'clock, the seniors assembled in front of Hol-
worthy Hall, in the oldest part of the yard, for the march
to chapel. Dean Willard L Sperry, of the Divinity
School, conducted the service. Following the service, the
commencement procession formed in the yard, and, led
by the band and the class officers, the men passed before
John Harvard's statue, doffing their caps in respect to the
founder ...*

B aker stood in the third row of men on the steps, waiting
not-so-patiently for the photographer to make his final adjust-
ments. The newly graduated students joked and cajoled, frustrating
the poor camera man as he begged for everyone to stand still.

"How soon do you think they'll give him his assignment?" Will
asked as we watched on.

"There's a meeting of all the navy guys in my cohort this afternoon."

"So soon?" He paused. "Wait. You said a meeting of all the guys?
Including you?"

I nodded. "Yeah, but I don't think it means I'm getting sent anywhere. I'm pretty confident I'll be here through commencement next
year."

Will blew out a breath. "Good. You scared me there."

"Nothing's going to keep me from seeing you walk across that stage, Mr. Shaw."

He elbowed my ribs. "I wasn't worried about graduation. I just wasn't ready ... you know."

To see me leave. I was thinking it too.

We'd only just found each other. In a world going mad with death, we'd actually found love, someone to hold and cherish, someone to see us through it all. We knew our time together was limited, that service would pull us apart—hopefully only for a time—but neither of us wanted that to come anytime soon. Another year together would cement our bond in ways neither of us could fully appreciate, but we wanted to find out for ourselves.

I didn't tell him there was still a chance I'd be shipped out with Baker. He'd be a nervous mess all afternoon, and nothing would change. If I got orders, it wouldn't matter if he had sweat over them or not. I didn't see any reason to worry him more than he already was.

Baker getting sent away was bothering me though. We hadn't spent much time together over the past few months because Will and I were always doing things, but Baker was still my best friend. He'd seen me through my first few years in the navy, and I looked up to him as a mentor as much as anything.

The thought of looking up to Baker made me chuckle. At six foot five, everyone looked up to him. He stood out in the graduating class lineup like a bowling pin among a line of tin cans. He was also the only man of the group not smiling like he'd just stolen another man's girl. I guessed his mind was preoccupied with the afternoon meeting. Mine sure was.

"Where's Arty and Janie?" I asked, hoping to steer the conversation to happier topics.

"Arty had some meeting with his secret team. I can't believe they made him miss commencement. The whole damn campus shuts down for this, but no, they had to meet. He was furious, and Arty's pretty funny when he gets mad. His neck turns red and he stomps around the room like some kind of cartoon character."

I chuckled. "And Janie?"

"She's here somewhere, probably flirting with one of the graduates. She's become quite the, um, how should I say it? Opportunist? She's probably lining up a man for some prewar morale boosting before he ships off, if you catch my meaning."

"Our Janie? Really?" I couldn't decide whether that was amusing or made me sad. Janie might've been wound tight at times, but she'd always been a good girl. Turning into some kind of campus charity girl made my stomach ache.

"Will he be able to tell you about it?" Will asked, abruptly changing the subject back.

"What? Sorry, I got lost in thought. Tell me about what?"

"Baker, will he be able to tell you about his assignment?"

I shrugged again. "Probably not. I doubt he'll even be able to tell me where they're sending him, much less anything about his mission. ONI hasn't been in the field operations game for long, but they've learned from all the rest about keeping secrets."

Will grunted, then held up a hand to wave Baker over. The photo was complete and the morning's graduates were scattering.

"Hey guys," Baker said, his rumbling bass vibrating through my chest. "Let's get out of here, okay? I'm hungry, and I'm tired of getting hit up with questions I can't answer."

"There goes my plan to grill him over lunch," Will quipped. I was pretty sure he was only half-joking and had planned to ask Baker what he thought would happen later.

"Those guys are military. I have to keep them in action. But you"—he pointed down at Will and leaned over in his most menacing pose—"you're a civilian. I'll beat the shit out of you till you puke on your shoes."

Most men, when faced with Baker's wrath, would've pissed themselves. To his credit, Will didn't flinch. He reached up and straightened Baker's tie and said, "There. All better. Thanks for leaning down so I could fix that. You looked ridiculous in that photo."

Baker's mouth dropped, then his lips twisted into his approximation of a grin. I nearly spat laughing. Will, not missing a beat, turned to me and said, "Lunch? We'd better go if we want to beat the rush."

And off he went, leaving Baker staring in his wake and me laughing through tears. It was the only time in all the years I'd known Baker that someone had gotten the upper hand on him so quickly.

---

A couple hours later, Baker and I returned from the meeting to find Will sitting on the floor in my dorm room, studying maps. I sat on the bed beside him and absently ran my fingers through his hair. He leaned into my touch and smiled up at me.

"More fucking training. You've got to be shitting me," Baker fumed.

Our heads snapped toward Baker.

"Easy. Shut the door," Will whispered urgently. "Someone will hear you—"

"It's not classified that I'm going to training," Baker grunted. "I can't tell anyone where I'm going or what the training is about, but that it's a training mission isn't a secret."

"Oh," Will said. "I don't get it then. Why are we pissed about this? You could be storming a beach or something."

"We may end up *behind* enemy lines—which might be worse, now that I say it out loud—but none of us will fight *on* the lines." He sat in the desk chair we rarely used while studying. The metal screamed under his weight. "We've been training since we got here, for six months. Thomas and I were in mostly desk jobs before, and I was looking forward to seeing some real action."

"Won't this get you ready for action?" Will asked.

Baker tossed his orders on my desk and blew out a frustrated sigh.

"Let me start over. I'm being sent to *conduct* training, not go through it. They're ordering me to become a trainer in one of our new special schools designed to—never mind. It doesn't matter what it's designed for. They want me to teach. I'm not a teacher."

"Instructor." "What?" His head snapped toward Will.

"I'm pretty sure they're called instructors, not teachers."

"Do you remember that chat we had about beating the shit—"

"Alright," I said, reining them back. "How long is this posting?"

"A year." "That's not terrible. And after that?"

"Who knows? If they like me in the role, I'd guess my orders would be extended. That's how it usually works."

Baker would be good at anything he was assigned. He was just that kind of guy: diligent, hardworking, smart—everything the navy wanted in an officer. If they'd assigned him to instruct, there was a reason—and a need.

"Did you talk to anyone about being in the field?" Will asked.

Baker nodded. "Captain Gelman ran the briefing today. I got a minute with him after, while your idiot boyfriend, or whatever you call him, was keeping the other guys away."

"And? What did he say?""He said I was too tall for field work.""What?" Will spat out, reeling in a laugh before Baker could get pissed again. "Too tall? Really?"

"Yeah. He said I'd stand out too much, that I had the blond hair and all, but there's no way someone my height could ever blend in, and that's the most important thing about ... it's really important. That's all. That's what he said."

Baker snatched up his orders and stood. "I need to go beat something. I'll see you guys at dinner."

The door slammed behind him, and my hand found Will's hair once more.

"He's really worked up about *not* going into battle."

"You should've seen him when he read his orders," I said. "Baker's been looking forward to seeing the war up close. The idea of sitting back and letting others fight really gnaws at him. He's a good guy that way."

A moment passed before Will asked, "Did you get any papers?"

"You mean orders?" I leaned down and kissed the top of his head. "No. I'm still here. The captain did talk about some specialized training I'll have to take over the summer, in addition to our classes, but that's it."

I felt the tension leave Will's body. In that moment, I realized just how afraid he'd been for me; for us. I had worried about the possibility of an early mission, but had been too wrapped up in my own head to see that Will was struggling too. I felt suddenly ashamed to have let him ache alone.

"Snail, I'm sorry," I said, dropping onto the floor and pulling him into my chest.

"What for?" his muffled voice asked.

"I was so stuck in my own head that I didn't even think how anxious you might be about all this. Just talk to me, okay?"

He rested his head beneath my chin, a spot that had quickly become his favorite. "I don't know what I would've done if they'd sent you away."

"You would've finished school and gone on your own assignment."

"I know. It's not that. I mean, it is, but ..." He sat up and turned to face me. "This whole thing has made me think about next year. It's all I can think about. We'll graduate, and they'll send you to God knows where, and I'll go somewhere else, and ... and we won't be together."

His voice caught as he spoke.

"Thomas, I just found you. I can't lose you, not so soon."

I grabbed his face with both hands. "Will Shaw, you will never lose me, no matter where we are. We might have to fight before we can be together, just like millions of other families broken by this war, but we *will* be together."

He looked so small in that moment. My heart ached at the pools reflecting in his eyes. I wanted to wrap him in my arms and make all his doubts and fears vanish, but he was right. We would be split up—not tomorrow or next month or the next, but we would be sent to different worlds. One or both of us might not make it back. But we couldn't focus on that now. We had to believe, to cling to the hope that we would one day hold each other and never have to let go.

Will seemed to read my thoughts as tears finally tumbled down his cheeks, and he fell into my arms.

## Chapter Thirty-One
# Will

There was a week of respite between commencement and the beginning of summer classes.

Janie headed home to spend the summer in New Hampshire with her parents. This would be her last summer before her senior year, possibly her last carefree months to spend with her parents before the chains of adulthood bound themselves around her waist.

Like Thomas and me, Arty had orders to attend summer classes and continue whatever secret research he'd been conducting. We had each been in our respective programs for over six months, and I had yet to get even a hint about Arty's assignment. All he would tell me was that his work would be vital in supporting men and women who were "the tip of the spear." That phrase struck me as odd. I knew he was probably working on innovations in weaponry or armament, something to enhance our troops' ability to overpower the enemy, but something in his words sounded more like a slogan than a mission.

Arty's mother practically begged him to return home for the week, arguing that their time together would be even more limited as life—and war—tore them apart. Mrs. Ableman made a point to invite me to join Arty, to relax and recover some sense of normalcy before beginning studies anew. She even played the little brother card, talking about how much Adam and Albert would love to see me again.

Arty agreed and traveled home that Monday.

Part of me craved the familial warmth of the Ablemans' home. Spending time with them conjured an odd mixture of emotions. Pain and sadness gnawed at my gut as images of my parents flooded my mind. And yet, the way Arty's family wrapped their arms around me, literally, gave me a sense of peace and comfort I found in few other places. Even wrestling or playing ball with the boys brought an easiness to my spirit I'd long forgotten.

But there was no way I would let anything interfere with the first free week Thomas and I would have together.

"Can you believe it?" he asked, stepping through the doorway into my dorm room that Monday, a duffel bag over shoulder. "We have a week, just us, barely anyone on campus, with our own room."

He dropped the bag to the floor and turned to face me, a fire blazing in his eyes. It wasn't simply hot, it was primal. There was deep hunger in his gaze, unlike anything I'd ever seen.

"Shut that damn door and get over here. You don't get to leave this room until we're both wobbly and weak."

For those over 18 who enjoy spice, visit https://dl.bookfunnel.com/v8pnpxqx3v for a scene that doesn't fade to black!

# Chapter Thirty-Two

# Will

O ver that term, Thomas and I had spent many hours alone, but never—not once—had we enjoyed the simple joy of waking in each other's arms. So, for seven precious days, we learned just how bright the summer sunrise could truly be.

On the morning following our *first time*, Thomas had laid on his back with my head nestled beneath his chin. His fingers traced circles on my back, occasionally rising to bury themselves in my hair and massage my head. My own ran across his chest as I memorized every curve and crevice.

I'd never known this feeling, this love poets penned about. I had never understood how inexplicably intoxicated the emotion could render a person, in broad daylight, when alcohol was nowhere to be seen. My skin tingled just thinking about Thomas. When we were together, my heart thrummed with joy. When we were apart, even for just moments as he returned to Andover to change clothes or retrieve a book, my whole being yearned for his return.

What madness was this, infecting my soul to its core?

Perhaps the oddest part was how little I cared. It didn't matter how ridiculously giddy I felt, or how parts of me tingled at the thought of him, at the thought of him pressing against or inside me. I didn't care how others saw us, what they thought, how they might react. My world was the two of us, and nothing else mattered.

At least, that's how my heart wanted to feel—or whatever one's heart did when infused with sunlight and ocean mist.

In truth, while I was elated, I'd never been more terrified. Before Thomas, I'd had nothing to lose. Nothing to risk. I had no parents, no brothers and sisters, no family to leave grieving and broken. My own existence meant nothing to me—or, likely, anyone else—beyond one's normal fear of the unknown beyond this life.

But now, there was something in my life worth cherishing, something worth guarding against all threats, something worth living for. Now, I had something precious to lose.

And that thought drove spikes of dread into my mind and heart.

I tried to focus on the newness of our love, on the beauty of finding each other in a world gone mad, but it was impossible to forget that madness. Its grip clung to the throats of every person old enough to see the world for the war-ravaged wreck that it was. I couldn't think of our happiness without also imagining the loss of it.

I wanted to just love him and be loved by him. I wanted to, so badly.

The door flew open, and Arty strode into our room, loudly signaling that my solo week was over. "Hey, roomie. Miss me?"

I wheeled my chair around and stood. "Of course, every day. The longing in my heart—"

"Alright, enough. My stomach is already a little weak from the trip over. It sure can't take all your gushing." He set his bag down and stepped into a hug. "It's good to see you too."

He stepped back and grabbed a bundle off the bed. "My mom made you these. She said she'd never seen anyone devour them like you had over Hanukkah."

He opened a tin to reveal dozens of jelly-filled donuts smothered in powdered sugar. I snatched one and tossed it in my mouth. "Oh, God, I think I might explode right here."

"Will!" Arty's eyes popped wide. "Seriously? You talk like that while my mother's jelly is in your mouth?"

I nearly spat donut across the room.

"That's *not* what I meant! You're impossible!" The red of his cheeks nearly matched the color of the donut jelly.

"How was the family?" I asked, once the donut was down and I could stop laughing.

Arty had moved to his bunk and begun unpacking his bags. "Good. Mom and Dad say hi. My brothers are mad at you."

"At me? What did I do?"

"Adam claims you promised to come home with me again. He said you specifically talked about visiting after graduation."

I groaned. "We did talk about it. I mean, at the time, I didn't have any reason—"

"Will, they're pests. Don't worry about it." He cocked a brow. "Besides, you *did* have a reason to stay here. How is Mr. Reason?"

A massive, ocean-sized smile burst onto my face, and I found myself wrapping my arms about myself in a giant self-hug. "He's good."

"Sweet fucking mother of all things holy and good. You're smitten. No, you're a thirteen-year-old girl." He dropped a stack of folded shirts into his dresser and sat on the bed. "Out with it. You two have been together for nearly half a year. Why are you suddenly ten times gushier than those terrible romance movies the girls all lose their minds over?"

I giggled. I fucking giggled.

Arty slapped his forehead. "Oh, this is worse than I thought. You may have to move out."

"What? Even though you carry on about Elizabeth the same way?"

He held up a palm. "Touché. I guess now this means we're square. Now, while you're still glowing, tell me everything."

# Chapter Thirty-Three

# **Thomas**

SUMMER SCHOOL CALENDAR

*Wednesday*

*The Consumer and the War-Forum Lecture. Auspices of War Service Committee and Social Studies Workshop of Graduate School of Education. Emerson D, two o'clock.*

*Modern Problems of Family Life: Seminar on Youth Standards in Wartime. Professor Joseph K. Folsom, Emerson 211, two thirty.*

*Social Union Tea. (Primarily for graduates) Warburg Hall, Fogg Museum, four o'clock.*

*Synthetic Rubber—Illustrated Lecture. Dr. Howard I Cramer, New Lecture Hall, eight o'clock.*

**Thursday**

*Current Events Talk. Professor Abbott Payson Usher, New Lecture Hall, four o'clock.*

*Poetry Reading. Professor Theodore Spencer. New Lecture Hall, eight o'clock.*

*Harvard Night at the Pops. Summer School Chorus. Symphony Hall, Boston, eight thirty.*

**RUSSIAN RELIEF OPENS DRIVE**

*Opening a new headquarters in Harvard Square, the
Cambridge Division of the Russian War Relief has
opened a drive to raise money through contribution,
and the sale of books and toys.*

S ome memories imprint on our minds, like a pleasant taste that
lingers on the tongue, while others are seared into our conscious
thought, like a hot iron charring flesh.

July in Cambridge was brutally hot.

Our morning runs were met with the rising sun and rapidly rising
temperatures. By the time we staggered back into the yard, every one
of us was drenched and dripping with sweat.

We were in the best shape we'd been in since we met, but the heat
was an enemy no man could defeat. It simply kept clawing until it
crept into every part of our bodies. Add humidity drifting up from
the river, and there was nowhere to hide.

"Can't we just sleep late and *dream* about running," Will huffed
one particularly hot morning.

I grunted, too overheated and out of breath to actually laugh.

"See you in a couple hours," Will said, wobbling his way toward his
dorm to clean up before starting his day's classes.

I stood there, hunched over with my hands on my legs, gasping
for breath but unwilling to let the sight of him vanish before it was
absolutely necessary. Will had captured me in every way. His mind
challenged me, his wit indulged the banter I enjoyed so, and his body
... God, his body enthralled me in ways I had only dreamed about.

But more than any of that, the Will Shaw I had come to love
was a deeply good man, a pure spirit whose intentions and desires

were unmarred by the turmoil of his past. Most would bear scars so deep as to alter their very nature. Will's strengthened him and made him more committed to being the best version of himself. I marveled at his determination, at his commitment to principles many of our generation tossed about as hollow words or phrases. He lived those ideals, and I loved him more deeply for it.

And I envied him his idealism.

I had yet to see battle, to truly know the horror of war, but my role within the ONI had shown me the darker nature of man. I'd seen classified intelligence on Hitler's operations, on his trains laden with countless innocent souls bound for his vile chambers. I'd seen images of his handiwork, both on the battlefield and in the shadows where he believed his actions were well hidden.

I had seen true evil, and it had left its mark on my soul.

I prayed Will would never know what my eyes had seen. My heart wept that time would share those images with the world. It would be necessary, if only to ensure we never allowed anyone to walk that demonic path again.

America had already lost her innocence. Pearl Harbor and the battles that followed ensured it would be many years before our people slept peacefully again. But to truly know what was happening an ocean away would shatter the soul of the nation.

I dreaded that day, and, in a strange way, longed for it.

Some secrets could never leave the darkness. These demanded the light of day.

Will had long since vanished when I shook myself free of the images leafing before my mind. Only a few from our run remained in the yard. How long had I been standing there?

My first class was one Will and I did not share, one he believed related to Soviet studies. It had nothing to do with the Soviets.

There were only three students. Each of us served in the navy, and each was deeply embedded in the ONI's operational division. Most of the men who worked within the agency were analysts, sailors who specialized in identifying enemy ships and planes, and offering tactical guidance on defeating those units. Some participated in the planning of naval battles or naval participation in amphibious assaults. A select few were sent to gather intelligence the analysts would assimilate for use.

Our instructor was a civilian who introduced himself as Mr. Hazard, a name we knew as pure sardonic humor, an earmark of all intelligence services.

When I finally graduated this eternal training, I would enter the war in secret, a nameless member of the operational division of the ONI, one of the men dropped into hostile territory and tasked with learning everything I could about the enemy's strength and intentions.

Staring at the space Will had occupied moments earlier, I begged to all that was holy for him to become an analyst for whatever clandestine group that had recruited him. Dropping me into scalding water was fine; the idea of Will tumbling into that tempest wrenched my heart.

Despite the throbbing of my legs from our workout, I jogged north across campus toward Andover House. I'd already wasted enough of the morning and would likely miss breakfast; I couldn't be late to class. Our military instructors were strict, but Mr. Hazard was an insidious bastard.

My hair was still wet and disheveled as I strode into the conference room we used for our classroom. One of my classmates was seated on the opposite side of the long table, diligently studying from a fat tome. Mr. Hazard stood at the head of the table.

"Jacobs," he said without preamble. "Report to Commander Jeffers in A-2."

I blinked twice.

The other student had lost interest in his book and stared up at me with curious eyes. He glanced to Mr. Hazard, then back to me.

Alarms sounded in my mind, and my pulse began to race. I'd never been rerouted from a class before and certainly not to report to another instructor.

"Now, son."

"Uh, yes, sir." I turned and stepped back into the hallway.

A-2 was the designation for the classroom we used for Commander Jeffers's German class. I'd expected to interrupt some other class in progress, but found the room empty, save for the commander, who was seated behind the small metal desk.

He glanced up as I entered.

"Thomas, come in," he said, tossing his glasses on the desk and rising. Tiny lines pinched the corners of his eyes, and his jaw tightened as he stared up at me. He stepped around and sat in a student chair, turning it to face another. "Take a seat."

I did as instructed and waited while he gathered his thoughts. I could almost feel a darkness fall across his eyes.

"Son, there's no easy way to tell you this. I know you and Lieutenant Commander Raymond were good friends."

Lieutenant Commander Raymond? Baker? Why was he talking to me about Baker? And why did he say we *were* good friends ...

"Thomas, Raymond died last week. The Germans picked up his radio signal and got to him before he could move."

"What? What are you talking about? Baker's an instructor at one of the training facilities. He was pissed they wouldn't let him—"

Jeffers leaned back. His chair groaned. He shook his head.

"But ... sir ... Baker didn't go ..."

I couldn't wrap my mind around any of this. Baker was safe, tormenting new recruits and teaching them how to survive. There was no way he could've been killed. Besides, even if he'd been sent on a mission, he was too good to die.

He couldn't be … gone.

Jeffers rose and placed a hand on my shoulder. "I'll leave you to your thoughts. There's no class in here for a couple hours, so you'll have some privacy."

The sound of the door clicking shut behind him barely registered.

How had this happened? How was it even possible? Baker wasn't an ocean away. He was somewhere near Washington, DC, somewhere surrounded by woods and the scent of pine. He was barking at younger men, pushing them. He was sharpening spears and readying them for the fight.

That's what he'd told me.

Then again, we were in the business of secrets. I'd kept everything from Will, and, while I believed him when he said he didn't know what his future held, I was sure he'd not told me everything he knew about his posting.

But Baker and I were brothers. We wore the same uniform. He trained *me*.

"Why?" I muttered, still numb and unable to move. "Why not just tell me?"

As if it would've made any difference.

I buried my face in my hands and let sorrow wash through me.

When I finally glanced up, Baker's lopsided grin and floppy blond hair was all I could see through my watery eyes. He'd taken the place of Jeffers in the seat opposite me. My heart leapt into my throat as I gaped at my friend and mentor. He smiled down from his towering height, a wizened gleam in his hazel eyes.

I reached for him.

My hand found nothing but cold, dry air.

# Chapter Thirty-Four

# Will

**FIRST FRESHMAN DANCE TO FILL LOW-
ELL HOUSE**

*Opening campaign on the social front for the Class of
1946 will be the Freshman Informal Summer Dance
scheduled for tomorrow night from eight to twelve
o'clock in the Lowell House dining hall. Artie Ross and
his orchestra will be featured, probably along with en-
tertainers from Boston, who will amuse the dancers
during intermissions.*

*Work may come before pleasure for most students, but
this dance is an exception. Formerly scheduled for Friday, a Chem A exam has been postponed on purpose*

*to let even the most industrious forget their books for a while ...*[1]

## BONDS

*In a special sale of war bonds and stamps at the UT last night, one anonymous benefactor offered to buy a $1,000 bond if the rest of the audience would buy $1,000 between them. The quota was quickly reached, bringing the total to $2,400 in ten minutes.*[2]

## THE MAIL: LETTERS TO THE EDITORS OF THE CRIMSON

*I wish to object to* The Crimson's *portrayal of the barber shop price situation. May I point out that only one of the Harvard Square barbers opposed the rise in prices. In answer to* The Crimson's *vivid prediction of students rushing across the river to Boston for haircuts ...*[3]

---

1. Ibid, September 2, 1942

2. Ibid, September 4, 1942

3. Ibid, January 5, 1943

A side from the news of Baker's loss, the summer months had passed uneventfully for us. The Germans had launched offensives in southern Russia and Africa, while the Japanese continued to molest China's mainland. We had hoped the tide might turn after Midway, but news reels reported little good news.

The campus filled quickly as the men—and now women—of Harvard flooded the yard. There was something invigorating about the beginning of a new school year. Freshmen arrived, wide-eyed and hopeful. Familial privileges often earned newbies a spot among the Crimson, but those who'd truly earned their place in Cambridge were easy to spot. Many of them had dreamed of attending the college for years, and the honor of stepping foot on the campus that first time was rarely lost on a single one.

During the break between terms, Arty had again returned home, giving Thomas and me another blessed week together. When the weekend prior to the start of the term rolled around, Arty had yet to return. By midweek, several days into our new classes, I began to worry. Janie hadn't heard from him, and none of his professors knew his whereabouts. I tried phoning his parents, but they didn't pick up—another concern to add to my growing list.

On Friday of that week, I received a letter.


*Dear Will,*


*I hope your new classes are to your liking, even the ones you pretend are about American literature. My enlistment assignment has brought me to a place I cannot name to do things I cannot say with goals I cannot describe.*

*How is that for being a good friend and sharing things?*

*Seriously, I received orders to spend this term in a research facility somewhere on the East Coast. I arrived here a few days ago, and it's the most exciting thing I've ever been part of. I wish you could see the things we're working on. We're going to win this war, Will. I swear it.*

*Maybe one day I'll be able to tell you about some of this, because it truly is fantastic.*

*Our dorm room is yours for this term. Yes, I know what that means for you—have fun, and please try to keep off my blankets. Don't think I didn't pick up on your activities last time! And forgive me for not saying anything sooner. They wouldn't let me.*

*I'll write when I can, though I doubt I'll be allowed to say much more than what I've said here. Write me back at the return address on the envelope. They'll get letters to me in the magical way the government does things, which means I may not see them until after the war. Still, I would appreciate it if you wrote.*

*If it's not too much trouble, could you invite Elizabeth to lunch or dinner with the group? She took this pretty hard, and I don't want her to be lonely. Plus, she was pretty upset that she wasn't sent on this trip too. At first, I was flattered, thinking she wanted us to be together, then I realized the slight had more greatly stung her professional pride. She's smarter than I am, by a mile. They messed up not sending her here.*

*I really love her, Will, and I still can't believe she's interested in a boy like me. That might actually be more amazing and unbelievable than what I'm working on.*

*Tell Janie and Thomas hello.*

*I love you all,*

*Arty*

Mixed emotions barely described how I felt reading Arty's words.

My eyes darted toward Arty's bed. Thomas and I had indeed tried to christen every inch of our tiny dorm room. Throw in our wanton desire to try every piece of furniture and position, and no corner of our room was safe. Poor Arty. I'd have to wash his sheets before he returned.

And his blanket.

And his pillowcase.

*I might have to get him a new pillow.*

My second thought was how relieved I was that Arty was safe. By his rambling, I knew he was in heaven with his assignment and likely spending most of his waking hours trying to out-nerd everyone around him. While I didn't know exactly what he was working on, I knew it was research for the war effort, and if there was anyone in America who could make a difference through research, it was Arty.

Or maybe Elizabeth.

He'd been right about her being smarter than him. Hell, she was smarter than all of us combined.

Arty's safety probably should've been my first thought, but he'd thrown me off with his blanket reference and the visual it had conjured. There was something about Thomas and his shit-eating grin and firm, toned body that utterly destroyed my brain's ability to produce rational thought.

My mind finally settled on the disturbing reality that one day—far too soon—Thomas would be sent to God knows where, Arty would likely end up in yet another secret research facility, Janie would probably go home to earn her stripes in her father's business, and I would be ... somewhere else. In that moment of disquiet, I didn't care that I had no clue where my future led, only that it took me away from Thomas and the friends who had become my family.

If a knock at the door hadn't interrupted my thoughts, I likely would have spiraled into a self-loathing pool of murk and despair. Thankfully, as was his wont, Thomas saved the day.

"Hey, handsome," he said, kicking the door shut behind him as he wrapped his arms around me and planted a slobbery kiss on my lips.

"You're so gross," I said, wiping his spittle with my sleeve, smiling the whole time. "I have news from Arty."

"Good news? Talk to me." He flopped dramatically onto the bed.

I read Arty's letter aloud, but had to pause as Thomas jeered at the part about the blankets.

"We're gonna do it doggy style all over his sheets just for that. He won't just come home to snail tracks, he'll have skid marks too."

"Thomas, you're disgusting," I said, trying—and failing—to stop myself from laughing. "His brilliant little head would spin and pop off. He might never be able to build bombs—or whatever it is he's building—again."

"But it would be hilarious." He reached out and pulled me onto the bed atop him. "Screw the world and the war, let's make Arty's head explode."

Two weeks later, a second letter arrived from Arty.

*Will,*

*This place is unbelievable. It's the most amazing place I've ever seen. We are working on some seriously incredible stuff that I can't tell you about ... still. Sorry.*

*What I can tell you is that most of the researchers here are in their forties or fifties, and they have the creativity and flexibility of a plank of wood. Who would've ever thought I would be the creative one of the bunch—of any bunch? But I am! I've come up with some new ideas for things, and ideas to tweak things, and they're actually listening to me. They're trying my ideas, and some of them are making it into the ~~field~~. Sorry, war. I don't know where that word came from.*

*I can't wait to tell you all about this—after the war, of course. It'll probably be then before we can talk about it, if we can even then.*

*I'm babbling, aren't I?*

*I'm just so excited. This is amazing.*

*Tell everyone hi and that I asked about them and that
I love them.*


*Arty*


I smiled as I folded the letter and stuffed it back in the envelope. I could see Arty vibrating as he penned those words, hear the childlike wonder in his voice. He was such a wonderful guy. It was good to hear how happy he was. It was even better to hear that he was fitting into a role that would be productive, useful, and, most importantly, Stateside. I was terrified when we enlisted that the least athletic, least prepared-for-battle friend I knew would end up on the front line. His success with his program, whatever it was, meant he would most likely spend his time in uniform in a lab without ever touching a rifle.

A stack of books loomed from my desk. I groaned thinking about the night to come. Our military instructors had indeed stepped up their training, especially the All Things German class with Herr Jeffers. When our coursework started in January, I'd expected the hard-assed Sergeant Major Stafford to be the bane of our collective existence, but he was a lightweight next to *Folterknecht* Jeffers. He began this term by telling us the rest of our time together—the entire year—would be spent exclusively in German. English was no longer allowed in his class. One of the army guys made the mistake of addressing him as Commander Jeffers and earned an eraser to the chest for his blunder. A cloud of gritty white chalk plumed and hung in the air for the rest of that class.

Thomas, already fluent in German, became Jeffers's ally in teaching us colloquial phrases. Who knew that breaking up with one's love interest might cause one to add "love bacon," the literal translation of *Kummerspeck*, the German version of "adding a few pounds."

My personal favorite was *Rotzlöffel*, a reference to a brat or smart-ass kid, but is literally translated as "a spoon of snot."

After that particular class, I made it clear that Thomas had better protect me from Jeffers and his tricks if he didn't want to experience his own love bacon.

The study of cartography and camouflage complete, Sergeant Major Stafford rotated out, presumably to some training site at a secret base on the far side of the moon. We didn't care. He was far from us and that was a good thing. We had grown weary of the study of his perpetual growl and the study of using leaves to hide in the woods. The topic might have been interesting, fun even, if we'd done some actual hiding in some actual woods, but talking about theoretical hiding with theoretical leaves was tiresome.

His replacement, Major Tillis, somehow possessed an even less cheery disposition than the good sergeant, and his course, covering weapons, their functions, and ranges, was even more dry. When he first introduced the topic, our entire cohort was excited for the chance to test-fire the best the US military had to offer. Then we learned the entire term was little more than memorization of charts and mathematical formulas, and our enthusiasm shriveled faster than an old man's libido.

And then there was German.

Like Hitler gobbling up countries, our German studies class consumed the hour previously held by Lieutenant Willard's codes and radio course, which our military sherpas promised would resume once we graduated and entered our proper training.

Monotony bore its way into our skulls with each passing hour. Our senior year, famed for its carefree "slide," became a battle to slay one torturous, boring beast after another.

Until the first week in October when Commander Jeffers, Sergeant Major Stafford, and Lieutenant Willard strode into our classroom, each sharply dressed in the class A uniform of their respective service.

"Boys," the commander said, "pack up and meet us at Harvard Square in one hour. The rest of this term is a field trip."

# Chapter Thirty-Five

# Will

Eight students, including Thomas and I, boarded a bus. We hadn't been told our destination, how long we would be there, or even what we should pack. I watched through the window as the last of our classmates handed a small duffel bag to the driver.

"Looks like he doesn't expect this to last more than a week," I mused.

Thomas leaned across and out the window. "Glad we didn't pack that light. I doubt we'll see campus again before the end of term."

I hadn't planned to pack much, but Thomas insisted we fill our trunks and duffels with enough clothes to last for weeks. It wasn't cold in Cambridge yet, but he made me pack all my heavy coats and gloves too. He didn't know any more about this trip than the rest of us, he was just more paranoid.

By the time the bus pulled away, the sun's rays were kissing the horizon.

Commander Jeffers walked down the aisle, stopping where the first of the students sat, then held up a folder. "It will take us several hours to reach our destination. In this folder are new identities for each of you. You will assume them immediately and use them for the duration of this outing. From this point forward, you *are* your new identity, even to the people on this bus. You may help each other learn your cover while on this bus, but once we step off, you may not use your real name until we leave the camp. Instructors will be watching everything, everywhere. Do not let us down."

He pulled a sheet from his folder and handed it to the first student, then proceeded, one at a time, to hand out the rest.

"Well? Who are you?" I asked.

Thomas's lips quirked as he glanced at the paper. Then he read aloud in English, layering the words in his thickest German accent:

*Cover Identity: Wilhelm Müller*

*Background: Wilhelm Müller is a twenty-three-year-old German national who grew up in Berlin. He hails from a family with a long-standing tradition of artists and academics. His father, a respected professor of literature, instilled in him a love for books and languages from an early age. Wilhelm attended a renowned university in Berlin, studying languages and international relations, which facilitated his fluency in German, English, and French.*

*Personality Traits: Wilhelm is known for his youthful enthusiasm, curiosity, and open-mindedness. He is genuinely interested in exploring different cultures and embraces the opportunity to meet new people and forge* connections. *His passion for literature and the arts is evident in his conversations, making him a vibrant and engaging individual in social circles.*

*Cover Story: Wilhelm's cover story portrays him as a recent university graduate working as a language tutor and part-time translator. He explains that he enjoys helping others improve their language skills and find opportunities to use his linguistic talents. Wilhelm expresses a desire to explore different cultures, which led him to study abroad briefly in the United States.*

*Residence: 43 Johannis Str.*

*Wilhelm is a family-oriented individual with deep-rooted connections in Berlin.*

*Father: Frederick (deceased)*

*Mother: Hana*

*Sister: Anna, lives in Bonn with her husband, Felix, daughter, Ida, and son, Alexander.*

"I'm a German college grad named Wilhelm? Seriously, my name is *Will*?" His nose scrunched like he'd stumbled across something foul.

I grinned and whispered, "If only they knew how appropriate that truly is."

His head spun, then he glared with wide eyes, a very Thomas version of a reprimand.

I rolled my eyes and read my cover identity to him:

*Cover Identity: Tobias Richter*

*<u>Background</u>: Tobias Richter is a twenty-three-year-old German national who recently graduated with honors from Humboldt University in Berlin. Born into a family of intellectuals and history enthusiasts, his father was a well-respected professor of archaeology, and his mother was an accomplished linguist. The family's love for culture and heritage deeply influenced Tobias from a young age, inspiring him to pursue a career in historical research and preservation.*

*<u>Personality Traits</u>: Tobias is known for his gentle demeanor, intellectual curiosity, and strong sense of duty toward his country's heritage. He is an avid reader*

*and a skilled researcher, delving into the intricacies of history with an unwavering dedication to accuracy and authenticity.*

*Cover Story: After graduating from Humboldt University, Tobias introduces himself as a young historian with a deep interest in preserving Germany's cultural treasures. He presents his aspiration to work as a researcher and curator in Berlin's most esteemed cultural institutions, aiming to safeguard historical artifacts and promote German history to the world.*

*Residence: Currently living in a hostel, looking for an apartment.*

*Tobias has no surviving family.*

"Let me get this straight. You're basically an art nerd?" Thomas smothered a laugh.

"Hey! Archaeology is cool ... I think. Shit, I don't know anything about art or archeology. How am I supposed to pull this off?"

He shrugged. "No idea. I can speak languages, but I've never been a translator. Guess we'll find out when we get to wherever we're going."

For the next few hours, we drilled each other, reinforcing our new identities in our minds and embellishing the backgrounds with details we thought made sense and wouldn't get confused. The instructors hadn't told us to add to our covers, but we couldn't see a way to avoid it. The sheets they'd given us were bare bones, at best.

We stopped at a local diner in some small town in the middle of nowhere. Sergeant Major Stafford gave us a generous half-hour to eat, relieve ourselves, and return to our seats.

It took another day and a half of bus-bound torture across roads that clearly cared little for the comfort of our posteriors to reach our destination. All eight of us were passed out as the bus lurched to a halt. I woke and rubbed my aching neck. Thomas's head still rested against the aisle cushion, his eyes darting rapidly beneath heavy lids.

When we moved again, the bus crept forward. I watched as two men in British military uniforms waved us past a guard shack that stood next to a heavy swinging gate. Signs with bright red lettering were nailed to the shack:

**PRIVATE PROPERTY: KEEP OUT.**

Beneath the words was a symbol that reminded me of the British Royal seal.

A few moments later, we stopped at another gate and were inspected by another group of heavily armed men, this time a team of six. Their shack was a cement bunker with holes that looked like archer's slits in a castle turret. The groaning of massive hinges heralded the opening of a far heavier gate. Unlike the simple arm from before, this barrier was one thick, solid sheet of dark metal.

Another neatly printed sign read, *103.*

"Time to wake up, ladies," Sergeant Stafford bellowed.

"What the hell?" Thomas muttered as his eyes fluttered open.

"We're on some kind of British base. We just passed through the second security gate."

"British?" His eyes narrowed. "Did we drive all the way to Canada? The Brits don't have any bases in the US."

I shrugged. "We might be. We were on the road long enough to cross the border."

"Listen up," Stafford called. "This place—and anyone you meet here—are figments of your imagination and never actually existed. You will never know where it is. When you leave, you will have no memory of anything beyond a very long camping trip on Harvard's dime. Do you understand me?"

"Yes, Sergeant Major," we replied.

He started to turn, then looked back with an evil glint in his eyes. "One more thing: no English until we return to Harvard. German language only."

Thomas shifted beside me and summed up all our thoughts: "*Scheiße!*"

# Chapter Thirty-Six

# Thomas

F our hours after our heads hit pillows in the communal barracks that housed all eight of us, Sergeant Major Stafford's pleasant voice blared louder than any bugle.

"Rise and shine, ladies. The sun will wake up eventually. We can't wait for her lazy ass. Breakfast in ten minutes. Remember, you are your covers."

"Did you know he spoke German?" I sat up on the side of my bed and rubbed my throbbing temples.

"I'm going to throw something in German if he does that again," Max, a rugged army guy bunked next to me, grumbled as he stood and stretched his back. I tried not to peek at his legs, but the muscles in his quads bulged, along with every other part of him stuffed into his white boxers.

A throat cleared behind me.

Will had an accusing brow raised when I turned. The asshole was fully dressed and looked like he'd slept a full eight hours. I was usually the morning person, but the bus trip had seriously messed with my body clock. I gave him a sheepish smile.

"*Frühstück*?" Breakfast?

I nodded and stood, thankful for the reminder to speak in German. Within only a few hours' sleep after a multi-day bus trip, I was lucky to remember my own name—even though it was no longer my name.

Shit, there was so much to remember.

I grabbed my cover identity sheet and followed Will and a couple of the other guys out the door. Comfortably fresh air tickled my skin as we walked from the barracks across to the mess. Given how far we'd traveled, I'd worried winter might bite us in the ass, but the autumn breeze was only slightly cooler than in Cambridge.

Breakfast consisted of two fried eggs, tomatoes, pickles, and a couple pieces of toast, in what I assumed was our host's attempt at a traditional German morning meal. Thankfully, coffee was also on the menu. It was stronger than the American stuff we were used to, but sated my craving for a boost before the day began.

There was an odd feeling in the mess hall as we ate. Students clustered in twos and threes at long tables. Despite our remote location on a place everyone called a "camp," each of us wore trousers and a sport coat, though no one bothered wearing a tie.

No one spoke, beyond the occasional request for salt or pepper to be passed. It felt almost as though everyone was afraid to speak. The heavy air of uncertainty blanketed the hall.

Instructors watched us from across the room, where they sat at one large, round table that looked to have been carved from a single piece of knotty wood. Sergeant Major Stafford, Lieutenant Willard, and Commander Jeffers sat with three other men I didn't recognize. Each wore dark blue, loose-fitting jogging suits, like ones we'd wear for our early-morning runs back on campus.

Finally, Jeffers stood and approached our tables. "*Guten Morgen.*" Good morning.

He waited for all eyes to turn his way before continuing in German. "Welcome to Special Training School 103. This camp will be your home for the next month. This session has two objectives. First, to immerse each of you in German; the language and culture. The second is to get you acquainted with living inside another identity. For many, becoming someone else is an awkward adjustment, but it will be the difference between survival and capture—or worse—when behind enemy lines. The slightest mistake or hesitation could cost you, and everyone associated with you, everything. It most certainly will jeopardize the success of your mission. You must *become* your cover.

"If you're going to make mistakes, make them here, in this camp, in this month. This is the time to learn. When we return in the spring, those same mistakes will incur harsh and immediate consequences."

He paused a moment, eyeing each of us in turn. "You will continue your Harvard classes, but will also participate in other activities meant to offer more direct experience with German people and situations. When not in class or attending an assigned activity, you have free run of the grounds. There's nothing for miles around, so explore all you like. Your barracks and the mess hall are also open to you at all hours, but all other buildings are restricted.

"We will challenge you at every turn. Our friends from across the pond are experts in counterespionage. You will meet them soon enough. Their mission is to make you fail. Do not let them succeed."

He glanced at a pocket watch. "The buildings are labeled with letters. Assemble in the classroom in Building B in fifteen minutes."

Then he did the last thing I would have expected. He snapped to attention and speared his hand in the German salute and yelled, "*Heil Hitler!*"

Eight stunned students stared up.

He glared down, then snapped, "Are you not loyal to your *Führer*? *Heil Hitler!*"

Reluctantly, chairs groaned against wooden planks as we stood and returned the salute, "*Heil Hitler.*"

"You must do better. You must *believe*. Whoever you were before you stepped onto this land no longer exists. You *are* your covers."

With that uplifting admonition, Jeffers turned and returned to the instructors' table, where he began casually sipping his coffee.

Our classes picked up exactly where they'd left off in Cambridge. The only difference was that each instructor spoke in German. Commander Jeffers's class kicked off the day and was easy enough to follow. It was, after all, the study of All Things German.

When Lieutenant Willard began the second period with a re-examination of German codes and ciphers, I watched Will's expression tumble from confident understanding to a blank sheet of incomprehension.

"I have no idea what a *Lautstärkeregler* is," Will whispered, despite Willard pointing to the dial with a pencil as he spoke.

"It's the volume control," I replied.

Most of the German names for radio parts sounded similar in English. For example, the aerial terminal in German was *Antennenterminal*. Knowing a little Latin mixed with basic German made most words easier to parse out. Unfortunately, once we landed in Europe, parsing anything could get us shot.

"You're going to have to help us all later. Look around." Will motioned with his eyes.

I scanned the room to find varying degrees of blank stares on each of our classmates. It wasn't only Will who was getting lost in the sauerkraut.

For our third class, Sergeant Major Stafford revisited our old friend cartography and camouflage. Unlike radio terms, the German words for even basic mapping terms had no relation to their English cousins. Come to think of it, they weren't even cousins. They were wholly unrelated bastards from a mother who'd slept with a bartender's milkman's second cousin's brother.

Even I was struggling to keep up, and I'd been learning German since I was twelve.

Stafford's evil grin never faltered.

Around one o'clock, we reconvened in the mess hall for lunch. Two women in simple smocks ladled us bowls of stew filled with diced potatoes, sausages, tomatoes, and a few other vegetables I didn't recognize. Fresh fruit filled bowls on our tables, along with hard rolls and squares of butter.

"Doesn't look like we'll hate the food. I think they missed the ration memo," one of the guys behind me said.

"Guess taking over all your neighbors means you can steal all their food too," another replied.

The weight of the statement, meant more as a light joke than mood killer, brought the gravity of our future missions into perspective once more. Even the simplest acts, such as eating a hearty meal, were threatened by the Nazi regime. The responsibility to succeed at our missions settled tightly about our shoulders as we again ate in silence.

"Report to Building C in ten minutes," was all the good sergeant said as the instructors stood and exited.

"What now?" Max asked.

I shrugged.

Will avoided my gaze, scooping the last of his stew into his mouth.

We walked across the small yard from the mess hall to Building C, a long, tin-roofed, single-story unit that looked like a storage facility for any factory in America. What we found inside made us freeze in the doorway.

On either side of the building, lining the long walls, a replica of a German street market had been erected, complete with vendors behind rolling carts, men and women strolling about, and armed German soldiers marching in pairs as they scrutinized each passerby. There must've been fifty people roaming about, mimicking daily life in Berlin or some other city within the German fatherland.

The mouthwatering scents of savory sausages and freshly made sweets blended with the tangy bitterness of burned tobacco. Loudspeakers concealed high in the ceiling played sounds of a streetscape: the roar of an engine, the honk of a horn, the bark of a soldier's order.

In an attempt to complete the realness of the scene, the ceiling had been painted as a mural of the sky, complete with puffy clouds and a distant plane flying overhead.

Everywhere we looked, the blood and black of the Nazi flag hung limply in the windless chamber.

"What are we supposed to do?" Will whispered.

I shook my head. "No idea, but I'm pretty sure we shouldn't just stand in the doorway. Let's look around."

Slowly, our group dissolved into pairs as we edged onto the cobblestones of the faux street, drawn in every direction by the myriad stores and actors.

"*Kann ich ihnen bei etwas helfen*?" Can I help you with something?

The shopkeeper's voice startled me so badly I nearly tripped over Will. The man was middle-aged, balding with black hair swirled poorly across his scalp, and wore the mustache typical of a Hitler-loving Berliner. A long table filled with books was spread before him.

"Do you have any more ... classic books?" I asked. "My girlfriend loves old romances."

The man's eyes tightened, a barely perceptible tick, then he smiled broadly. "Of course, of course. They are in the back. One moment, please. I have just the books for you."

"Your girlfriend?" Will whispered once the man was out of earshot. "Now you have another cover to maintain, making up new people."

"And here I thought you were jealous."

His eyes darted around, then up to me. "Funny, but risky, even for you. You know they're watching us."

"You're right—"

The man returned, ending whatever lame admission I was about to make. He really was right. I just enjoyed making him squirm.

"I am sorry. I only found this one book. Do you think your girl would like this?"

*The Scarlet Letter* stared up at me. I flipped it upside down and dropped it onto the table, leaning across to hiss at the man.

"American? Seriously? You want me to buy an *American* book?"

The man nodded over my shoulder, and two soldiers in the uniform of the German SS stepped up behind us. I could feel Will's spine stiffen.

"And how would you know this is an American work, young man?"

Will took a step backward. The soldier closest to him moved with lightning speed, whipping the rifle off his shoulder and pointing it at Will's chest. "Do not move."

"Answer my question. How do you know this book?" the seller asked.

"I attended university ... at ... um—"

"Where? Where did you attend *university?*" the man sneered.

"Humbolt," Will interjected, his voice lacking the hesitation I couldn't shake from mine. He ignored the soldiers, casually perusing the books on the table as he spoke, like nothing at all unusual had just happened, and the business end of a gun wasn't pointed at him. "We attended Humbolt here in Berlin. Our literature studies were quite extensive."

The bookseller scoffed, and one of the soldiers grabbed me by the arm.

Will turned and raised a brow, like he was annoyed by the soldier's impertinence.

"You might know our family names. We are rather well known here in Berlin. Wilhelm is a Müller. I am a humble Richter." There was so much condescension lacing his name when he spoke, I thought he might actually spit on the soldier. Immediately, the bookseller's eyes widened, and the soldier's grip released.

"Herr Müller, forgive me. There are so many undesirables around these days. One can never be too careful. Take this book as a gift from me."

Will snatched the book before I could reach for it, then tossed it into the seller's chest.

"Take that American filth and burn it before I have these soldiers search your shop. It's the least my father would do. Come, Wilhelm, let's be away from this place."

Will grabbed my arm and shoved me past the guards as they glared at the startled shopkeeper.

We'd made it past two more shops before I leaned over and asked, "Who's your father supposed to be?"

Will shrugged. "Isn't there a high-up named Richter? I know there's at least one major asshole named Müller. I was guessing he wouldn't know who their kids were."

"What if that Müller doesn't have a son?" I asked.

"Guess we would've been screwed. You needed a save." He turned away to look at a butcher's offering.

My pulse still hadn't slowed, but Will looked like he was having the time of his life. His German still needed work, but he blended in more comfortably than I ever would have imagined. For the first time since we'd met, I began to realize why he'd been handpicked to join his program.

That afternoon, one of the British officers who'd introduced himself as Whitehall assumed command of our training. The three instructors we'd grown used to retired to some other building, leaving us at the mercy of Brits who had long since lost the meaning of that word. Their classroom sessions were brief, to the point, and followed by hours of practical exercises aimed at sharpening our German and assimilation skills to a fine edge. Failure to maintain cover was met with the butt of a fake soldier's rifle or a night losing sleep on the cold floor of a concrete box.

By the third week in November, our German proficiency had risen sharply, and each of us wore our cover identities with ease. Still, the instructors came up with new and inventive scenarios every day, never replicating the same streetscape or other encounter.

Will quickly rose to the top of our class. The ease with which he conversed with the actors was nothing short of remarkable. And yet, as the sun set on America's Thanksgiving Eve, he slipped up, using a reference to one of Harvard's buildings rather than those found on the campus of his alter-alma mater. The two SS soldiers we'd foiled in our first meeting hauled him away.

When he didn't show for dinner, I assumed they were giving him the interrogation lesson.

When he still didn't arrive at breakfast the next day, I began to worry.

Commander Jeffers was halfway through his lesson on the Second Reich when the classroom door opened and Will stumbled in. His eye was blackened and his cheeks were angry with cuts and bruises. He held his side as he slumped into his chair.

Brighton, one of our other British instructors, followed him into the classroom, silencing whatever Jeffers was about to say.

"Men, Mr. Shaw just enjoyed an evening of Name That Traitor. It's a little game the Germans play when they capture a member of an enemy cell. They'll use any means necessary to get you to turn on your radio operator, your host, or any other member of your team.

"This is not a painless game, but Mr. Shaw played brilliantly. His face bears the fruits of his labor. When you return in the spring, each of you will be captured at some point. You must know what it feels like in order to prepare yourself. It will not be pleasant, but it is necessary."

He met Will's exhausted eyes. "Well done, Mr. Shaw. It will be an honor serving with you."

"Thank you, Brighton," Jeffers said with a tone of dismissal, but the barrel-chested Brit didn't move. His eyes scanned each student before landing on me.

"Mr. Jacobs, come with me, please."

Will winced as he glanced back. I couldn't tell if he was sore, fatigued, or trying to communicate something, but his eyes held more than I could identify in that brief moment. I rose and followed Brighton out of the classroom.

A moment later, I sat alone at a table with four chairs in a small conference room, wondering if it was my time to experience the Germans' not-so-fun game. When the door opened, Lieutenant Jeffers strode in, pulled a chair around so he could face me with nothing between us, and sat. His face was drawn, his eyes downcast.

"Lieutenant, what happened? I can see—"

Without a word, he stretched out his fist and opened it, revealing a silver signet. A simple anchor with no lettering or other markings adorned its face. I ran a finger over its smooth, unetched sides.

I would know that ring anywhere.

"This is ... was ... Baker's." My voice caught. I couldn't pull my eyes from the anchor.

"One of our agents got it back to us. We do our best to return something to families when ... well, when this happens. Baker didn't have any family, so we thought you might want it."

I looked up through watery eyes.

Jeffers held my gaze, then nodded once and rose. I felt his hand on my shoulder as my eyes drifted back to the ring in my now-shaking fingers. "Take your time, son. When you're ready, rejoin your class."

# Chapter Thirty-Seven

# Will

Thomas made it through the rest of our camp experience without enjoying the butt of a rifle or a night in isolation. I wasn't sure how he'd managed that, given how easily he'd given himself away almost every time we strode down the cobblestones of the next fake town. Most of the other guys weren't any better, earning quick rebukes or brutal arrests to end their day's simulation. I was glad we had another term before facing the real world, but wondered if it would truly be enough to prepare us for SS officers with lifetimes of ferreting out fraudsters.

The night before our return to Cambridge, Thomas and I stole away from the others. It wasn't uncommon for individuals or small clusters to take walks, especially at night. There was something invigorating about the crisp night air and full moon that was hard to put into words. The strolls allowed time to process the day's activities. More, they renewed our spirit.

I couldn't begin to guess how many acres of bare land surrounded Camp X, as we'd come to call our temporary home. Rows of trees lined imaginary boundaries, and it was impossible to tell whether thick woods or more open fields lay beyond.

When we'd first arrived, the vast emptiness of the landscape felt eerie, somehow claustrophobic in the enormity of the nothingness. Most of my life had been spent in densely packed American cities. It was strange to feel closed-in by a lack of buildings and people.

Now, the open fields with their limitless ceiling of the deepest night sky felt welcoming and warm, like a favorite blanket wrapped about the shoulders on a wintry night. As we strode toward a stand of boulders at the far end of one tract, brittle grasses crunching beneath our boots, I knew there was more in Thomas's desire for a walk than simply exercise or a moment of peace. I could feel something brewing in his mind.

It made my heart stir like an uneasy stomach after a heavy meal.

Still, I said nothing, enjoying the simple closeness, the togetherness we'd each craved but eschewed due to the ever-present scrutiny of our peers and instructors. If he had something on his mind, he'd bring it up when he was ready.

Thomas and I had no secrets.

Well, we did, actually.

I had no idea what he did for the ONI, though I was fairly certain the navy wouldn't waste resources sending an analyst to field training. That ruled out desk jobs. Beyond that, I had no clue what he was training to do or where they might send him. My heart prayed he would go somewhere safe, like Washington, DC, and focus on counterespionage or something equally mundane here at home. I wasn't sure I could handle knowing he was being dropped into hostile territory—like Baker.

It was also clear that he had no idea to which agency I was assigned or how they might use me once our training was complete. I was confident he had no clue because *I* had no clue. There hadn't been a single conversation, not with an instructor, recruiter, or anyone else from the government, about my future, since that initial chat with Major I'm-Sure-That-Wasn't-His-Name in the campus recruiting office. I'd tried to put that out of my mind, but attending months-long camping trips at places nicknamed X put things into sharper focus. I was now nervous about where I might be dropped, or planted, or whatever they would call it when it happened. I wasn't exactly frustrated by the lack of communication, but it was becoming more unsettling as my eventual graduation neared.

Thomas climbed atop a boulder, finding the perfect spot where he could lean against another with his back toward the distant camp, hidden from the sight of anyone who might also take an evening stroll. He patted the stone next to him like it was a comfy cushion, and I clamored up and sat next to him.

My butt had barely settled when both his hands clasped my face and pulled me into him for a deep kiss. I resisted at first, alarmed that we might be discovered, but quickly lost the ability for rational thought as the man I loved poured himself into his passion. How could the moon become fuller simply by the pressing of lips? Somehow, it drew nearer to us, filling the sky with her yellow glow, smiling down as we enjoyed each other for the first time since leaving Cambridge.

"Guess you still love me," I breathed as our lips parted.

He responded by pressing himself into me once more.

I moaned, my whole body suddenly alive and hungry for his touch. Damn the cold. I wanted his skin against mine.

"God, I want you so bad," he muttered.

"I want to feel you rubbing against me, take you inside me," I growled.

Something rustled in the distance, and he pulled away, sitting up straight and listening. A long moment passed before he relaxed.

"We shouldn't ... we're too close to camp." He peered over the boulder to ensure no one was nearby.

"I hate this hiding, always waiting to be caught," I grumbled.

He grinned. "Funny thing for a spy-in-training to say. Sure you're in the right business?"

"That's not what I—"

"I know, babe," he said. "It's still funny though, when you think about it. We should be the best spies ever. All we've ever done is hide who we really are. We've had a lifetime to train for all this. Add some German, and *voilà*!"

"Isn't *voilà* French?"

He speared my side with his fingers, and it took everything in me not to cry out at the sneak attack.

As he settled back into place beside me, satisfied we were still alone, I took his hand and entwined our fingers, stroking the back of his hand with my thumb. It was such a simple act, but one of which we'd been deprived for far too long. I realized in that moment just how much I'd craved his touch.

"I miss this," slipped out in a sigh.

We sat shoulder to shoulder staring up at the moon. He tilted his head to rest against mine. "Me too, babe."

He squeezed my hand, and I felt a ring press into my fingers. Raising our hands, I saw in the moonlight that he wore Baker's silver anchor. I reached up and traced its lines.

"I miss *him* too," he said, and I could feel the pain in his faltering voice.

I waited, sensing how special this moment, this memory, was to Thomas. I scooted down so my head could rest on his chest as I gazed up at the stars. He seemed to drift into some distant past, his voice an echo when he spoke.

"He talked me into joining the navy, you know."

"Really?"

I felt his nod.

"I was so young and stupid. He was already a lieutenant with several years on me. I hate to say it, but my family got me a commission before I ever set foot on a college campus. It's not supposed to work like that, but war and money changes a lot, I guess." A sardonic grunt slipped free. "He'd say I was just stupid now."

I turned my body to face him sideways and nested my face beneath his chin, as he drew me as close as he could. He was so strong, yet in that moment, he seemed more vulnerable than any wayward child.

"Baker got me through basic and all the bullshit they put us through. Be glad you don't have to do any of that. It sucked."

I ran my hand along his chest, more to feel and comfort him than out of any passion or desire.

"He was an ONI recruiter back then. I didn't have a clue. Hell, I didn't even know what the ONI was. When I joined, I had these images of sailing across the ocean under a flapping flag, the sea misting against my face as massive guns fired over the horizon. He told me I'd probably end up in a map room underground somewhere, studying troop positions or something equally boring."

I watched as his fingers absently twisted Baker's ring as he spoke. He'd done that a lot lately, fiddled with that ring. He did it when presented with a complex or challenging problem, but mostly, I knew he did it when the past intruded on his present. The ring had become part of him, like Baker had been. I smiled weakly, imagining an aged version of Thomas, gray and withered by time, still fiddling with that ring ... and remembering.

By the time our bus pulled back onto campus, unmarked snow blanketed Harvard Yard, as most of the students had retreated for their holiday break. Thomas and I walked to our respective dorms, laden with the clothes and supplies we'd taken to Camp X, but with nothing that might indicate we'd been anywhere other than a sanctioned college destination.

A folded note atop my bed greeted me as I opened my door.

*Will,*

*I got back the week after Thanksgiving, excited to tell you all about where I've been (at least, the parts I can tell you), only to find our room abandoned. Where have you gone? I checked around, but no one seemed to know, only that you, Thomas, and others of your classmates were seen boarding buses a couple months ago and hadn't been seen since.*

*How rude.*

*Wherever they've taken you, hope it's at least half as fun as my little field trip was. Let's see, I can tell you we worked on some weapony stuff. That's a term, isn't it? Weapony? Oh, the theme for everything we're working on is "miniaturization." It doesn't matter if we're working on a radio or a tank, the question is, "How can we make it smaller?"*

*How cool is that?*

*I'm in heaven. This is so much more interesting than architectural plans for apartments or commercial buildings like my father wanted me to study. I might've shot myself if that was to be my life's work.*

*That's really all I can tell you about my work. Sorry. Guess even my explanation is miniaturized. (That's funny, don't deny it.)*

*I've gone home for Hannukah. Elizabeth is with me. This is her first time meeting my parents, so keep your fingers crossed. Hell, cross your toes too. Grab a rabbit's foot. Hop on one leg. Whatever it takes. God, I hope they like her. How could they not, right? She's perfect. Did I mention how much I love her? She's like sunlight on a … never mind. I was about to get all vomit-inducing. That's how Thomas described it last time we were all together. I guess he's right. I just can't stop talking when she's around ... or when she's not around and I think about her. She's just ...*

*\*Puke\* I know. Sorry.*

*Speaking of vomit-inducing, how is Thomas? Did you play basketball while you were away? I hope so; you need practice. It puts you in a much better mood.*

*If you can, you should come join us. I know my family would love to see you, especially my brothers. If you're not there, they'll nag me to play ball outside in the snow, and I think we both know how well that would go.*

*Please, come save me.*

*If you can't come, we'll understand. I'll be back after the new year for our last term.*

*Can you believe this will be our last term? Will, we're seniors! We're about to graduate. Where have the past four years gone?*

*Alright, my father should be here now, and he gets really mad if I make him wait in the car. Call me if you can. We miss you.*

*All our love,*

*Arty*

*PS. I can't believe I almost forgot—JANIE GOT EN-GAGED! Did you know she was even dating anyone? I'm not sure she knew until a massive diamond found its way onto her finger. She swears we're going to love this guy, but I have my doubts. You know how she is. Hurry up and come home so we can judge him ... I mean, meet him.*

I folded the letter and tossed it on the desk, chuckling at Arty's squeaky-door voice ringing in my ears. Basketball. Seriously? Arty had concocted that code word for "special time alone" between Thomas and me in case our letters were ever read. I wasn't sure it would fool anyone, but it made me smile.

Basketball, indeed.

There had been no balls in hoops. Or anything else in hoops.

Our code word might need work.

Then a thought struck: Arty was home for the holidays, for two weeks. As much as I wanted to see my roomie and best friend, that meant Thomas and I had two weeks with no classes, no assignments, no military anything ... and no Arty in my room. I scrambled to change out of my bus-worn clothes, determined to run all the way to Andover to share the good news, when a banging on the door nearly scared the piss out of me.

The moment I opened the door, Thomas barged in, kicked the door shut behind him, and threw me by my shoulders onto the bed.

"This feels familiar," I said with a grin.

He tore off his heavy coat, then yanked his shirt over his head, unveiling his hardened chest and stomach. "No more talking," was all he said before nearly knocking the air out of my lungs as he leapt on top of me.

The bed screamed in protest.

I didn't.

# Chapter Thirty-Eight

# **Thomas**

**BUSY SCHOOL WILL RETRAIN OFFICIALS**

*The Harvard Business School has agreed to expand its recently announced War Production Retraining Program, in compliance with a request by war industries, the university announced today.*

*In this connection, the Business School has stated in a recently published explanation that training of an unprecedented character is to be given to men already employed in war production. After a fifteen-week course, men who demonstrate ability are to be put in more responsible positions in the companies which sent them ...*

## BC, HIGH SCHOOLS AVOID OIL FREEZE

*With the oil shortage threatening to close school doors at Boston College and several local high schools, temporary relief was obtained yesterday when the navy released some of their reserve supply of the precious fuel for civilian consumption. Harvard seemed reasonably free from danger of a freeze. Exhaust steam from the Cambridge Electric Company, which warms Crimson buildings, is coal-generated, and so far not closed off by war conditions ...*

## RACQUET MEN WIN TOURNEY

*Jack Barnaby was a happy man this Christmas, with good reason. His pet project, the Varsity Squash Racquets Team, had just taken over the finals of the Invitation Intercollegiate Squash Tournament. Run by the University Club in New York, the tournament has in the past been an excellent crystal ball for gazing into coming intercollegiate competitions ...*

"That might've been the best two weeks of my life," I said, kissing Will's neck and pulling him closer. He loved it when

I held him close, his back against my chest so I could nibble his neck and ears.

A low rumble sounded, something like a massive panther in play mode. I could feel it vibrating against me as I squeezed him tight.

I nibbled his earlobe, and he stretched his neck, giving me better access.

"God, I love it when you do that."

Then I bit down harder.

"Ow. I used to love it," he said, reaching back and rubbing his lobe between two fingers. "No fangs, mister."

That forced me to flip him onto his back and bite his nipple.

"Alright!" he squealed, shoving me back and jumping from the bed, a broad smile belying any irritation threaded through his voice. "Enough of you. I need coffee, and time for my body parts to heal before you get hot and hungry again. If your googly eyes don't give us away, me walking bowlegged for the next month might. Thanks for that."

I gave him a mock salute. "Anything for the cause, sir."

He grabbed a sock off the floor and flung it at me.

"Abuse! That's naval abuse!"

"When I abuse your naval, you'll know it, sailor ... and you'll probably like it anyway, you sicko."

He leered. "Come, try me. Now I want to find out. Do you spear it with your tongue or try to stick your—"

I ducked as he threw the other sock.

"We've basically been naked for a whole fortnight. If I have to eat out of another box, I'll go mad. Come on. Breakfast is calling."

"You're so forceful when you're hungry. I love it," I said, getting to my feet and wrapping my arms around his still-naked form. I pressed a kiss to the back of his neck. "God, I love this man."

He spun around, wrapping his arms about my neck and kissing me deeply. "I love you more than life, but not more than breakfast. Now, get dressed before my love morphs into something more basic, like a hunger killing."

I snorted and slapped his ass, earning yet another squeal and a hop.

Arty would return to campus this afternoon, and, while Will's roomie was fully accepting of our relationship and had basically adopted me as another brother, he likely wouldn't be open to seeing us doing naked things in front of him, especially when he learned how often we did said naked things on his bed ... and his sheets ... and against his desk ... and, well, everywhere else we could find in their tiny dorm room.

It really had been the best fortnight of my life.

That evening, Will, Arty, Elizabeth, Janie, and I sat around a large rugged table in the corner of a pub only a few blocks from campus. Two soldiers sat slumped at the bar, one swaying so badly from his drink I thought he might topple at any moment. The bartender looked ancient and was probably the owner of the joint, making a living offering respite to students and military personnel stationed at Harvard. He eyed his swaying guest, drying the same glass for nearly a quarter-hour. A lone bard strummed the melancholy of the times from a corner lit by nothing but a thin candle.

The cacophony that was our table stood in contrast to everything about the place. Janie's mouth was a blur—almost as blinding as the rock she must've shown us a dozen times in as many minutes. Every other word was about some guy named Taft.

Taft?

"Like taffy?" Will asked..

"No, silly. Taft, like the president."

"Wait. Your fiancé is dead?" I needled, earning a grin from Will and a punch from Janie.

"No, he is very much alive. He's an attorney in Boston with a firm with four names, I can never remember them, they all sound alike. But they sound very official and important too."

"Oh," Will said dramatically. "I see. Very nice."

He got a punch this time.

Elizabeth leaned in, offering a sincere, sympathetic smile. "He sounds positively wonderful, but Janie, I have to ask, how old is Taft? I thought you were more interested in university boys than, well, older men." She spoke her last words almost in a whisper, as though they hinted at scandal.

"He's thirty-one," Janie said rapidly, muffling her voice a bit.

"Thirty-one?" Arty bellowed loud enough for the swaying drunk to turn with raised brows.

Janie straightened her spine. "Yes, thirty-one. That's a perfectly acceptable age, thank you very much. He knows what he wants in life, unlike the children here at Harvard."

Will chuckled. Arty crossed his arms.

"I have a pretty good handle on what I want in life," he said, grasping Elizabeth's hand like it might run away if he let go.

"I'm good here too," I said, elbowing Will, but not giving the bartender or anyone else more to go on. "The navy has her hooks in me. I'll probably be a lifer."

"Yes, yes," Janie said, now flustered. "That isn't what I meant at all."

Will rescued her, placing a hand on hers. "Janie, we're just teasing. We're very happy for you. Now, when do we get to meet this mystery man?"

Her cheeks colored. "Well, I suppose we should ... do something. I mean, we could get together ... Taft is very busy. You know how it is."

As I listened to the banter of this close-knit family, I couldn't imagine what pain-riddled mother in the throes of birth would burden a boy with such a name as Taft. It made me think of the petty boys in boarding school determined to win the game of "my daddy has more money than your daddy." If only they'd known who my daddy, or my great-great-granddaddy, was. Thankfully, they didn't, and I liked it that way.

"Janie Lynn, are you embarrassed by us?" Will feigned offense.

She blanched. "No, Will, of course not. I never—"

Arty piled on. "Then why haven't we met this love of your life? Exactly how long have you know the dead president?"

"Arty, be nice." Elizabeth patted his arm and gave Janie a nod.

"He's not dead!" Janie pouted.

"Your name is Janie Lynn?" I asked.

Will, Arty, and Janie turned and gaped at me. A heartbeat, then two, and all three of them burst out laughing. Elizabeth and I shared a blank stare, which only made them laugh harder.

"We just call her that when we're pretending to be her angry parents. It's not her name. She's not from some bumpkin town, Thomas. Really." Arty reached across Elizabeth and patted my arm like she had done his a moment earlier.

"Five months," Janie said in a small voice.

"Oh," was all I could think to say. This conversation had bounced faster than most of our basketball dribbles, and I was struggling to keep up.

"Five months!" Will and Arty shouted in unison.

"What about five months?" Elizabeth asked.

"How long they've known each other. Keep up, dear," Arty said.

"When did he propose?" Will asked.

"So your name isn't Janie? Or it isn't Lynn?" I asked.

"He *did* propose, didn't he?" Arty scowled.

"YES!" Janie shouted. "He proposed. How do you think I got this ring?"

"You could've bought it. Lots of nice stores in town." Arty shrugged as if solving a crime.

"Or a pawn seller. They have nice things sometimes. Are you sure the dead president didn't get it on the cheap? Maybe cash in gas coupons for a ring?"

"Gas coupons?" Janie gasped. "This is a diamond!"

"So he says," Arty chimed in.

"Arty," Elizabeth warned.

"You never said when he proposed," Will reminded.

"Had to be before the pawn shop," Arty said.

Janie screamed and threw her hands over her head.

The entire bar fell silent. Even the guitar player froze and stared. The drunk teetered and landed in a heap, while his friend turned and gaped at the screaming woman. The bartender finally set his glass down.

Janie sucked in an exasperated breath. "We met five months ago. He proposed on the second of December. Taft comes from a family of attorneys in Boston. He has a war exemption on account of his eyesight, or, more accurately, his lack thereof. He is tall, handsome, and perfectly respectable, unlike the rabble sitting around me. I will introduce you at a time of my own choosing and not a moment before. Is that all?"

Whoever had paused the film of our lives inside the pub apparently found the switch and movement resumed. The guitarist strummed, the drunk stumbled to his feet, and the bartender found another glass to dry.

As for our group, Arty changed the subject as though nothing odd had just happened, blurting, "I'm leaving again next week and won't be back until commencement."

And just like that, those around our table sat frozen and gaping again.

# Chapter Thirty-Nine

# Will

“Wʜat do you mean you're leaving? You just got here."

Arty had stunned everyone into silence, which, for our group, was a lot.

Elizabeth stared with doting eyes, her hand resting atop his. She was the only one at the table who did not appear shocked.

"My posting has been accelerated. The original plan was for me to complete my studies, graduate, then join active service. That's changed, partly because the war effort is ramping up, but more because, well, I kind of made a splash at Matchbox."[1]

Thomas and I exchanged baffled glances.

"You made a splash? What does that even mean? And what's a Matchbox?"

"A matchbox is a small cardboard container—"

---

1. While there were many secret research facilities throughout the US during WWII, engaging scientists, professors, and businessmen and women across many disciplines, Matchbox is a wholly fictitious location based on the author's wild imagination of one such facility.

"Arty!" Thomas ground his teeth. "This isn't the time for jokes. Talk to us."

I looked at Thomas out the corner of my eye. He'd leaned forward suddenly and become oddly intense.

Arty paused a beat, examining Thomas, then seemed to mentally shrug. "Matchbox is where they sent me last term. It's a developmental facility for specialized items used in the war. Like I told Will, most of the teams there focus on making existing tools or items smaller. Miniaturization is everything, and, apparently, I'm quite good at it. Shrinking is my thing."

Janie leaned across and patted Elizabeth's arm consolingly. "I'm so sorry, dear. Sex isn't everything."

I nearly spat beer all over the table.

Arty sneered, which only made Janie's self-satisfied grin widen.

"As I was saying." He turned back toward us. "The head honchos at Matchbox asked the army to move up my timeline so I could continue the work I started last term. We're making some incredible advancements."

"I'm so proud of Arty," Elizabeth said, lifting his hand to her lips while never taking her eyes off his. "He's making a real difference."

"Which agency are you working for?" Thomas asked.

The question surprised me. First, because Thomas never asked about assignments or missions. He was the ultimate keeper of secrets where one's service was concerned. And second, because we sat in a public place where anyone might overhear our conversation, his query felt like a violation of every non-disclosure speech we'd ever been given.

Arty didn't flinch. "The OSS—Bill Donovan's Office of Strategic Services. Specifically, the Research and Development Branch they started last fall."

My mouth opened, and for some insane reason, refused to close.

Thomas somehow leaned forward more. "That's the new intelligence service Roosevelt created, isn't it? Donovan was Coordinator for Information before this, right?"

"Coordinator *of* Information—the COI," Arty corrected, though I doubted Thomas misspoke without intention. It felt like he was testing Arty. Why, I couldn't guess. "But yes, he still is, technically, though he also leads the OSS using the code name C, an abbreviated version of the official title."

Thomas made to speak, but Arty raised a palm. My mousy friend had somehow grown since I'd seen him last, and he commanded the table's attention. Where had my little Arty gone?

"Before you ask, none of that is classified. It's all in the congressional record and has been reported by the media. If you two ever left our dorm room to read a newspaper, you might've seen it."

Janie snorted. "Fat chance. You should've seen—"

"Janie!" I snapped, glancing up at the drunk and his friend at the bar. "Shh!"

She followed my gaze and blanched, them mouthed "Sorry" across the table.

Arty cleared his throat. "Guys, what I'm working on will help the men—and women"—he gave Elizabeth and Janie a pointed look—"of the OSS a real advantage when they face the enemy. I really am helping keep our people safe and able to carry out their missions."

I sat back and ran a hand through my hair, suddenly overwhelmed by what Arty had told us, but more by the confident, straightforward manner in which he'd said it all. I'd never been prouder of my friend than in that moment.

"Arty, that really is amazing," I finally said.

I glanced at Thomas. He was still glaring, his face a mask of emotionless steel. I nudged him under the table with a knock of our knees. "Isn't that great, Thomas?"

He seemed to wake from some enthralling dream. "Oh, yes, quite. I mean, wow, really, Arty, that's great. Just great."

Every eye at our table focused on him, as though searching for the Thomas we all knew. The imposter who'd just thrown up on his own shoes was clearly not him.

"Anyway," Arty said, saving us from the interminable silence. "That's why I'm leaving tomorrow. They're letting me come back for the week of commencement so I can walk, but then I have to go back for my permanent posting."

He paused, then looked at me, a quirk forming at the corner of his mouth.

"Sorry, Will, I won't be wearing army green."

"What? Why not?"

"We wear lab coats." His face practically split as his proud smile beamed across at me.

The next morning, as the sun painted the Cambridge sky hues of brilliant gold, our little band assembled on the edge of Massachusetts Avenue to bid farewell to our beloved Arty. Janie's face was streaked with tears. Elizabeth's smile never faltered. Thomas snatched our scrawny friend off the ground and swung him around with his feet dangling above the ground, like some youngster bidding adieu to his parents as he headed off to summer camp. I choked back whatever threatened in my throat and held Arty close. "I love you, Arty. You know that, right?" I whispered in his ear.

"You're the brother I never had, Will. I love you too." He squeezed my whole body against his. "I'll see you in June, okay?"

He pulled back and I nodded, unwilling to trust my voice.

I wasn't sure why, but that moment felt important, more so than others. We had done this before, at the end of nearly every term, always knowing we would return to campus, see each other again, share silly stories and spit beer once more. For some reason, as the sun shone through breaths that lingered on the bitter breeze, my heart lurched at our parting.

I missed Arty the moment his car drove away.

The eight of us sat in our Andover classroom, wondering where Commander Jeffers might be. In all the time we'd been enrolled in our special studies, none of our instructors had ever been late to class. Not even once.

Jeffers was now ten minutes late.

At thirty minutes past, Jeffers strode into the room and stood before his desk, his eyes landing and pausing on each of us in turn. The silence of that moment was almost as chilling as his lingering gaze.

"There has been a change of plans."

The sound of men leaning forward in rickety wooden chairs was the only thing breaking the silence as we waited for his next words.

"This cohort's orders have been ... revised. Report to the corner of Kirkland Street by Randall Hall in four hours. There is no need to pack clothing, but you will want to bring personal items. We're headed back to that special place you visited last term."

He paused as the rustle of anticipation passed through the room.

"The original plan was to conduct your full field training this summer, but conditions on the ground have necessitated an advancement of that schedule. You may hear others on campus receiving similar orders within their respective programs or assignments. The whole of government, by order of the President, will now move at a far more rapid pace. The Brits were closer to collapse than we originally believed. They survived without us, but just barely. The rest of Europe hasn't been as fortunate—if you can call any of this fortunate. Now, it appears Hitler's aims are headed East as well. The ambitions of our enemies know no bounds and even less reason. The President has decided it's time we brought the entire might of America to bear—which includes each of you."

He sucked in a breath, then blew it out. It looked like the weight of the world had landed on his shoulders.

"Gentlemen, I'm sorry, but your college days are officially over."

# Chapter Forty

# **Will**

The bus ride north had not become shorter over the holidays. January snows slowed our progress further, and the bus's poor heater struggled to keep up with the rapidly declining temperatures. Even the crusty Sergeant Major Stafford remained buttoned up in his heavy coat for every frigid mile of the trip.

That we knew what to expect helped make it less tedious. Some of the men brought cards or other games, while others wrote letters or read books to pass the time. A few practiced the German they'd likely not used over the holiday break.

Thomas, out of an abundance of caution, sat a few rows behind me, only visiting a few times each day during what dragged into a week-long drive.

I stared out the window at the sea of snow. The weather had become so difficult that I saw very few cars as we drove out of the States, and even fewer once we crossed into Canada. It was as if some master painter had cleaned his brush and smeared the canvas of the world with pure white, and no one dared mar his masterpiece.

When we arrived at Camp X, I shivered beside the bus, waiting alongside the others to retrieve my pack. Stafford stepped up and clamped a meaty paw to my shoulder.

"Shaw, you have a guest." I turned, startled. Stafford simply motioned with his head for me to follow, then turned and strode toward Building E, one of the smaller cabins on the side I hadn't entered before.

Thomas hadn't stepped off the bus yet, but as we strode away, my neck tingled, and I looked back to catch his lingering gaze and a questioning quirk of his brow through the window.

Building E was smaller inside than I'd expected. It was little more than a one-room office with a side chamber for file storage. I recognized the thin, unassuming man in spectacles seated behind the metal desk immediately.

"Major?"

Stafford excused himself, slamming the door shut behind me. I nearly jumped out of my boots.

"Sit." The major motioned to the only other chair in the room. He surprised me by switching from German to English. "When you leave this room, continue referring to me as the major. To those not in our organization, I am an army recruiting officer, nothing more. Understood?"

I nodded, having no clue why.

"Inside our agency, I am Manakin."

I cocked my head. "Uh, like those figures in department stores?"

He barked a laugh, the first sign of emotion I'd seen from the man. "That's a manne*quin*. A lance-tailed manakin is a bird. The males generally form pairs called partnerships. They support each other, combining their voices to attract females. In a sense, they are a recruiting team for the avian kingdom."

I couldn't stop the eye roll that spread to my whole face.

"Don't mock. It's the best they could come up with. Most of our code names are birds of some kind. The more agents we add, the harder it is to get creative. You live with what you get."

"I'm afraid to ask," I muttered, not realizing I'd done so aloud.

"Oh, you already have a designation, my friend." He grinned as I groaned. "But let's take a step back. You've likely wondered what all this training would lead you into, just who you would be working for, all that?"

I nodded. "Yes, sir. No one's told me anything since we first spoke. I could guess some things based on the training, but that's about it."

"Good. That's as it should be." He leaned back, and his chair screamed louder than our dorm room seat. Apparently, office furniture hated the Canadian cold almost as much as we did. "In June of last year, President Roosevelt signed an order officially establishing a new department whose aim was initially to gather and analyze intelligence. Since then, the OSS has grown and evolved, both in scope and mission, to include more ... how shall I say ... *active* measures."

"OSS?" I interjected. "That's Arty's—"

Manakin raised a palm. "Never speak of others in the organization."

"But he's just—"

"It doesn't matter if he's a janitor in a shithouse. Secrecy is our shield. *Never* speak of another. Got it?"

His voice left no room for argument, so I nodded.

"You will be among the first of a new class within the Special Operations division. In short, Will, you are now a spy for the United States of America."

He let that sink in a moment before continuing.

"We had to get your basic proficiency up to snuff, German and all that, before beginning your real training. That starts now. When you walk away from this camp for the final time, you will be assigned missions that are critical to our war effort. Most of these missions will occur within enemy-controlled territory. Some may involve a small team, while others will be solo missions where you are on your own. The training you are about to receive will determine whether you are successful in your assignments or if you return home in a box. Actually, it's more likely you wouldn't return home, but would be tossed aside with other refuse by our enemies."

He spoke like he was describing a day at the beach, like there was nothing ominous or morose at all in being killed and discarded. I tried to slow my pulse, to rein in my breathing, but the room began to close in around me, and the air grew stale and thin. Somehow, the chill of Canada's winter became a sweltering sauna as sweat trickled down my forehead.

Manakin missed nothing and nodded. "Good. You get it. Take your training seriously. Perfect your German. Above all, hone your hand-to-hand skills. I hope you won't need them, but my hopes are worth less than a German mark in London."

He paused, then asked, "Questions?"

I had so many swirling about my head that it was impossible to choose. I could barely see clearly, much less think. I started to speak, then stopped, then ran a hand over my head.

He stood. "Fine. I leave tomorrow. If you think of any, come see me. Your instructors will know where to find me."

He motioned for the door, so I stood and began to leave.

"Oh, Will, one more thing ..."

I turned.

"Your code name is Emu."

The days blended together, one brief glimpse of sunlight after another.

On our first night, one of the Brits who called himself Thames stood before us with classic English formality. "The one-page legends you were given in autumn were designed to introduce you to living with a cover. Now, you must learn everything about yourselves. When living behind the lines, you will be tested, even when you do not realize it. The smallest detail may stand between you and a bullet to the head. Your principal task, for the rest of your time at this facility, is to become the identity in these folders. We will challenge you at every turn. Answer anything wrong, and you will feel it. Hesitate, and it will hurt."

He handed each of us a dossier full of pages, detailing our identities in excruciating detail, down to the names of our childhood friends, our favorite sporting teams, the color of our mothers' eyes, and so forth. No detail was left to the imagination. There were even multiple forms of forged identification bearing our photos and false names. Flipping through the pages, I knew it was critical but wondered how we were ever supposed to memorize it all.

The next day, our training began in earnest, but, like the passage of the Canadian winter, it was hard to keep track of one day to the next.

Mornings of that first week focused on learning the parts of a rifle, how to disassemble the piece then slam everything back into place as quickly as possible. The moment the instructors were satisfied we had the basic understanding of one weapon, they shifted to the next. We even learned to take spent casings and make bullets. I wasn't sure how we would do that in the field without all the right components, but the staff drilled the knowledge into us nonetheless.

I never knew there were so many types of rifles, pistols, and other firearms. We were taught each with precision, but were expected to practice toward mastery in our own time. The Brits explained that the breadth of knowledge they had to impart was too great to allow time for the honing of basic skills in class.

My head usually hurt by lunchtime.

Afternoons began with a review of all things radios and communications, something we'd spent two entire school terms studying. These sessions became interesting when new devices developed by military research arms were introduced. Each unit laid before us was smaller than the one previously discussed.

I smiled when a palm-sized camera landed on the table before us and wondered if Arty had played some role in bringing the tiny lens to life.

When weapons training shifted toward explosives, our years of theoretical exercises became deathly serious and unmistakably real. Firing a rifle at a single enemy was one thing, but building a bomb was another thing entirely. We were learning to kill and destroy.

It was during one of the explosives sessions that I wondered if Arty's handiwork had again graced our tables.

"This is a mole," the instructor said, giving us a moment to study the components laid before us: a small black box, a thin silver rod, a pair of thumb-sized canisters with glass bulbs on one end, and accompanying wiring. "A good place to wreck a train is in a tunnel. It takes time to clean it up and it holds up traffic. The trick is to explode your ordinance while the train is in the tunnel. That is where the mole comes into play."

He pointed at the strange canisters. "The mole is a set of photoelectric equipment which, when plunged into sudden darkness, initiates an explosive charge. The components of a mole are its eye, which is the photoelectric cell you see there, a relay unit, and an electric detonator."

He went on to explain how a mole was attached to the underside of a train where it could see the tracks. The cell built up an impulse from an accumulation of daylight. When the daylight was suddenly removed, the impulse was released and transmitted to the relay unit, where it was amplified into a charge sufficient to detonate an explosive.

Our instructor then lowered a screen and motioned for another of his team to darken the classroom and begin playing a reel. We spent the next twenty minutes watching an OSS-produced movie demonstrating various ways to position and deploy a mole. Some created maximum damage and were designed to destroy material or personnel. Other locations aimed only to disconnect a car at the coupling without damaging whatever contents might be inside.[1]

To call that afternoon sobering was an insult to those who'd given up alcohol.

After dinner, we drilled in German language skills. Several new instructors arrived, one Swiss, another Austrian, a third from the fatherland itself. Each spent grueling hours correcting enunciation and accents, depending on where our respective cover identities originated.

I'd never been so utterly exhausted. There were few unstructured, uninstructed moments.

When my head finally hit the pillow, the world truly went dark.

---

1. The Mole, Office of Strategic Services production, c. 1942

# Chapter Forty-One

# **Will**

O SS-produced films became a staple of our post-dinner evenings. The agency must've commissioned Hollywood to produce dozens of them, covering everything from basic fighting maneuvers to conducting a house search. A week into our second stay at Camp X, a pattern emerged. Whatever topic was covered in the film one evening would consume our lessons and exercises the following day. When the instructors played films titled *How to Get Killed in One Easy Lesson*[1], followed by *Resisting Enemy Interrogation*[2], we knew the next days would be brutal.

Around four o'clock—I didn't have time to check, and my mind was a haze of sleeplessness—four British instructors dressed in black from head to toe barged into our barracks, banging batons on trash can lids. The eight of us jarred awake and leapt to our feet.

---

1. Training Film TF21-1020, Signal Corps production, United States War Department, 1943

2. Training Film TFI-3383, First Motion Picture Unit production, Army Air Forces, 1943

"Dress," the lead Brit barked as the others tossed banana-colored jogging suits at our feet. When we didn't reach for them fast enough, one of the Brits smacked his can lid, then hurled it into the wall. "NOW!"

In moments, eight bananas stood in a row in Building B. The classroom had been cleared of desks and chairs, replaced by a series of padded mats. The four who'd awakened us were joined by a fifth man, also dressed in all black. This new instructor only rose to the shoulders of the others, but was barrel-chested, with arms so large I thought they might've been trying to escape his shirt.

"I am Sergeant Allen. Over the course of your training, I under-stand you have each studied martial arts. Some of you engaged in boxing. Both work if you have the space and an opponent kind enough to follow rules, but your missions will rarely afford either. It is time you learned how real fighting works."

He turned to one of the other instructors. "Bear hug. Attack."

The man moved without hesitation, arms outstretched, wedging Allen's meaty arms against his sides, and he wrapped the man in a tight embrace. I was sure Allen was done, and there would be a lecture about the efficacy of the bear hug, but the sergeant moved so quickly I missed how he broke the hold and brought the much taller man to his knees. Allen glanced up, eyeing each of us, and said, "Breaking a bear hug is easy, if you know how. Today, we teach you this, and many other techniques. Unfortunately, there is no kind way to train this sort of unarmed combat. Once you learn a technique, my team will attack without mercy, as your enemy would. Some of you may end the day in the infirmary. Despite how this day will appear, I assure you, our goal is to teach you to survive."

A few of the men around me shifted uncomfortably. I didn't dare turn my head, but thought I saw Thomas glance toward me from the end of our line. With the exception of the man beside me, who seemed to thrum at the idea of physical combat, a shroud of dread clung to each of us.

"You"—Allen pointed to the first student in our row, a lanky guy who spoke with a thick New York accent—"step forward."

Once the student was in place, Allen turned back to us. "Unarmed combat is a method of attack or defense, whereby an unarmed man uses a combination of releases, holds, throws, and punches, all coordinated into a scientific routine. It can deal accurately and quickly with a ruthless opponent who knows no rules. To be effective, it must be practiced until the movements become instinctive."

Without warning, Allen flew into a series of punches, taking the poor student to the ground faster than he could throw up his arms. I couldn't hide a wince as the student groaned from the mat, though I suspected Allen held back most of the strength in his blows.

"Other essentials are surprise, speed, smoothness of execution, and determination to go through with the attack until the opponent is completely under control. Back in line." Allen stretched out a hand and helped the wary student to his feet.

"Next." The sergeant pointed to me, so I took a couple steps forward. "Let's start with some key attacks, holds, and releases." He turned to me. "Thank you for volunteering. I will try to be gentle."

The glint in his eyes belied any hope of receiving this man's kindness.

"Here are an opponent's vulnerable points." He grabbed my shoulders and lifted his knee as he held me in place. "First, the cock."

Thankfully, he didn't demonstrate the pain of that vital part.

Then he flattened his hand and made karate-chop motions. "Then, the neck, the chin, and now, the arms. The forearm," he said, grabbing my wrist and twisting my arm around to force me down to my knees, while mimicking a chop into the joint of my elbow. "While an opponent is in this position, the back of the neck and the kidneys are exposed." One chop, then another.

"And the base of the spine." His elbow dug into my spine near my waist. He stood me back up. "Now comes the side of the neck." Chop. "And the Adam's apple." Chop. "Lastly, the shins and instep." His boot slammed on top of mine, then his toe pressed against my shin.

I thanked all that was holy that he'd only demonstrated all those hits and hadn't actually landed any, but then wondered, based on his uplifting introduction, how long that mercy would last.

"Now, let's put some of these together so you see how effective they are when smoothly executed."

*Great*, I thought. *Just what I was hoping for.*

"Back in line," he said to me, without executing a move. "I need an instructor who knows what's coming for this part."

*Thank you, Jesus.*

As soon as I'd settled back with my classmates, another instructor stepped up, and Allen thrust his palm into the man's chin, almost holding his head, but also shoving it, bending the man's whole body backward until he fell onto his back on the mat.

"See? There was little he could do to stop himself from falling. Once his torso was exposed, I could have done any number of things with a boot, elbow, or hand to fully disable him."

For the next hour, we paired off with a classmate and practiced the basic moves as Sergeant Allen called them out. Our opposing student was instructed to not resist, only to allow practice on offensive movements. The other instructors roamed among us, lifting or lowering our palms, correcting techniques.

Once satisfied we'd all mastered the basic movements, Allen began calling out combinations, first in twos, then threes, then random numbers that became challenging to remember.

Finally, Allen ordered a halt and lined us up again. "Time to cou nter."[3]

He spent the next twenty minutes showing us how to defend against the offensive maneuvers we'd just learned. He stepped through using the vulnerable points on an opponent's body, such as the thumb joints, to break free of a hold.

The next session stretched forever, lasting far longer than the first. We drilled the motions of attack and counter, first slowly, then slightly faster, finally at full speed. It felt like choreographing some intricate dance, and I suddenly gained respect for the actors in Hollywood who made fight scenes appear so realistic on screen.

"Enjoy your lunch, ladies. When we return, each of you will take turns with my team, attacking and defending."

February 1943 proved to be one of the most painful, sleepless months of my life. Six to eight hours of every day was dedicated to hand-to-hand combat techniques by our not-so-gentle British teachers. The first few bruises were disconcerting, but as the weeks rolled on, became as much a part of our camp life as the ever-present Canadian snow. A few of the guys in our cohort struggled with their fighting skills. One, unable to bring himself to be aggressive toward anything other than a pen and paper, received a broken arm and several bruised

---

3. Unarmed Combat, British Foundation Pictures Limited production, British Army Home Guard, 1941

ribs one afternoon. He didn't return the next day . . . or the next. We later learned he had been discharged from the program and sent back to fulfill his service to the nation on a different assignment.

Our group of eight was now seven.

March might have heralded spring back home, but we barely noticed a change in the wintry chill. Still, many of our activities left the heated comfort of the buildings and thrust us deep into the snowy, wooded surrounds of Camp X. Concealment training, which had been only theoretical in Sergeant Major Stafford's classes, became strikingly real as we sheltered beneath piles of brush or stands of snow.

I'd once heard someone offer advice to a hiker: If stuck in high altitude, where it's bitterly cold, sleep under the snow to shelter from wind and freezing temperatures. I wasn't sure what masochist crafted that pearl of wisdom, but the air beneath the snow where we shivered was just as bitter as any above. I came to dread the lessons in camouflage almost as much as our hand-to-hand sessions.

In late March, just before the weather did begin to warm, a week was dedicated to poisons. We learned dozens of ways to identify, mix, and deploy toxic substances. Some rendered an enemy immobile, while others killed them outright. Some were painless and silent, while others took an excruciating amount of time, allowing time for interrogation before the subject expired.

Many weeks after silence fell over the battlefield, we huddled in Building C to watch a newsreel of the Russian victory over the Nazis in Stalingrad. It appeared Hitler had finally overextended himself, wresting with the Russian bear and a winter that was mightier than any German armament. As elated as we were to finally receive good news from the war, the death toll in Russia quickly sobered any celebratory mood we might've entertained. The narrator threw out numbers that seemed incalculable in my mind, impossible to reason or reckon with, each representing whole cities, small countries of humans no longer alive.

While sobering beyond imagination, these reels also steeled our resolve. Each of us, to a man, swore to play our part in cleansing the world of the Nazi scourge. Our missions might not have been known, but our paths were as clear as the winter sky.

By the time we finally boarded our bus and said farewell to Camp X on May tenth, there were more than two hundred men—and women—training at the facility at any given time, with dozens of black-clad instructors putting them through their paces. We'd seen cohorts of twenty enter and leave in two- to four-week rotations. Considering the year and a half of language, cultural, and other training we'd received, that begged the question: How could they possibly be prepared to enter the field with so little training?

We didn't dare ask. Questions about other trainees were met with stiff and immediate rebuke.

When not secluded with our group, everyone wore masks like we'd seen in the training films, even the instructors. Clearly, the Allies were committed to enhancing their intelligence services at a scale never before seen.

As the bus pulled through the gates for the final time, the sun shone brightly, reflecting against the tin roofs, and our British trainers, now our comrades in arms, snapped to attention and saluted as we drove away.

I'd never been so glad to put a place in the rearview mirror.

I was still so naive.

# Chapter Forty-Two

# Thomas

We arrived on campus two days later and were informed that, while other students of Harvard scrambled to prepare for final exams, we had already faced the worst the college could offer. Our studies were complete.

"Wait," one of our surviving seven asked. Our second trip to Camp X had chipped away the veneer of awe that had surrounded our illustrious instructors prior to January. "So, we're free until commencement?"

Commander Jeffers nodded. "You've earned a little leave. Once you receive your assignments, I doubt you'll have much opportunity for leave until the war's over. Enjoy a moment to breathe—and heal."

Heal.

He'd said a mouthful with that one word. I had bruised muscles I hadn't even known existed before this trip. The idea of sleeping late in the morning and allowing my body to finally recover was more than I could've hoped for. I stepped away from the bus to peer onto the campus proper, reorienting myself to the real world.

Harvard had been home for so long. It was comfortable and familiar.

Now, it felt distant and strange. The students strolling through the yard made sense, as did the historic buildings and ivy. Then I realized what felt odd.

It was us. *We* no longer fit in the perfect Cambridge picture.

Our training might've been designed to mold rough clay into the perfectly formed intelligence officer, but it had also reshaped how I saw the world around me. These were the students and teachers, the staff and others, who, without even knowing it, demanded my thumb be added to the scales of war, hopefully tipping its weight in their favor, however great or slight that shift might be. These were the people I was meant to protect. These were my classmates and my family.

And yet, I was no longer one of them. I was no longer Thomas Jacobs.

I had been reborn into a man who lived in shadows most of these people never knew existed. Regardless of the outcome of the war, or of my service in it, my life had been given over to their cause ... and they didn't even know it.

I briefly wondered if the others were having the same out-of-body experience as they stepped foot on campus again. The whole thing felt surreal.

Will's whisper from behind startled me. The warmth of his breath on my neck made tiny hairs stand at attention with an electricity they hadn't felt since the new year.

"So, from May twelfth until May twenty-seventh, we have no classes, no training, and I don't have a roommate. Think we'll get bored?"

The others were still milling around the bus, so I didn't turn, but I was pretty sure he could see my smile through the back of my head. It felt like it wrapped all the way around.

"We might. That's an awfully long time to be stuck together with nothing to do."

"Oh, I'm sure we'll come up with things to do. Things I've dreamed about for almost five months. I might explode—"

"Stop that!" I hissed playfully, turning to face him. "You keep talking about exploding and I won't make it back to your dorm room with clean trousers."

His laugh was so sudden and loud that others turned.

"Come on, you dummy, grab your pack," I said aloud, slinging my bag over my shoulder and grabbing one of his. "I'll help you carry your stuff to your room. You pack like a woman, you know that, right?"

"Thanks, strong man." He wiped the grin away, then muttered low for only me to hear. "A woman, eh? Move your ass so I can show you what a man can really do."

It had taken a week or so for my mind and body to truly feel whole again. Will had taken care of my spirit. That part of my soul was happy, exhausted, and drunk on love most of the waking moments of those days. I'd never known how one man could be a slave to heal the deepest wounds, those not seen in the flesh, but that's what Will was for me.

That's *who* he had become.

On the Monday before our Thursday commencement, Will and I lay abed, arms and legs tangled together, sheets and covers discarded at the foot of the bed. I'd been awake for some time, enjoying the feel of his head on my chest and his breathing across my skin as he continued to sleep. Will had proven quite the champ in the sleeping-in game. Years of navy service had drilled that luxury out of my system.

Keys rattled outside the door, and my heart jolted like it had sprinted off the block.

Will jarred awake. "What—"

I covered his lips with my fingers until he heard the key sliding into the lock. His eyes flew wide, and he dove for the covers. I wasn't sure how that would help, but I lay frozen, watching his effort.

The door flung open, and Arty stopped in the doorway. "How did I know I would find the two of you naked? Do you *ever* wear clothes?"

He slipped inside and leaned back to close the door behind him.

Will draped the sheet over the lower half of his body, stood, and pulled his roommate into an awkward embrace. The sheet fell away the second Will's arms wrapped around Arty.

"Uh, Will, you're naked again," Arty squeaked, as his hands patted Will's shirtless back.

Will hugged him tighter and laughed. "Shut up and hug me back. You're my brother. You've seen me naked plenty of times."

"Uh, yeah, but I've never *felt* you naked."

I barked a laugh. "Pretty hot, isn't it? I especially love it when—"

"Thomas! Stop!" Arty finally freed his arms enough to shove Will back. Then he noticed me standing by the bed, stark naked and slightly aroused, though it was more my body's normal greeting to the morning sun than any true arousal.

A hand flew over his eyes forming a mask.

"Eww. Thomas, you're growing. I'm going to wait for you to put on some clothes, alright? Just tell me when you're dressed."

We shuffled through the room. He waited.

"Alright, we're decent," Will said.

Arty dropped his hand to find us, still naked, on top of each other on the bed again.

"Oh, God, make it stop," Arty huffed as he turned. "I'm going to breakfast. Janie got back this morning too, and is meeting me downstairs. It would be great if the two of you found clothes and joined us."

With that invitation, Arty fled the field.

Will and I burst out laughing.

"Was that cruel?" I asked, trying to decipher if the feeling in my gut was guilt or amusement.

"Absolutely. Cruel and unusual, as the law students would say, but perfectly hilarious."

He pecked my neck, then pushed himself upright.

God, the sight of that man naked made my heart soar.

"Come on," he said. "I want to see the two of them, and I'm starving."

"You did work up an appetite; twice, if I remember correctly."

He planted fists on his still-naked hips and wiggled his man bits. "If you have trouble remembering how many times we did *that*, I worry for you in the field, mister spy man."

I laughed and tossed a pillow, causing him to step aside and bang into his desk chair. "Ow! That's enough of you. Let's go eat."

# Chapter Forty-Three

# **Will**

I will never truly understand the power of friendship.

We hadn't seen nor spoken with Arty, Janie, or Elizabeth in nearly half a year, but somehow, as if by magic, the moment our eyes met again, time rewound to before we'd parted. It felt as though we'd never left each other's side, and the banter and laughter flowed as freely as it ever had. Though Arty's smile wasn't quite as wide as I'd remembered, not reaching his eyes as fully as it once had.

Then again, I'd noticed the same about Thomas. When we were alone, he allowed himself to shed all masks and simply be, but when others were around, even those we'd come to cherish as family, his gaze never fully relaxed.

I wondered if I did the same now. It was hard to see myself as others might, but I felt more ... serious.

Maybe we were all just growing up, becoming the adults we were meant to become. I hoped it was simply that, and not the war's dark shawl cloaking our vision with a weight we might never shed.

At least our friendship hadn't changed.

"Where is this mystery man of yours, Janie? You know the committee must approve before you tie the knot." Arty nodded soberly, as would any judge adjudicating a murder.

"He's a proper gentleman, I assure you," she said, not quite answering the question. "I'm sure there will be time for you to meet soon."

Everyone at the table knew what would follow commencement. More precisely, we knew how little we knew what would follow our graduation. Arty, Thomas, and I would receive orders sending us God knows where. Our little family would disperse and not see each other again for ... possibly forever. We might never meet Janie's fiancé, or see them wed, or see any of their life that followed.

My heart seized at that thought.

Thankfully, Janie refused to leave the present in exchange for our uncertain future.

"You two," Janie said in a low voice, pointing at Thomas and me with a fork laden with fried potato, "spent five months together this term. Out with it. I want details."

Color flooded my cheeks, as though she'd caught us in some tawdry position.

Thomas didn't flinch, speaking with an oddly firm gentleness. "You know we can't talk about our training."

She cackled. "Don't give me that line. I can see in the crimson on Will's face that more happened than just training." She leaned in. "Was it romantic wherever you were?"

I finally found my voice, bumping knees with Thomas beneath the table, signaling for me to handle this offensive.

"It was very romantic," I said with layers of heat dripping from my voice. "We barely spent a moment apart ... or in clothes."

Janie squealed and clapped like her child had just finished a recital. "I'm so happy!" she bellowed.

"Shh," Arty cautioned, his eyes darting to the tables around us.

Janie covered her mouth with both hands, giggling through her fingers. Her eyes never stopped twinkling and shifting between the two of us.

Thomas's knee rubbed more so than bumped mine, letting me know he not only approved of my little white lie, but that he was amused—and possibly aroused—by it.

A jolt shot up my spine as his touch lingered, and we shared a glance.

"That's the look I was waiting for," Janie hissed from across the table, still a bit too loud. "You two are so—"

"Utterly disgusting," Arty cut her off. "Can we talk about something more pleasant, like the war, famine, or disease?"

Elizabeth smiled dutifully, giving Arty the same longing look I'd just given Thomas. Janie, undaunted, slapped Arty playfully on the arm. Then her raptor's gaze took in Elizabeth ... then the two of them together ... then their gaze.

She squealed again, this time unrestrained by anyone in the dining hall . . . or on campus . . . or on the Eastern Seaboard. I covered my ears in mock pain.

"Arthur Wendel Ableman, you are smitten!" she declared.

Before he could protest, Elizabeth's hand rose and cupped one cheek, then she leaned over and kissed the other. Arty locked eyes with her, and I watched the entire world disappear. He could only see her as he melted into a pile of heartwarming goo right there at our table.

"Aww," the three of us not caught in the spell called in unison—a call echoed by two nearby tables who had more members in their chorus, therefore much greater volume.

Our puddle of goo turned redder than any Harvard pennant, but his eyes still lingered on Elizabeth.

Thomas's knee pressed into mine and held there.

I thought my heart might burst.

# Chapter Forty-Four

# **Will**

The morning of commencement, Thomas, Arty, and I were crammed into our dorm room. We'd packed most of our things, filling trunks and duffels, but our lack of luggage organization made navigating the already small space challenging. Thomas's navy white choker poked above his black gown[1], giving him an air of regality our simple shirts and ties lacked; though his lopsided grin matched the flop of his hair in a perpetual bemusement I'd come to love.

He'd never been more handsome.

I reached up to straighten the tie he wasn't wearing. He'd been looking down, twisting the silver ring he never removed, a habit begun the moment he'd first slipped it on.

"I wish he could be here," he said quietly.

I took his hand, kissed it, then pressed it to his chest. "He is. He *always* is."

---

1. Many servicemen wore only their dress uniform to commencement, eschewing the traditional cap and gown.

Thomas squeezed my hand, and I felt his chest fill to overflowing, then release. He brushed my hair back from my brow and let his fingers trail down my cheek. "I wish we didn't have to report in tomorrow," he said wistfully.

We'd each received a sealed envelope in our campus mailbox. The outside held no information beyond our first name typed in crisp newsprint black. The card inside mine contained seven words:

*Report to Andover 103 Friday at 0800.*

Thomas didn't report until 1030 hours, which meant each of us likely met with our instructors privately. I'd tried not to obsess over what that meant.

Would we receive our first real orders? If so, how quickly would we leave? Deploy? I wasn't sure what the correct term was. That sort of thing wasn't in our training.

Then I realized something else. Technically, I had been in the military this past year and a half. My orders had been to attend college and act normally, as if there was another option given the complete lack of information they'd offered me.

Would I be expected to wear a uniform tomorrow? I didn't own one. Was that the sort of thing they gave out or assigned or whatever?

Again, I was clueless.

I wanted to ask, but when I peered up into Thomas's eyes, I could tell his thoughts were still with his lost friend, and I didn't want to disturb his memory.

Arty, not understanding the import of the moment, had no such issue. "Come on, you two, we're going to be late."

"Do we have to do the whole procession thing?" Thomas groaned, kissing my fingers then freeing his ringed hand from mine and lowering it from his chest.

"YES!" Arty and I said in unison.

"We need time to get Elizabeth and Janie. They're waiting at their houses for us," Arty said.

"That means we have at least another hour, if we're on Janie time," Thomas quipped.

I snorted.

"I will drag the princess out of her house whether she's ready or not. We're not missing our own commencement. Now move!"

Arty was fiery.

Two girl retrievals and one procession later, we sat in a mass of men and women that flooded Harvard Yard. One entire section of wooden folding chairs was filled with men in uniform. Thomas, in his cap and gown, stood out as an oddity among their order.

As we sat together, a sea of hopes and dreams, my mind latched onto the word that brought us together: commencement.

In its usual context, the title for the day meant little more than a graduation, a recognition of those who had studied and labored, of those now ready to take their place in the world as Harvard graduates.

On that day, it carried far more weight.

It truly was a commencement, a beginning, the start of a journey whose path was as obscure as its end. We had spent so many hours worried about completing our coursework or successfully navigating our training that we'd rarely given appropriate consideration to what lay before us, to what we were beginning.

I wondered if all graduates felt that way as they stared into the caps of their peers, somehow glimpsing their future arriving with every blink of their eyes. Did every student's heart suddenly shudder as they strode across the stage and left the cocoon of their collegiate career behind?

We were commencing something far greater than any of us imagined.

---

At 0755, I paced before the door to Andover 103.

Arty had insisted Thomas continue sleeping in our room with me even though he was back and snoring softly only a few feet away. His one request was that there be no naked fun while he was in the room. Thomas's wicked streak reared its head, as he wanted to shatter Arty's rule just to embarrass the poor lad, but my better nature and loyalty to my friend won the argument. While there was no naked nookie, there was wonderful, naked sleep beneath the sheets.

I slept fitfully that night, and Thomas's eyes were open and staring blankly at the ceiling each time I stirred. We didn't speak, but were clearly sharing the same thoughts and trepidation.

When I finally surrendered to the day's early light, my mind raced and an uncontrollable heat pulsed across my skin. I'd been nervous when Thomas and I first met, but this was nothing like our childlike infatuation. This was true fear.

"Will, come in," Commander Jeffers said as the door cracked open. He wore his dress uniform, crisp with gold gleaming on his buttons and sleeves.

I had expected us to chat alone. I had not expected to see the major who'd recruited me sitting behind the teacher's desk.

Slowly, I stepped in.

"Thank you, Commander. That'll be all for now," the major said in clear dismissal to the officer of superior rank.

I hadn't meant for my brows to rise, but the major's smile told me he'd noticed. "I'm not really a major," he whispered. "Don't tell anyone."

I nodded nervously.

"Sit." He motioned to the desk opposite.

"Will, without ever setting foot in enemy territory, you have become one of the most highly trained members of the OSS. The luxury of time isn't one we often enjoy. Most only receive cursory training before mission assignment. You and your cohorts received the fullest preparation our government could offer."

He paused expectantly, though for what, I wasn't sure.

"Um, thank you, sir," I offered.

His smile tightened. "There was a great deal of debate over your class's training. Some argued we were wasting resources. Thankfully, C thought otherwise."

"C, sir?"

"Sorry, Bill Donovan, President Roosevelt's Coordinator for Information. He goes by the codename C for short. It's not a secret like an agent's name. In fact, the press has fun plastering it everywhere."

"Oh," was all I could manage.

"Bottom line, C believes in our mission. Your average agent will have missions similar to yours. Unfortunately, the average agent doesn't last long. Our theory is that a better-trained spy will be more effective—and die less."

I blinked a few times. "I certainly hope so, sir."

"Yes, I hope so too, son." He grinned. "That's why we invested so much time in you boys."

He opened a folder sitting on the desk and flipped through a couple of pages.

"Each bird in the Greenhouse—that's you seven—will leave next week on different assignments. Some of you will form teams, while others will act alone or be tasked with recruiting teams once in place. None of you may share information about your respective assignments. Do you understand that?"

"Yes, sir." They had made that crystal clear a year ago. Why he was beating that long-bolted horse was a mystery.

"Good." He scanned a page, then closed the folder, stood, and held it out to me. "Your first mission is outlined here. Good luck, Emu."

*If you enjoyed Crimson, please <u>leave a review filled with stars</u>.*
*Your feedback fuels an indie author's soul and helps others find*
*our work.*
*Thank you.*

# Reference

**C**amp **X** was the unofficial name of the secret Special Training School No.103, a Second World War British paramilitary installation for training covert agents in the methods required for success in clandestine operations. It was located on the northwestern shore of Lake Ontario between Whitby and Oshawa in Ontario, Canada. The area is known today as Intrepid Park, after the code name for Sir William Stephenson, Director of British Security Coordination (BSC), who established the program to create the training facility.

The facility was jointly operated by the Canadian military, with help from Foreign Affairs and the RCMP, but commanded by the BSC; it also had close ties with MI6. In addition to the training program, the camp had a communications tower that could send and transmit radio and telegraph communications, called Hydra.

The origins of Camp X lay in the British drive to maximize support for the war effort from the United States, which was neutral at the time. William "Wild Bill" Donovan, appointed in July 1941 as US President Franklin D. Roosevelt's Coordinator of Information, was keen to develop a cadre of secret agents, and Camp X was designed to help. William Stephenson (now widely known as Intrepid—although this was never, in fact, his code name, merely a telegraphic address he used after the war) was the principal facilitator of the project. Stephenson had arrived in New York in 1940 as station chief for in the United States and used his wide network of contacts across Canada to locate and purchase a suitable site.

The camp opened in early December 1941, and over the next few months trained several of its staff in the arts of secret warfare. The almost simultaneous US entry into World War II following Pearl Harbor meant that Donovan could openly establish his own schools. Donovan initially depended on the resources available at Camp X, including its syllabus, which provided the basic template for training American agents.

By the start of World War II, President Roosevelt realized the need for some sort of coordination for the gathering of intelligence. He chose General William "Wild Bill" Donovan to be the leader of the Office of the Coordinator of Information (COI), established on July 11, 1941.

COI was not created soon enough or well-established enough to avert the major intelligence failures that preceded the attack on Pearl Harbor six months later. Donovan moved to rename COI the **Office of Strategic Services** on June 13, 1942. It was also transferred from an office reporting to the White House to reporting to the Joint Chiefs of Staff (JCS).

Strategic Services Operations' department titled Special Operations (SO), modeled on the British Special Operations Executive (SOE), carried out missions dropping small teams of officers to train and assist resistance fighters, as well as commit acts of sabotage, destruction, and general mayhem.

# Also By Casey Morales

# About the Author

Casey Morales is an LGBT storyteller and the author of multiple bestselling & award-winning MM romance novels. Born in the Southern United States, Casey is an avid tennis player, aspiring chef, dog lover, and ravenous consumer of gummy bears. Learn more at AuthorCasey-Morales.com.

About the Author

9 781960 165114